THE PARTY

In front of everyone, Jonathan Tate turned into a baby zebra.

Louise's eyes widened, and Larry looked down where his son used to be.

"Sam, what..." Larry's agitated tone finally broke the silence in the room. "What is this? Where's my son?"

"That's a zebra," Gladys declared, turning to Abner. "I dare you to tell me it's not!"

Louise looked at Samantha pleadingly. "Samantha... how is this possible?"

It was as if a million thoughts were transmitting between Samantha and Darrin in one helpless glance. They'd been together so long, knew each other so well, he could tell exactly how she wanted to handle this.

"It's possible, Louise," Samantha started, "because Adam...and Tabitha...and I...are witches."

Out of nowhere, thunder roared as if a tropical storm were moving through the house. Gusts of wind whipped up and lightning flashed wildly, and before Samantha could even try to shield her kids, every mortal in the room was gone.

Vanished.

"Mother, where's Daddy?" Tabitha asked, the panic in the girl's voice rising.

"I don't know," Samantha replied, clutching Adam in one hand and the chain of her "S" necklace with the other, the breath nearly taken out of her. "Oh, my stars..."

"I, Samantha, Take This Mortal, Darrin"

Adam-Michael James
author of "The Bewitched Continuum"

an unofficial story based on
the television series created by Sol Saks

A BRIGHT HORSE PUBLISHING BOOK

I, SAMANTHA, TAKE THIS MORTAL, DARRIN
An unofficial story based on a television show created by Sol Saks

Story © 2017 by Adam-Michael James. All rights reserved.

Published by Bright Horse Publishing.

Printed by CreateSpace, an Amazon.com company.
www.createspace.com

Cover concept by Adam-Michael James.
www.adammichaeljames.com

Artwork by Dan Parent.
www.danparent.com

Additional graphic design by TechnoMedia.
www.technomediapei.com

Follow Adam-Michael James' *Bewitched* books on Facebook at
facebook.com/bwcontinuum

ISBN-13: 978-0692979266
ISBN-10: 0692979263

First edition: November 2017

10 9 8 7 6 5 4 3 2 1

TABLE OF CONTENTS

AUTHOR'S NOTES

Television audiences during *Bewitched*'s original 1964-1972 run had a complex, interesting world going on outside their living rooms. The civil rights movement was in full swing, the sexual revolution was ramping up, Women's Lib poured gasoline on their bra-burning; even gay men joined the wide-ranging parade of people standing up for their right to be who they were and live their lives accordingly.

On its surface, *Bewitched* was a cute little sitcom about a cute little witch whose powers – and relatives – caused more than a fair share of magical problems for her mortal husband week after week. But dig a little deeper...from its quaint beginnings to its campy endings, the show, at its core, was always about prejudice. And overcoming it. While witches deemed mortals inferior, and at least one mortal looked upon most other witches with disdain, Darrin and Samantha Stephens were an example of enduring the opinions and misconceptions of others and staying true to themselves.

Not to be left out, even the show's witches, albeit fictional, got a chance to buck stereotypes. From the very pilot, we were told witches don't ride brooms, don't have warts on long, crooked noses, and don't wear pointy hats. As Samantha said as early as the 1964 episode "The Witches Are Out" (#7): "we're just like anyone else – almost."

Flash forward 50 years past that pilot to 2014, when I got to release what many have called my phone book sized *Bewitched* reference guide – *The Bewitched Continuum* – in time for the show's golden anniversary. There are those who have termed my fascination with the Stephenses "obsessive", but what can I say; I'm a man of few passions, and when I'm passionate about something, I give it my all. So I delved into the continuity of all 254 episodes – though continuity was not a requirement for series of that time – and compared and contrasted to my heart's content.

Another thing not part and parcel for a departing show then was lensing a final episode. Now when a show goes off the air, you know before it even returns in the fall: "DON'T MISS THE COMPELLING FINAL SEASON!" *Bewitched* didn't have that luxury. It wasn't unusual; a quick Googling shows that the series finale was "invented" by *The Fugitive* in 1967, but didn't really make itself known again in any major way until *M*A*S*H* left the airwaves in 1983.)

There seem to be a few conflicting thoughts as to whether or not *Bewitched* was aware it wasn't coming back for a ninth season – however, there's at least an implied hint in Season 8's ending "The

Truth, Nothing But the Truth, So Help Me, Sam" (#254), in which Samantha giggles that Endora "just loves happy endings" and Darrin gives Samantha a kiss on her infamous nose as the last scene fades out. Of course, one of the things *Bewitched* is most known for, aside from switching Darrin from Dick York to Dick Sargent mid-stream, is the number of early-season episodes that were remade in some form or fashion in the later years.

And so, "The Truth...", which was itself copied nearly word for word from Season 2's "Speak the Truth" (#50), became the barely audible swan song for a show that had topped Nielsen ratings and captured the hearts and imaginations of people around the world. While writing *The Bewitched Continuum*, I thought: What if I did up a series finale for them? And out of that came a two-parter I called "I, Samantha, Take This Mortal, Darrin" (#255-#256) – a flip on the pilot's title, "I, Darrin, Take This Witch, Samantha" (#1).

But I didn't want to just create another mad scramble with Samantha and Darrin trying to explain away witchcraft by building a convenient slogan around it. I didn't want to have Endora put another spell on Darrin, or simply retool an original episode the show hadn't gotten around to themselves. What I did want was to have the show come full circle: to bring back beloved characters, have characters interact who never shared a scene, and up the ante for the Stephenses in a way that hadn't been done – not to mention address many of the observations I'd made about the show in *The Bewitched Continuum*. Most importantly, I felt it wouldn't be a proper send-off without polishing up the messages of acceptance and equality that Elizabeth Montgomery and Bill Asher layered into many episodes, either subtly or directly.

And oh, I had a lot of fun dreaming up how I would wrap the show. It came pretty easily, actually. Two episodes, four paragraphs – and that was it. Mission accomplished.

Today, however, like the audiences who watched *Bewitched* first-run from 1964 to 1972, we too have a complex, interesting world going on outside our living rooms – and computer screens. Only instead of slowly, ultimately moving forward, as in those days, there seems to be a concerted effort to drag the world backwards and return us to a state where inequality and intolerance are the norm. That may be a movement some want, though hardly all. But what can one guy who can tell you which season what *Bewitched* sound effect originated (probably to the episode) really do or say about any of it?

If Elizabeth (I know she preferred to be called "Lizzie", but I just can't bring myself to!) were alive, she would be speaking out against the idea that any one group of people is superior to another. If *Bewitched* were first airing in today's world, you can bet that Samantha would have a lot to say about the rights of others, the rights of everyone. After all, did she not once tell Tabitha, "all men are brothers, even if they're girls"?

And here I had this series-ending idea touching on these very subjects just sitting there. As I have learned over and over the past several years, "never argue with the muse." It's insisting *Bewitched* indeed has one more story to tell, and 2017 is the time for me to tell it.

So I took my final episode concept from *The Bewitched Continuum* (see pages 571-572 in that book) and figured I'd just flesh it out a bit. That's how it started, but that's not how it ended. I found myself combining ideas in ways I hadn't predicted, connecting dots I hadn't even paid attention to, and finding moments of humor in places you wouldn't think it was hiding. I had a general outline – which grew, naturally – but much of what came out of me was spontaneous; I often finished a scene with details and directions that weren't obvious to me when I first sat down to write it.

I had even more fun novelizing these "episodes" – and they're full of more Easter eggs than the White House lawn (which would have made a better analogy even a year ago, admittedly). The more intimately you know the show, the more you're going to delight at the references, though certainly anyone with a more casual investment in *Bewitched* will be able to follow along. What I didn't expect I'd do was create backstories for the Stephenses based on hints that had been dropped over eight seasons. It came as a sudden inspiration in the tub – on the screen in my head, I could see Darrin staring down at Madison Avenue, telling me his history. It was all I could do to dry off so I could record these ideas before I forgot them!

Well (or is that, "Well?"), everything snowballed from there. I wrote the first pages on my birthday (July 2), and much of the first half while recovering from trigger finger surgery; making a fist was hard, but I could still type. Then, I was quite literally sitting down to begin the final chapter (which turned into three) when my mother called from Florida asking me to get her out of the path of Hurricane Irma. I had no choice but to drop the *denouement* and take several road trips with mom, her oxygen machine, and her cat, to get out of Irma's way. (That series finale: my mom's place stayed in one piece!)

As I said in *The Bewitched Continuum*, this is not an official ending to *Bewitched* by any means, and it's only my idea – you might envision the show tying up with a different ribbon. But I truly feel mine is in keeping with the spirit of the show, and if we ever needed reminders of what Samantha Stephens stood for season after season, we need it now.

I hope you'll make use of the extensive endnotes at the end that explain what episode a particular passage is referencing – and what observation from *The Bewitched Continuum* I built a story point around. Also, I got a kick and a half out of researching mainstream and obscure funk tunes that might have been on the stereo at 1164 Morning Glory Circle; to listen to the "soundtrack" of this "final episode", visit youtube.com/user/amj26 for a video that streams all the songs and describes how they connect to what you're reading.

I want to thank Irene Doyle for indulging my muse's desire to channel 1972 in a photo shoot – the hippie result of which is on the About the Author page. A shout-out goes to Wayne Cox, my high school friend from Fort Pierce Central, who suggested giving my wonderful little kitty girl, Shadow, a cameo; Shadow's been having a catfight with melanoma the past three years and is still ahead by a paw! Also, mega thanks to my stepsister, Cindy Harris, for her help with proofreading.

I bow at the feet of Blair Sweeney of TechnoMedia, whose skill and imagination again created graphic art ideas I'd never think of.

And what would this book be without the incredible artwork of Dan Parent, artist and writer for *Archie* comics? Oh, my stars! His likenesses of the Stephenses are pure magic and nothing less.

Finally, I offer a big "thank you Mums!" to Bill Lane Jensen, my unofficial editor and very official *Bewitched*-o-phile; he knows the show as thoroughly as I do and let me know when I needed to quote Dr. Bombay and say "in layman's terms, I made a boo-boo!"

Time now to zap you back to a pair of Saturday nights when the regular ABC schedule just might be pre-empted by two episodes that, to this writer's mind, bring *Bewitched* to a proper close. I really hope you enjoy it; I wrote *The Bewitched Continuum* for myself, but "I Samantha, Take This Mortal, Darrin" I wrote for my fellow hardcore fans, because I know you'll all get the in-jokes. But take heart – you don't have to be a hardcore fan to get the confirmation of *Bewitched*'s central message that's worth repeating in closing: "All men are brothers, even if they're girls." And don't ever let any of those foolish mortals tell you otherwise.

Yours magically,
Adam-Michael James
November 2017

Part I

"Airdate": April 1, 1972
Episode #255
(30 minutes)

1 Promotional Activities

Darrin Stephens looked through the blinds from his office on the 32nd floor[1] of the Clark Building[2], peering at the congested traffic of Madison Avenue. At times he still marveled at how he'd gotten here. Growing up in the suburbs of St. Louis, boy Darrin used to stare at the radio, less entranced by the antics of the Lone Ranger or Fibber McGee and Molly than the catchy commercial jingles that bookended each program. All through high school until he graduated *cum laude*[3] with a bachelor's degree from the University of Missouri during television's sporadic beginnings, Darrin rarely thought of anything but breaking into the world of advertising. He even incurred the wrath of a senior year girlfriend, Mary Jane Nilesmunster[4], who was livid about him being too focused on his ambitions to focus on her. Ambition had been like a magnet to Darrin, pulling him through internships in Kansas City and Chicago before inexplicably attracting him to the Big Apple.

After a few unremarkable turns at less than inspirational agencies, Darrin one day found himself in the foyer of Manhattan's McMann and Tate, shaking hands with head honcho Lawrence Tate. Darrin recalled how "Larry" once had hair as fiery as his temper[5] – but that fire also expressed itself through a passion for the business. Larry's get-up-and-go was contagious; under Larry's tutelage, Darrin reached further for the stars than he knew he was capable of, racking up success after success and earning a reputation as a force to be reckoned with despite his young age. From that standpoint, Darrin Stephens might have been content with such an existence indefinitely.

At no point, however, could Darrin begin to conceive he would one day be married to a witch. Not the kind he'd read about in stories or watched on the silver screen, but a real, live, beautiful sorceress who could make the unachievable achievable with a twitch of her perky nose. Darrin thought back to his honeymoon, which happened in a posh hotel not far from this office, seeing vividly the wedding night confession Samantha backed up by moving an ashtray across the table and making an Old Fashioned appear in his hand, straw and all.[6] Darrin smiled as it occurred to him that Samantha's greatest feat had probably been saving him from a loveless relationship with social climber Sheila Sommers. And instead of zapping or twitching or incanting, all Samantha had to do was run into him in the revolving door thirty-two floors below.

Of course, every married man has to make some adjustment, as Darrin remembered thinking to himself post-confession. But he couldn't have predicted that adjustment would include being turned into objects and animals, or having spells put on him that changed his behavior and placed in him one embarrassing situation after another – much less finding himself rescuing Samantha centuries in the past[7] or needing to be rescued himself during the early days of the Salem witch trials.[8] There had been witchcraft in every nook and cranny these past eight years, doled out by Samantha's imposing parents, Maurice and Endora, temperamental and jokester relatives like her cousin Serena and Uncle Arthur, and even well-meaning witches like beloved Aunt Clara and the Stephenses' maid, Esmeralda. There were days Darrin looked in the mirror while shaving and wondered how he wasn't in a rest home somewhere.

Yet when Darrin saw Samantha's smile, that twinkle in her eye, the way she had faced down her parents and even the mighty Witches' Council on his behalf, there was no question. Darrin loved this witch and was loved by her in a way no mortal could, he was sure of it. While he held to his insistence that witchcraft not be practiced in his house, which was his and Samantha's agreement from the beginning, Darrin had come to develop a certain reverence for the amazing powers his wife and her kinfolk possessed. That was quite a bit of progress considering he started out claiming witchcraft was nonsense[9] and famously flying into a rage because Samantha had magically flipped pancakes.[10] When Darrin finally got really honest with himself, he realized he had only felt threatened by witchcraft; after acquiring powers of his own a couple of times[11] and seeing it was simply what such powers were used for that counted, he had entered into a private sort of gentlemen's agreement about magic. And, unlike the days when he'd had panicked daydreams about producing supernatural offspring[12], it didn't even matter anymore that his children, Tabitha and Adam, were indeed capable of magic themselves. Despite the constant ups and downs, Darrin had long since been of the opinion that what he and Samantha had built together since their 1964 meeting was more powerful than witchcraft.

Darrin's intuition, honed through years as an ad man – and as a witch's husband – told him everything was coming full circle in this moment. He had just come off a challenging but satisfying two weeks doing up a campaign for the Montgomery Industries account. He knew, after witnessing Larry's champion brown-nosing for so long, that it was necessary to take any of his boss/friend's compliments with a grain of salt the size of a small planet. After all, Larry was apt to go along with whatever a client said in any given moment. It wasn't that way in the early years[13], but Darrin had adapted. So Darrin's eyebrow had raised when Larry became unusually circumspect about this client's reaction to his work.

"Darrin, we're not paying you all this money to keep tabs on the window washer."

Darrin turned away from Madison Avenue to find Larry standing in the doorway of his office. By his own admission, Larry could be volatile, rash, and a blowhard[14], but he also had an impish side to him. Darrin couldn't quite tell if he detected a slightly upturned curve in Larry's white mustache.

"Just charging my creative batteries," Darrin replied, smoothing his plaid suit jacket. Having been fired over a dozen times by Larry and threatened with termination even more often[15], Darrin tried to cover his involuntary defensiveness with levity. "Wouldn't want this car to stall in the middle of the freeway. Speaking of which, I've had some additional thoughts about the Asher Automotive account – "

"Well, just pull off at the nearest exit and find yourself a parking garage, because you and I have to talk." Larry seemed especially grim as he habitually seated himself on the corner of Darrin's desk.

Darrin slowly took his chair, suddenly aware of the varying patterns in his office's wood paneling.

"I finally heard back from ol' Allen Montgomery," Larry began. "In particular, he's weighed in on your campaign for Montgomery Industries' line of nightclub wear."

"Yes, I've been trying to envision a member of the old guard getting hip to a slogan for platform shoes," Darrin replied, suppressing a sudden urge to smile.

"'You'll be on top of the world at the disco,'" Larry quoted dryly. "Certainly wouldn't've been my first choice."

"I could have said 'You'll rise to new heights.'" Darrin's joke fell flat.

"You know, Darrin, you've come up with some very unusual slogans over the years. And by using some very unusual tactics. Dressing up like Little Lord Fauntleroy[16], doing magic tricks with dog food..."[17]

"Yeah, well...I guess you could say I'm drawn to the unconventional."

"To say the least. I don't remember that being a trait of yours when you first started with us, but it's become increasingly noticeable. And Darrin, in the business world, traits like those have consequences."

That familiar sinking feeling settled in the pit of Darrin's stomach. He estimated it had been about two years since Larry had actually pink-slipped him[18], which was darn near a record. And wonder of wonders, this wasn't even due to Endora's interference.

"The quality of your work can no longer go overlooked," Larry said soberly, standing up. "That's why your services at McMann and Tate will no longer be required."

Darrin wracked his brain, trying to determine what he had done to earn this latest place on the unemployment line. Or what he had done to goad one of his witchy in-laws into arranging it. If not Endora, it could be Maurice, or maybe this was one of Arthur's jokes – the possibilities seemed endless.

"However," Larry added, "your services at McMann, Tate and Stephens will most absolutely be required."

Darrin had to hold on to his swivel chair as Larry's glower was replaced with one of his celebrated cat-that-ate-the-canary smiles.

"Rendered you speechless, eh? I just couldn't resist the temptation to yank your chain a little first. Funny, huh?" Larry let out a guffaw, but his face blanked at Darrin's non-reaction. "Wasn't it?"

Darrin squared his eyes. "I'm just reminded of those times you dangled this same McMann, Tate, and Stephens carrot – "

"Only to have me tell you the signs would read that way in a few years – if you behaved."[19]

Darrin nodded. "Not six months ago, if I recall."

"Touché. Listen, you son of a gun[20], I'm only going to tell you once. Remember the time I told you I hated losing accounts because it made me feel rejected?[21] Let's just say I've also come to realize there are times I feel threatened by your talent. Sort of an extension of the rejection, if you will. So...maybe I've taken it out on you on occasion by firing you and otherwise holding you back. Tell anyone I admitted that, though, and I'll deny it."

Darrin half wondered if Larry were still under the influence of the truth spell Endora placed on the unicorn pin he'd gifted Samantha with just last week.[22] "*Now* I'm rendered speechless."

"Old man Montgomery has awarded us the advertising for everything Montgomery Industries produces, based on the platform shoes slogan alone. That's upwards of $15 million in billings – the biggest take in our history. So grab that carrot, Darrin, because it dangles no more." Larry strode to the open door and waved someone toward it. "And if you don't believe *me*..."

In walked Howard McMann, Larry's often silent but undeniable partner.

Darrin got to his feet in two seconds flat. This was on par with visiting royalty.

"Hello, Stephensy[23]," McMann said in greeting before stopping himself quizzically. "Sorry, Stephens. I don't know where the sudden urge came from to call you that."

Darrin did. He hoped that's all McMann would remember about the night they nearly put Larry on the unemployment line themselves because of Endora zapping Darrin's ambition into overdrive. "Good to see you again, Mr. McMann," Darrin smiled, deciding not to call him "Howard" as he had done while bespelled.

"It seems, Howard, that Darrin here is having a hard time believing his ship has come in," Larry explained.

"You've been with us, what – eight, eleven, thirteen years?[24] Who pays attention to these things," McMann told Darrin, looking about as baffled as he had when Darrin spouted hippie lingo during that last meeting at the Stephens house. "You've been toiling away in the same job all that time. It's true; we're fixing that today. Just gotta process some paperwork and everything around here will read 'McMann, Tate and Stephens.' Everything. From the logo in the reception area to the stationery." McMann nudged his head toward Larry. "Get a move on that, Tate."

Half deflecting, fully sincere, Larry reached for Darrin's hand. "It's been a long time coming, old friend."

Darrin had one flash of bitterness as he recalled this would have come a lot sooner if Larry hadn't quashed the same promotion because of that printer's error that listed Omega National Bank and Trust's assets as $100.[25] Pushing the thought away, Darrin clasped his friend/adversary's hand. "I'm looking forward to finally being a partner, Larry – Mr. McMann. Advertising, and the public, have changed a lot since I started, and I will do my best to keep taking this agency into the '70s. And beyond."

McMann took his turn shaking Darrin's hand and added a pat

on the shoulder. "I know you will, Stephensy – there I go again. Anybody getting thirsty in here?"

"I'm sure Betty can come up with some of your special coffee," Larry offered, rolling his eyes. Darrin bit his lip thinking of McMann's penchant for joe laced with high-octane rum.[26] "Come on, Howard, let's give our new partner some privacy."

"Gonna be interesting, having a three-man show instead of two," McMann noted as he headed out the door with Larry. "By the way, Tate, I've just now noticed. Why were all our offices remodeled?[27] And who paid for it?"

Larry grimaced as he trailed behind his superior. "That was almost two years ago – have you not been here in that long? I just wanted to keep up with the times, you know, and I thought you wouldn't mind..."

Darrin chuckled watching the scrambling Larry's exit. The more things changed, the more they stayed the same. Except Darrin had a major change to report to a pretty blond witch residing at 1164 Morning Glory Circle. Darrin punched the ten long-distance digits into his new pushbutton phone with an almost uncontainable pride as its circuits connected him to Westport, Connecticut.

2 Witch Nobody Can Deny

Samantha Stephens placed her last dry dish in her cupboard and breathed a sigh of contented relief. As she had done virtually every day of the nearly three thousand days of her marriage, she looked around and turned her thoughts to her to-do list of domestic duties. Dishes? Check. Laundry? Check. Vacuuming? Well, she had just done that the other day, but it wouldn't hurt to run through the house again. Samantha had long ago learned to take a certain satisfaction in an orderly domicile; hers would be the envy of any mortal housewife in Westport. In Connecticut. Maybe in the entire United States.

Pulling the old yet reliable pink vacuum cleaner out of the utility closet and hauling it through the saloon door to the dining room, Samantha couldn't help thinking she was probably the only witch who took any joy in activities like this. How many times had she heard from any and all supernatural relatives that she should be living in a flash of color, in the sparkle of a star?[1] She hardly thought about that now. Taking care of Darrin and the kids had become second nature. And Samantha didn't want it any other way.

Samantha uncoiled the vacuum cord, plugged it in, and was ready to switch on her helpmate when the phone suddenly insisted on her attention. She followed its ringing to its usual place on top of the living room television set and picked up the receiver. "Hello?"

"Sam, you will never guess what just happened."

"For you to call in the middle of the day with a statement like that, either there's been a business triumph, Larry fired you, Mother's at it again with one of her spells, or there's a rhinoceros in your office," Samantha told her husband jovially. "Shall I start playing Twenty Questions?"

"You'll only need one. Remember me mentioning how Larry's been playing it close to the vest about my work on the Montgomery Industries account?" Darrin asked excitedly. "How weird he's been behaving?"

"I'm sure he's assumed the latter about you any number of times," Samantha surmised. "And that's two questions."

"Well, we both win. Allen Montgomery loved my campaign. So much so that McMann just walked in here and made me a full partner. Larry could barely keep it a secret. I am now working for McMann, Tate and Stephens!"

Samantha's jaw dropped. "Oh, sweetheart, that's terrific! I am so, so proud of you."

"Thank you, honey. Maybe Larry finally got the idea I'm indispensable when you zapped up my own agency a few months back," Darrin grinned. "If so, I may have to thank that hippie warlock Alonzo for pushing me out of the firm."[2]

"Or maybe Madame Maruska planted the seed. You know, that theatrical cosmetics maven you thought was Mother?"[3]

"Yeah. I'd forgotten she insisted on making the agency 'McMann, Tate and *Steffens*' before she'd work with us. I don't think the subject ever came up before that."

"'Don't play fair' indeed," Samantha smiled, recalling the slogan that won over Madame Marus-*ka*. "How does it feel, finally getting this promotion?"

"Part of me won't let it sink in. Is it on the up-and-up, is it some plot by one of your parents, cousins, great-uncles? I think it'll be a few days before I can fully embrace it. Plus, whenever I tried to fly out of the nest before," Darrin remarked, "you found a way to plunk me back into it."[4]

"True, though never out of a desire to keep you stuck; I hope you know that. Larry's trigger-happy, but he's the best friend you have. Like Louise is mine. I just would have hated for us to be cut off from them. Besides, it was inevitable Larry would come around on his own one day."

"And now he'll have to deal with me as a partner instead of a subordinate. It's even better than ending up a vice president to his president."

"Weren't you vice president at McMann and Tate when we first met?" Samantha wanted to know. "I have a vague recollection of seeing a plaque with that title on your door then."[5]

"Huh. If I was, it was for so short a time I don't remember."[6]

"There's no question about your title now," Samantha beamed.

"And it's most worthy of celebration. How about getting everyone together for a party? Maybe a week from Saturday night?"

"When you say 'everyone', you mean only everyone with a hundred-year life span, right?" Darrin hoped. "No offense to your friends and relatives, but if we're going to make merry, it should be decidedly non-magical merry-making."

"Oh, you can count on that, sweetheart. I can't tell if my family would find this reason to celebrate or stamp their feet in frustration – and this isn't the time to find out. I'll put them on alert, then start making some calls the mortal way. Please tell Larry and Mr. McMann they are definitely invited."

"I sure will. I should be home at the usual time. Unless that hour-long drive out of Manhattan[7] doubles again, as it is wont to do."

"We wanted to live out of the city," Samantha shrugged. "Feel like anything fancy for dinner tonight?"

"All I feel like is our own private merry-making ahead of the party. After Tabitha and Adam are asleep for the night, that is."

Samantha could practically hear Darrin's wink over the phone. "I'm tempted to twitch Interstate 95 clear for you," Samantha admitted, "but I'll see you when you get here. And Darrin...I really am proud of you."

"I don't know if it's true what they say about 'behind every great man,'" Darrin rhapsodized, "but behind this man there's a great witch. 'Til tonight, then. Love you."

"Love *you*."

Samantha slowly hung up, her mouth again agape. She scanned the living room – every cushion, every lamp, every book on the shelf suddenly took on new meaning. It may be a quarter of an acre of crabgrass, as Mother once put it[8], but it was her crabgrass.

In fact, the first time she had seen this quarter acre had been with Endora. Samantha wistfully remembered how they had magically decorated the empty property, starting outside and working their way in, attracting the attention of across-the-street neighbor – and champion snoop – Gladys Kravitz.[9] Oh, Morning Glory Circle had changed since 1964. The whole world had, really, and those changes were reflected in every corner of this house. Gone was the old olive green woven carpet and the couch with the matching floral pattern; in was tan shag carpet and a kaleidoscope of golds, oranges, and browns, all part of the renovations the Stephens house had undergone a couple of summers ago.[10] Samantha was a little disappointed that she and her family hardly ever used the staircase she thought would be great to install in their new kitchen.[11] But the one thing that hadn't changed under this roof was the love that she and Darrin shared. Scratch that, Samantha thought: their love was probably even stronger.

Samantha wandered to the mirror in the foyer – she never could quite decide whether she wanted a mirror or a painting in that spot[12] – and studied her modern appearance. She smoothed her straight hair, appraised her knit blouse, and decided that she fit into her 1972 surroundings. Not that she hadn't undergone her own renovations over the years. From glamorous to demure, button-down shirts to sleeveless dresses; from bouffants and ponytails to teased 'dos requiring a gallon of hairspray, Samantha had definitely kept up with the times during her marriage.

Of course, Samantha concluded as she wandered past the couch onto the reinvented patio (she still missed the gazebo[13]), she had kept up with any number of times long before her marriage. The Pilgrim chic of her childhood in the late 1600s[14], the Revolutionary War fashions of early witchhood, the impossibly tight corsets and endless petticoats of the Victorian Age. She had especially enjoyed the sudden radical transformation into the flapper period of the 1920s. Indeed, she had been quicksilver[15], a state of being Mother constantly beckoned her to come back to.

Endora had been right about raising Samantha as a proper, well-bred witch.[16] How could one not be that with the Shakespearean Maurice as a father? Samantha learned from her parents an appreciation of art, theatre, ballet...and all mortal fineries. As well as a few fineries mortals hadn't thought of yet. And the travel! Every major city, every emerging country, every interesting place on this planet. And others. Whatever Samantha needed or desired, she could easily bring into existence. It was a good life, and Samantha had known it.

Yet somehow, through every century, Samantha had felt like something was missing. She didn't dare mention it to Maurice of the volcanic temper; when she first became aware of that sense of dissatisfaction, she confided it to Endora, but stopped when her mother reminded her there was nothing a witch could possibly feel dissatisfied about. And so, Samantha blossomed into the kind of witch many warlocks fell for. She dated several, including George[17] and Rollo[18] and Ashley Flynn[19] – excellent prospects all, but fish she ultimately threw back into the sea. Samantha didn't mean to earn a girlhood reputation as a gadabout. It was just that, in these fine specimens of warlock, she couldn't find what she didn't know she was looking for.

As girls, lookalike cousin Serena had told Samantha she had

unusual taste.[20] Samantha pooh-poohed this; she figured that since her parents had abandoned traditional marriage for a more open arrangement[21], this particular apple hadn't fallen far from the magical tree. And on Samantha would have gone, putting mortal jet-setters to shame and needing no jet to do it – until she decided to experiment with moving among mortals. Little things in the beginning: walking in and out of restaurants physically, picking up objects instead of levitating them, flying with the aid of mortal inventions (she'd have ended up on the *Hindenburg* if she could have gotten out of the party Endora insisted she attend). Samantha became fascinated when she discovered there was something fulfilling about having all the powers of the cosmos at her disposal – yet not using them.

Then there was the day Samantha strolled down a busy street in New York City[22], looking all around her, amazed at how easy it had become to pass herself off as a mortal. It might have remained a lark had she not decided to make a detour into the Clark Building – she'd been sure there was a boutique in its lobby whose mannequin wore a dress she'd admired – which put her on a collision course with a dark-haired human male in the revolving door.

A casual enough encounter, prompting the requisite apologies. But later, in a department store, she literally ran into the same man again – twice. Annoyance had turned to laughter, and though this fellow wasn't handsome in the classical sense, there was a warmth in his crooked smile that Samantha found appealing. She agreed to have dinner with him, drawing back when she learned he'd only been in the store to find a gift for his girlfriend, the elite Sheila Sommers. However, Samantha soon saw that her new beau felt about Sheila the way Samantha had felt about Rollo and the rest; an attractive, acceptable enough partner, but falling short of igniting the spark that many – mortal and witch – proclaimed too lofty an ideal to reasonably attain.

Over the next several weeks, Samantha found out there was magic, and there was *magic*. So she became the wife of Darrin Stephens, Missouri-born[23], Manhattan-residing advertising executive.

In retrospect, Samantha conceded she should have told Darrin she was a witch from the start. Maybe she'd sensed in this otherwise wonderful man a resistance to anything out of the ordinary. Darrin clearly wanted to do for himself – a large part of why he rejected Sheila and her rich family.[24] Samantha couldn't be sure Darrin wouldn't reject her as well, but, feeling married people shouldn't keep secrets from each other, she summoned her nerve at the start of their honeymoon and demonstrated her powers for him. If all went south, she could always pop out of their posh hotel room and return to her witchy life, even if it were a life she no longer felt enamored with. Fortunately, Darrin accepted her supernatural status, though it would be years before Samantha could do any magic without him having reactions that ranged from rattled to downright furious. For the most part, Samantha understood. She had agreed to a life of love, honor, and no witchcraft[25], and that was what she tried her very best to give him.

Naturally, passing for a mortal and functioning as one were two entirely different things. Cooking had been especially challenging; Samantha remembered presenting Darrin with plenty of burnt offerings in those early days.[26] Then there was driving; Samantha had gotten used to it, but the letters on the gear shift still baffled her.[27] Despite her initial stumbling, Samantha surprised herself with what a quick study she could be.[28] Occasionally, her first impulse was still to twitch at something, much like being fluent in a second language yet defaulting to one's native tongue. Yet mopping, scrubbing, ironing – she didn't even have to think about those anymore.

While Samantha may have been pleased with her adjustment, Endora always let her know that her own sentiments were exactly the opposite. How many times had Samantha endured Mother railing about a daughter of hers choosing a life of mortal drudgery? Somewhere in these lectures, Samantha had detected a note of genuine concern, particularly regarding the fact that Samantha and Darrin aged differently.[29] It was true: Samantha knew she would outlive Darrin – that one day, hopefully not for decades, she would have to face a life without him. Samantha eventually came to the conclusion it was similar to a mortal having a dog or cat – just because you know you're going to live longer than your companion, do you deny yourself all the love that's there to give and receive?

Of course not. And of course Darrin wasn't Samantha's pet, though her parents often thought of him as such and physically rendered him so. It was several years into her marriage before Samantha realized that, through building a life with Darrin and creating a family with Tabitha and Adam, she had found what she'd always craved during her witchy existence – the stability that Endora and Maurice's open marriage didn't provide.

But the carpet wasn't going to get vacuumed this way. Samantha reached for the cleaner's handle, then stopped herself. Hmm. Maybe she should start inviting mortal family and friends to Darrin's promotion party first before continuing housework. Where was her address book? Had she left it by the other phone in the kitchen?

Yes, there it was, next to the containers of flour and sugar on the counter near the washing machine. As Samantha moved to retrieve it, out of the corner of her eye, she saw her cookie jar disappear.

"Okay, who's the wise witch?"[30] Samantha asked of the ether. Yet, instinctively, she knew her near-omniscient family couldn't be bothered with a couple dozen cookies. And Tabitha wasn't due home from school for an hour... "Oh, Adam," Samantha said to herself, looking at the ceiling. He must be up from his nap.

Samantha had to get these calls made. But she couldn't do that and keep an eye on Adam at the same time. So, as she had many times before in similar situations, she took a breath and called out:

"Yoo-hoo! Esmeralda!"

An apron materialized, hovering effortlessly. A disembodied voice accompanied it. "Yes, Samantha?"

Samantha let out a half amused sigh. "Esmeralda, you know perfectly well Darrin isn't here. And that he's not nearly as averse to your presence as he was when you first started with us."[31]

The rest of Esmeralda popped in with the apron. "I know, but since I conjured up George and Martha Washington the last time I was here[32], I thought I should play it safe."

"Relax. With it being Easter this weekend, as long as you don't sneeze up the Easter Bunny – or anyone else associated with the holiday! – you'll be fine. Would you mind looking in on Adam while I make some phone calls? He's experimenting with his powers again," Samantha added, indicating the missing cookie jar.

"Aw...isn't he wonderful?" Esmeralda marveled.

"Yes," Samantha allowed. "When his powers were tested, I told Darrin it would be harmful to forbid Adam to use them[33] – something Tabitha reminds me of all the time. Cosmos knows we forbad her. Now, instead of outright telling the kids they can't practice witchcraft, we're trying to teach them there are times and places for it. This just isn't one of them."

"I'd be happy to dash upstairs and make sure Adam doesn't get a tummy ache from too many cookies." As the yoo-hoo maid turned to see to her duty, she stumbled and nearly fell, grabbing the kitchen island for support. "Oh, *dear!*" she exclaimed.

Samantha rushed to her domestic's side. "Are you all right?"

"I will be," Esmeralda assured, struggling to stand up straight. "It's just these shoes that Mr. Stephens gave me – what did he call them, 'platforms'?"

"Mmm-hmm. From his latest account."

"I know they're supposed to be fashionable and flunky – "

"I think you mean 'funky'."

"Whatever they are, they're hard to walk in!"

Samantha wrinkled her nose merrily. "In that case, I think it would be all right if you popped directly into Adam's room. And incidentally, those very shoes are the reason that Darrin is being made a full partner at McMann, Tate, and Stephens!"

"He is? That's super!" Esmeralda's expression became a blank. "What does that mean?"

Samantha only said, "It means you can have more platforms if you want them."

"Is there a spell for mastering these things? They'd certainly catch the eye of Ramon Verona."[34]

"Your warlock crush? Is he back on the market?"

Esmeralda shrugged. "No...but you never know when he might be."

"Come to think of it, Esmeralda, you've never said what happened with your old boyfriend, Ferdy. I thought you two got engaged last year."[35]

"Um...we did, but..." Esmeralda stammered.

"I'm just confused, because when we saw you in Pisa months later, you went out with Darrin's client, Count Bracini.[36] Remember him?"

Esmeralda hesitantly offered a sheepish confession. "Oh... things were going very well with Ferdy...until I sneezed while we were necking and accidentally turned him into a kissing fish. He's swimming around Thailand or somewhere; hopefully I'll remember how to change him back before some tuna boat catches him. Now, I'd better get upstairs if I'm going to catch Adam."

"Well, I'm glad you're on duty again. After you regained your confidence doing that magic show a while back[37], you left as if you weren't working for us anymore. So I wasn't sure what your intentions were when you took the kids to the park the very next week."[38]

"Why face the world alone when you actually have friends somewhere?" Esmeralda successfully zapped up a bottle of Pepto-Bismol. "Adam may need this. See you in a while!" And with that, Esmeralda and her platforms were gone.

Samantha tittered to herself. Back on track, she made a beeline for the kitchen phone and grabbed the address book, thumbing through it. "I'd love to invite some folks we haven't seen for a while..." Suddenly she inhaled sharply, remembering. "But not before taking care of my un-guest list. Mother?"

The kitchen remained quiet. No formidable red-haired witch

popping in wearing one variety or another of global costumes. But Samantha didn't feel like playing hide-and-seek. "Esmeralda?" Samantha called up the neglected staircase. "I have to run out for a minute...will you keep Adam company and fix Tabitha her snack when she gets home from school?"

"No problem!" came the voice from Adam's room. "And remaining cookies accounted for!"

Samantha gently tossed the address book on the counter. "If the mountain won't come to Mohammed..." Snapping both fingers, the ordinarily ordinary housewife popped out.

* * *

Somewhere in a vast spiral of colors, clouds, and stars[39], Endora stood in front of a mirror that hung in mid-air. Though whether this atmosphere counted as air was doubtful. After centuries – ahem, millennia – of breathing in the best the universe had to offer[40] (just one more advantage of a witch's metabolism), Endora could hardly stand descending to Earth anymore. Not because she minded visiting her mortal-marrying daughter, but because of that icky brown oxygen mixture humans filled their lungs with. The world had been such a lovely place just a couple hundred years ago; how did these limited creatures manage to do so much damage in so short a time? At least humans were good at *something*.

No sooner than Endora noticed she was still wearing her usual green-and-pink flying suit did she zap herself into a hot pink rubber ensemble with huge matching sunglasses. Breakfast in Sweden, and now Endora was about to meet up with a contingent of British Royals in Africa.

"Mother?" bounced Samantha's voice off the atmospheric continuum.[41] Since her daughter's tone didn't seem especially urgent, Endora waved the summons away. She'd pop in on Samantha later. Chances were, all she wanted to know was if Endora had cast a spell on Durwood. And Endora hadn't. Not today, anyway.

Endora wandered around her ethereal abode, knowing there was something else she needed for this excursion. Only the finest surrounded her, naturally – Louis XIV *everything* was still considered highly fashionable in her circles.[42] Even Endora's lovely little tuxedo cat, Shadow, lolled in a bed made of pink cashmere and daintily raised her paw to zap up a jewel-encrusted saucer full of the richest cream.

Unlike Samantha's closet-sized excuse for a domicile, there was no need for a television or radio or record player. Any entertainment could be magically piped in, and there wasn't much to keep up with in the mortal world unless it affected witches – which hadn't been much of a concern since about 1700. Still...there was something about Samantha's house, over and above the fact that Samantha and Tabitha and Adam were there. A coziness, an intimacy? Endora couldn't place it, and would have denied it to anyone who had the gall to explore it.

Oh, well. Certainly whatever she needed in Africa, she would just materialize when she got there. Endora was about to raise her arm to initiate her departure when Samantha suddenly appeared next to the ornate tortoiseshell bureau.

"Oh, good, I caught you at home," Samantha said with just a hint of sarcasm.

"My darling daughter!" Endora exclaimed. "This *is* a red-letter day. So rare that you make the trip here when you want to see me. Ironic, considering this was your home for centuries."

"It's not like that'll ever slip my mind, Mother. If it'll make you feel better, yes, it's been a while since I've been...*up* this way. Didn't you hear me calling?"

"I considered sending one of those response balloons you get such a kick out of,"[43] Endora relayed gleefully. "But I can't stop to talk now, dear. I'm whitewater rafting in Zambia. And I should have been there ten – oh, I know what I'm forgetting!" Endora conjured up a large purple paddle. "I assume they'll provide the raft. Care to join me?" Endora stopped herself. "Oh, you don't still get seasick, do you? I'll never forget how green you were when we helped open the Panama Canal..."

"And that was before Dramamine," Samantha said, scrunching her face. "Look, I won't keep you from your African outing. I just wanted to share a bit of news with you – and a request. Darrin's been made a full partner. From now on, the agency will be McMann, Tate, and Stephens!"

"Who, what, and where?"

"You know what I'm talking about," Samantha scolded. "You've been to Darrin's office enough. Causing shenanigans, usually."

"All right, What's-His-Name's[44] been promoted. What am I supposed to do, zap up a parade?" Endora's eyes brightened. "Disneyland is about to open their Main Street Electrical Parade. I could have them do a dry run in his reception area."

"This is a very big deal, Mother, for Darrin and for me. Can't you at least fake being impressed?"

"Impressed? Oh, Samantha, that husband of yours should have

owned that whole building by now. And really – coming up with trite phrases to manipulate people into buying what they probably don't want anyway? He's not curing world hunger or anything."

"Sometimes I wish there was an incantation for that."

"There is. But as you yourself have pointed out on more than one occasion, spells affecting mortals on a mass scale go against our ethics.[45] Besides, if we did it all for them, they'd never learn anything. Of course, that implies they actually *do* learn..."

"Mother, I did not set foot on Cloud 8[46] to start a debate on mortal cognitive abilities. I just wanted to tell you about Darrin's promotion...and about the party I'm throwing to celebrate it."

"A party! You might recall when Webster made his dictionary, he was going to put my picture next to that word. Would have had to be hand-drawn, though; those early cameras were abominable. Oh, mortal parties are categorically dull...but I suppose I could make an exception for McMann, Tate, and Stubbins. What time, dear?"

"No time, at least not for you."

"You mean you don't want me there to mark Durwood's infinitesimal bit of advancement?"

"If you'd like to congratulate him, I'm sure he'd appreciate it. But it'll have to be done privately. The house will be filled with mortals – and we could really do without another evening of magical cacophony, especially on your part. I'm going to have a very serious talk with the kids, and I'd be eternally grateful if you could use those superlative powers of yours to let the rest of the family know to keep clear next Saturday night as well."

"Come now, Samantha! Don't you think I have better things to do than play Witches' Postal Service?"

"Admittedly, 'neither snow nor rain nor heat nor gloom of night' fits us better," Samantha grinned. "Please, Mother. It's just one evening."

"I suppose if I don't comply I'll never get to Zambia," Endora pouted. "All right, Samantha. The things I do for you."

Samantha hugged her mother and gave her a kiss on the cheek. "Thank you. I just want the party to be perfect. By the way, whitewater rafting? Since when have you taken that up?"

"Darling, it's going to be an Olympic sport in Munich this summer; didn't you know?" Samantha shook her head. "If I like it, there's still a few months to ensure myself a place on the team. Now, I simply have to fly. I will send out the word to everyone as soon as I get back." Endora placed two fingers astride her nose. "Witches' honor."[47]

"Thank you. Have fun. Don't capsize out there!"

"That's what your father told me the day I was planning to set sail on the *Titanic*," Endora confessed. "You'll have your witchless party. Though with Derek there, 'witless' is more like it. Ta, dear!" Endora and her paddle vanished into thin air.

"My witchless party," Samantha said to herself as she gave Shadow a parting pat. "Good!"[48]

The next moment, the nebulous brights and darks of Cloud 8 were left to mingle in silence.

3 Répondez, S'il Vous Plâit

"Aw, that's too bad, Kermit! You've been like a bat in a cave since you left to head up Wayne, West and Adams," Darrin said as he absently tried to uncoil his phone cord. "Yeah, Tabitha and Adam are doing great; thanks for asking. How are Robin and Alfred adjusting to the new school? Glad to hear that, old man. Listen, we'll miss you. Let us know when we can collect that rain check. Samantha sends her love to Gertrude! 'Bye for now, Kerm."[1]

Darrin hung up, thinking how great it was that Kermit and Gertrude were still married. They had gotten together not long after Darrin and Samantha had tied the knot themselves – with Samantha's encouragement. Darrin remembered he hadn't been the most congenial about that courtship because he'd been sure Gertrude wasn't human. He didn't know to this day if Gertrude was part of the coven, but he'd realized that was unimportant ages ago. It wasn't such a bad club to belong to, at least on the less chaotic days.

Grabbing a manila folder and rising from his desk, Darrin strolled past the reception area, catching a glimpse of the building maintenance crew prying off the staid "McMann and Tate" placard he'd looked at for years and readying to replace it with the funkier up-to-date design of "McMann, Tate, and Stephens." Even having had the weekend to absorb it, the news still hadn't completely registered.

Larry emerged from the adjoining hallway. "Admiring Wilson's handiwork?"

"Keith designed that? I like it. Very bold."

"He knows what's 'today' even more than you do. McMann was very keen on having Keith revamp our logo. After I suggested it to him, of course."

"Keith in his office?"

"Just came from there. You two almost done brainstorming on the York and Sargent account?"

"Yeah, I've got a few tweaks I want to run by him. Plus deliver an invite to the party. Have you told Louise yet?"

"Oh, yes, she's all excited. And that scent in the air is my credit cards melting from her not being able to decide what dress to buy and charging all of them instead."

Darrin chuckled. "Louise always has been a decathlon shopper.[2] I'd better get this to Keith," he added, holding up his folder. "Will you make sure that Mr. McMa – I mean, Howard – knows he's invited? And Margaret[3], too, of course."

"Sure thing. Geez, I've talked to McMann more in the past few days than I have in the past few years," Larry noted. "I'm not sure I like it."

"Hey, you can always make me your liaison."

"Consider it your first assignment as partner. I'm off to the art department."

"See ya later, Lar."

Darrin ventured down the hallway on the other end of the agency, an area to which he admittedly hadn't paid too many visits. He was stopped no less than four times by well-wishers and their handshakes and back pats and kudos. Finally, feeling as though he had just chopped his way through an appreciative jungle, Darrin arrived at the slightly ajar door of one Keith Wilson.[4]

Keith looked up, hearing Darrin's gentle rapping. "Come on in, D!" Keith said exuberantly, bouncing up from his desk and extending a hand. "What's with this knocking stuff, man? Now that you're a partner I thought you'd just barge on in like our friend Tate."

Darrin bypassed the handshake and slipped Keith some skin instead. "I start doing that, you have my personal permission to smack me upside the head with your guitar."

"Naw, that hard head of yours'd put a serious dent in my axe. Dorothy may not mind," Keith laughed, "though she's been real patient about me jamming with the guys in our garage. Whatcha got, more on our York and Sargent gig?"

Darrin handed Keith the folder. "Yeah, just some additions to what we went over last week. Larry set our presentation for the 14th, so we might as well get straight on all this early."

"A taskmaster already," Keith teased. "But we'll knock their socks off. How's Sam?"

"She's a busy girl, I'll tell you that much."

"Yeah, I thought I heard some rumblings at the water cooler about an upcoming soirée. What, my invitation get lost in the mail?"

"You're looking at it. Saturday night at seven. Make sure to bring Dorothy."

"And Lisa?"

"Tabitha would sulk for weeks if you didn't. Too bad we don't all live in the same town – Tabitha and Lisa would love to go to school together."

"Don't I know it. I think they're over that whole 'sisters' thing," Keith surmised, thinking back to two Christmases ago when the girls pledged their sibling solidarity, "but Lisa still talks about Tabitha all the time." Keith picked that moment to return to his desk so Darrin wouldn't see the quizzical look that had come over his face.

"I'm glad we're still able to bring them together so much. Besides, maybe the girls can entertain Adam while we grown-ups are entertaining ourselves."

"Especially if the champagne flows the way I think it will," Keith added knowingly. "This shindig'll be hotter than what the secretarial pool is planning here at the office for sure...if you'll allow me the pleasure of bringing some of my records. Me and Dorothy've been picking up some really with-it discs lately."

"I'll tell Sam to warm up the phonograph," Darrin smiled. "I'd better get back to my office before Larry changes his mind about putting that new sign up. Brilliant logo, by the way."

"I never argue with the muse. She and I were designing that for a friend, after all."

That moved Darrin. "Let me know what you think of the campaign suggestions, and we'll look forward to seeing you all on Saturday."

"Cool. I'll give Dottie a call right now and make sure she Magic Markers it into our calendar," Keith winked.

"Right on." Darrin flashed Keith a peace sign as he left.

Keith took a satisfied breath as he reached for his phone. Spinning the rotary dial appropriately, he couldn't help noticing how easy and comfortable his family's friendship with the Stephenses was. Darrin was practically the only co-worker who had developed a real bond with him, who wasted no time in suggesting they bring their daughters together.[5] To be fair, Larry, whom Keith had expected would be a member of the old boys' club, had once told a client to stuff it when said client wanted Darrin off his account, thinking he had a black wife in Dorothy. Thanks to Darrin and Larry, Keith felt exceptionally appreciated at McMann and Tate, and he had no doubt it would be the same at McMann, Tate, and Stephens.

Unlike too many people, from ad execs to subway riders to grocery store clerks, the Stephenses always treated the Wilsons with respect despite their difference in skin pigment. For the girls particularly, that difference simply wasn't a factor. So why did it still bother him a bit that Lisa had said –

"Hello?" Dorothy's voice filtered through the receiver.

"Listen to how much sugar comes across in just that one word," Keith greeted.

"Mmm-hmm. I know you're not calling in the middle of the day all smooth and what-not to tell me you're working through dinner again," Dorothy sassed playfully.

"Woman, do I always call you with news like that?" Not a word. "Okay, maybe I do. But not this time. Remember I told you about Darrin getting promoted?"

"Of course! He really deserves it."

"Sure does. Sam thinks so, too, 'cuz she's throwin' him a big ol' wingding Saturday night. And we're all invited."

"Oh, honey, that's wonderful!" Dorothy exclaimed. "I don't see enough of Samantha. And I love how close Lisa and Tabitha have become." This time Keith was silent. "Don't you agree?" Dorothy added purposefully.

"Yeah, they're tight, and it's great, but..."

"Are you ever gonna let that go? I've told you a hundred times, Lisa was just funnin' when she said Sam and Tabitha are witches. It's kid stuff, like playing Barbies. Or Mary Tyler Moore."

"I just don't know that witches are the best role models for our daughter."

"You'd prefer Shaft?" Dorothy joked. "Let's just go to Sam's party, toast Darrin's success with something exotic and delicious, and let the kids be kids."

"You got it," Keith declared...though he wasn't entirely convinced.

* * *

Frank Stephens squeezed the receiver so hard he was amazed he didn't break it. "Hey, Sam, that's sensational!" the boisterous man bellowed. "Well, you bet we'll be there! I'm not at all surprised – when Darrin was a kid, he'd sit at breakfast coming up with slogans for cream of wheat. Not that we could get him to eat the stuff," Frank guffawed. "Oh, Phyllis will be ecstatic. I'll tell her when she comes back in from talking to that fool bird. You believe she still uses that name Tabitha gave him – what is it, Mr. Marvelous? I've never been able to convince Phyllis that Tabitha didn't have a full conversation with him.[6] Anyway, tell Darrin since he's a partner now maybe he can find his ol' Dad something to do in that agency of his. Even in retirement you can only go on so many cruises! Sure. See you then, Sam."

Frank couldn't have been prouder if Darrin had become President of the United States. Maybe that was a bad analogy; Frank didn't entirely trust Nixon. Hopefully there would never be another president who made enemies of the press or engaged in espionage for political advantage. At any rate, Frank was secretly thrilled that his surname would be emblazoned on a New York advertising agency. He'd once had his own ideas about becoming an ad man; marketing ideas had swirled in Frank's head that time Darrin created a dancing bear, though that didn't pan out.[7] Neither did Frank's concepts for an alcohol-dispensing vending machine.[8] Both products had been ways of living out the dream he'd shelved when taking a job at General Motors' St. Louis Truck Assembly after it opened in the 1920s, not long before proposing to Phyllis. Making Chevrolet trucks was steady work that fed and clothed his boy, not to mention put him through school, and Frank's decades at the plant allowed him and Phyllis to live comfortably now that they were in Westport.

Hard to believe now that Phyllis had spent years unable to decide whether to put down roots here![9] She'd claimed she wanted to be near Darrin after his unexpected marriage to Samantha, but every time they tried to settle on the East Coast, Phyllis would get uncomfortable with its faster pace and insist on returning to Missouri; thankfully, Frank had obeyed his instinct to keep the house back home and simply rent here. This three-year stint in Connecticut was the longest so far, and Frank shared Phyllis' enthusiasm for watching grandkids Tabitha and Adam grow up. Yet it seemed like Phyllis' already peculiar behavior became more pronounced whenever she was around their son's family.

Couldn't be helped, Frank figured – Phyllis did have a departed sister who thought she was a lighthouse.[10] And he'd heard enough stories about their grandmother, who allegedly had supernatural powers.[11] So it wasn't a complete surprise when Phyllis insisted she'd seen Samantha while they were vacationing in an English castle[12], nor was it the time Phyllis claimed Samantha's voice came out after she spoke.[13] The instances where Phyllis was sure she was losing her mind[14], however, and announced she possessed powers of her own[15]

– those were more cause for concern. Oh, well. Frank loved Phyllis regardless, and they were getting older. Who knew how senility might affect *him*?

Maybe it already was. Whenever Frank remembered how he had seen an apple floating to Tabitha[16] and a pair of glasses floating in mid-air[17], he did his best to bury the memories. Today he did it by calling out to his wife. "Phyllis? How about giving that bird some privacy? I've got some exciting news for you."

Phyllis strolled in from the patio, regal as ever. "What is it, Frank? Oh – Mr. Marvelous says hello. Actually, 'Hi, there, baby.' For some reason, he's never mastered 'hello'."

"Forget his feathers and think of the feather in our son's cap. Samantha just called: Darrin's been promoted. His agency is becoming McMann, Tate...and *Stephens*."

Phyllis' face brightened considerably. "Oh, it's just what I've dreamed of for our son!" Phyllis wasn't given to extravagant displays of affection, but she pulled Frank into a single firm hug. "It's about time they gave him a chance for advancement over there. Poor baby."

"Baby? Come on, Phyllis, he's forty-four.[18] Listen, we're invited to Darrin and Sam's party Saturday night – unless we've got something else going on."

"What something else? I'm home almost all the time since I stopped giving two days a week to the League of Women Volunteers.[19] Did Samantha say if we need to make anything?"

"I guess we just make tracks – to their place."

Phyllis frowned. "Is Samantha's mother going to be there?"

"How should I know?" Frank replied, exasperated. "You're not still jealous of her. Phyllis, I flirted with her once, when she and I first met.[20] Can't you forget it?"

"Memories linger, dear," Phyllis remarked snidely. "Frank...do you realize we've barely seen Darrin and Samantha the past twelve months?"[21]

"Sure, but Darrin just earned a promotion. You know he had to put the time in to do that."

"And Samantha always talks about how busy she is with the PTA[22] now that Tabitha's in school. What took so long to enroll her?[23] I don't know that I believe Samantha saying she changed her mind about home schooling."

"What difference does it make? We're going to see everyone and congratulate Darrin in person. Ya know, Saturday is still four days away. Might be enough time to come up with some new products Darrin and I could go in on together. I'll bring him a slew of ideas!"

Phyllis stared at the heavens. "I'll bring the sherry."[24]

* * *

Louise Tate hefted two-and-a-half-year-old Adam Stephens in her arms. "My, you're getting to be so heavy, aren't you! Such a great big boy now." A breathless Samantha made her way out of the kitchen to meet her friend and son in the living room. "I can't believe how fast he's growing, Samantha," Louise gushed.

"Thanks for watching him for a moment. He's at that stage where he takes off running as soon as his feet hit the floor."

"Jonathan did the same thing. Makes me miss him at this age! I don't miss the diapers, though. So, do I dare bring this tyke down to earth?"

"We'll have to risk it. Set him down next to that mountain of Hot Wheels cars and let's see how long that lasts."

"You know, Samantha, it's too bad Tabitha only started public school this year," Louise said as Adam's bum met the carpet. "She and Jonathan could have been in the same grade together. But don't mention that to Jon. He's started that phase where he thinks girls are yucky."

"That'll be over in a few years, tops," Samantha commented distractedly. "Louise, how is it Thursday already? Oh – don't let me forget to thank Larry for ordering the food for us. Without that I'd never be able to pull this together in two days."

"Honey, don't thank Larry," Louise said, waving her hand. "He's making Mr. McMann pay for it."

"And people say there's no consistency in life." The frazzled Samantha unconsciously paced in front of the couch. "Let's see... Larry confirmed the food, I've pretty well invited everyone on the list...I feel like I'm forgetting something. I know I'm forgetting something."

"Decorating, dear, remember? The reason you asked me to come over?"

"Wow, I'm sorry, Louise," Samantha told her long-time friend as she brushed back her hair with her hand. "I've put together hundreds of dinners for McMann and Tate clients...a few dozen parties...but this one – I just want this one to be perfect. I feel like balloons aren't spectacular enough. There should be some kind of theme. What would really say 'partner'?"

"Well, you could string up lassos for cowboy partners, hearts and diamonds for bridge partners – or stars and stripes for the kind of partners on *Love, American Style*."

"I use the latter example, I'll have to stash the kids in the attic and buy a Twister mat."

"Okay, how about this – Darrin's on his way up, so maybe you could get helium balloons and tie them to his easel, let them lift it off the ground..."

The doorbell cut through the advertising wives' blue-skying.

Samantha peeked behind the couch; wonder of wonders, Adam was still entranced by the little metal vehicles.

"You're being very good. Would you keep being good and mind Aunt Louise while I answer the door?"

"Yes, Mommy," Adam answered, nodding his head full of dark curls.

Louise patted Samantha's shoulder as she approached the door, then knelt down to distract her son. "What do we have here?"

Samantha was more than a little surprised to find a more-than-familiar woman on her doorstep:

Gladys Kravitz.

As if no time had passed since her arrival on Morning Glory Circle, Samantha observed a measuring cup in her neighbor's hand.[25] "Why, Mrs. Kravitz! Darrin and I wondered if you'd moved. We haven't seen you or Mr. Kravitz in...well, it's gotta be a year or so."[26]

"Hi there, Mrs. Stephens," the bubbly red-head replied, just a hint of suspicion permanently locked in her brow. "Abner decided he wasn't enjoying retirement, so he rented one of those motorhomes and we drove all over the country. Then right after he won the Daily Double and bought this with his winnings – " Gladys flashed the diamond ring that she had already called Samantha about the day Abner gave it to her[27] – "we spent a few weeks with Abner's sister Harriet in Passaic. Remember her?"

"Harriet! Now that's a blast from the past. She was here just after Tabitha was born, if I remember right."[28]

"She remembers you, too, Mrs. Stephens! Boy, does she remember," Gladys added, looking away slightly. Samantha decided not to pursue it. If memory served, Harriet had seen a few witchy things of her own during her long-ago visit and Samantha was sure the snoopy Kravitz in-laws had compared notes.

"So, what can I get for you, Mrs. Kravitz? Something the corner store ran out of?"[29]

Gladys suddenly thought of the cup in her hand. "Oh! Yeah! I'm making Abner some *kourabiedes* – Greek sugar cookies! But we only got back yesterday and I haven't had a chance to go shopping."

"Not to worry; we've got sugar to spare. Come on in and I'll fill this up for you." Samantha saw Louise rise where Adam was still busy playing on the floor, hopefully too distracted to test his powers in front of her or Gladys. "Louise, you've met our neighbor from across the street, haven't you? Gladys Kravitz, this is Louise Tate, the wife of Darrin's boss."

"Darrin's partner now," Louise lovingly corrected.

"This'll just take a jiffy. Be good, Adam!" With that, Samantha scurried into the kitchen.

"I do feel we've met before," Louise told Gladys after an awkward silence, "though it escapes me exactly when."

"I think I recognize you, too," Gladys surmised. "What is this about Mr. Stephens being a partner?"

"Didn't Samantha tell you? Darrin got bumped up to partner with my husband at the agency."

"Isn't that wonderful! I'll be sure to congratulate him next time I see him. Abner got promoted at his factory once, when we were first married. He went from sorting nuts on the conveyor belt to sorting bolts."

Louise smiled as though she had Vaseline on her teeth, hiding her relief when Samantha emerged with a heaping cup for Gladys.

"Here we are! Now you can make your cora – curry – well, it's all Greek to me," Samantha tried to joke.

"Thanks much, Mrs. Stephens. I've been going through a Greek phase ever since Harriet took us to this Mediterranean restaurant in Hackensack," Gladys announced as Samantha walked her to the door. "Next week I'm going to attempt *baklava*."

"Yes, I know how you like your phases." Samantha slipped, hoping Gladys would let that one pass. She could still taste the soybean brownies Gladys had foisted on her and Darrin during her vegetarian period.[30] "Please tell Mr. Kravitz we said hello."

"If I can get a word in while he plays chess with himself[31], I will. Oh, and he'll be happy to hear about Mr. Stephens' promotion. Mrs. Tate told me."

"We're all pretty happy about it. Louise and I were just trying to figure out what decorations to put up for our party – " Samantha eyed Louise, whose look said, "You opened that door, honey, not me." Samantha's first impulse was to wiggle her way out of inviting Gladys; this was a woman who had told reporters[32] and soapbox derby committees[33] about the witchcraft she'd witnessed. Yet, this was also a woman who had been a part of the tapestry of the Stephenses' lives ever since they moved to the neighborhood. Samantha could barely believe what issued forth from her mouth next. "Mrs. Kravitz...if you're not busy Saturday night, why don't you and Mr. Kravitz come by for our celebration?" Louise's expression stayed diplomatically neutral.

The normally talkative Gladys had trouble putting a sentence together. She could think of only a handful of times she'd been invited to a Stephens occasion. "Well, Mrs. Stephens, if you're sure..."

"I insist. The festivities start at 7:00. And it'll be a little dressy, so don't be afraid to gussy up."

"Don't be afraid? Mrs. Stephens, I haven't gussied since LBJ!"

"Then we'll see you Saturday. And let me know how your Greek dessert comes out."

"I'll bring some – if Abner doesn't eat them all first!"

Louise watched Gladys skitter excitedly across the street before Samantha closed the door. "Samantha, I think now I remember when I met her. It was here," Louise realized, gesturing toward the living room. "Didn't she go on at length about human frogs?"[34]

"So I've been toad." Samantha snickered to Louise, hoping "human" frog Fergus F. Finglehoff and his girlfriend Phoebe were happy in the swamp.

* * *

On the subject of frogs, Maudie Peabody carefully eyed her second grade class as they finished up their vocabulary worksheets, particularly one still relatively new student she had once labeled a "frog freak."[35] What was it about that Tabitha Stephens? First she absconded with a frog from the class terrarium, then she broke records acing a standardized test in thirty seconds before rattling off answers to aptitude questions most adults couldn't answer.[36] Naturally curious, Mrs. Peabody had followed Tabitha home and caught her levitating a ball. The girl's mother had declared they were witches, then backtracked and said the family were magicians – which caused the principal, Mr. Roland, to insist on Mrs. Peabody taking a sabbatical she narrowly talked him out of. Since then, the child "prodigy" had progressed in her schoolwork as any 7-year-old might have. But her teacher smelled a most definite rat.

Ringing interrupted her thought process and delighted the two dozen students. "That's the lunch bell. Class dismissed. Turn your worksheets in at my desk as you leave." No wonder Mrs. Peabody was a little grumpy. For her, "lunch" usually meant sneaking half a sandwich in between getting ready for the first grade class which occupied her afternoons.

Tabitha, not needing supernatural powers to tell that her teacher constantly had her under surveillance, politely delivered her paper and got out of there as fast as she could.

Boy, being a witch was great, but it sure caused problems. After her dubious beginnings at Towner's Elementary, though, Tabitha was determined to keep the promise she made to her mother – and especially her daddy – that she would conduct herself like a regular mortal kid.

Which wasn't always easy. "Hey, Dumb Name Girl," a boy called to Tabitha in the hallway. Anxious to avoid another confrontation, Tabitha tried to pick up her pace. But the boy jumped in front of her.

"What do you want, Charlton Rollnick?"[37] Tabitha's defenses went up. She'd already gotten in trouble for retaliating against Charlton's bullying by turning him into a bullfrog. Yet she'd zap him again if she had to.

"Bet you think you're smarter than me now that you skipped to the second grade while I'm still in first."[38]

"I didn't want to skip," Tabitha insisted. "Everyone made me."

"Oh." In that one syllable, there was a distinct change in Charlton's tone.

"I gotta go eat lunch now," Tabitha said, waving her bag and taking a step to escape.

"It was more fun when we were in the same class," Charlton confessed. "None of the other girls like terrariums like you do."

"I guess."

"Listen," Charlton said, his posture stiffening. "My mom's making corn dogs for dinner tomorrow night. You could...come over if you want to. I mean, because of you, I don't have to take piano lessons anymore."

Tabitha considered this. Until she remembered what tomorrow was. "I can't, Charlton. My parents are throwing a party on account of my daddy got promoted at work. I'm gonna get to see my friend Lisa. She's my...*tem-po-ra-ry* sister.[39] You wouldn't understand. Plus I'll probably have to watch my baby brother."

"Yeah, okay," Charlton answered quickly. "More corn dogs for me." If the kids were older, they might have known to define the awkwardness between them as a "pregnant pause." Charlton unpaused it. "You go on the jungle gym?"

"Sometimes."

"I could show you how to get across the parallel bars faster."

Tabitha shrugged. "Okay."

Charlton and Tabitha exited the hallway side-by-side. Which, in their absence, became a quiet place, as most of the kids were outside eating.

Quiet except for the slight shuffle of a sensible shoe.

Mrs. Peabody had heard Charlton's voice outside her door and instinctively sprang into action, assuming trouble. She would have retreated from the doorway once she saw the Rollnick boy was discoursing amicably with her unofficial star pupil, but her ears pricked up when Tabitha leaked intel about her parents' party. It occurred to Mrs. Peabody that, as a good educator, she was responsible for assigning homework. And she knew just at whose home she wanted to work tomorrow night.

4 The Party of the First Part

"Cheers!" The Stephens living room was garlanded with raised glasses. The Stephenses, Tates, and Kravitzes all offered champagne salutes; Keith and Dorothy Wilson[1] clinked their flutes with those of Darrin's parents, while kids Tabitha and Adam Stephens, along with Lisa Wilson and Jonathan Tate[2], were allowed to toast with cola. Long-time secretary Betty Wilson[3] was there alongside two of her former agency co-workers, Betty Ashmont[4] and Betty Moorehead[5]. The mood was giddy, and Darrin felt a little embarrassed by all the attention, yet he also felt proud – and very loved.

"It's probably cliché to launch into *For He's A Jolly Good Fellow*," Larry Tate bubbled, "and shouting 'Hip, hip, hooray!' would be cornier still. So I will only say it's a new era for McMann and Tate – mostly because we're having to add 'Stephens' to the name. This party is for you, Darrin, and in the spirit of festiveness, I feel compelled to tell you what Howard McMann told me when I became partners with him."

"Which was?" Darrin asked.

"Don't mess this up." Chuckling echoed among the adults. "Okay, that's not exactly how he said it, but there are children in the room." The laughter became more hearty and ribald.

"I always said Larry would celebrate anything[6]," Louise commented quietly, leaning toward Samantha. "This is definitely one of his better reasons for it."

"So," Larry continued, "another toast. To McMann, Tate, and Stephens – and many years of fruitful success."

"McMann, Tate, and Stephens!" the gathering roared. More clinking, more sipping, more smiling.

"And let's not forget revenue. We're not in the ad game for our health!" Larry was both kidding and serious, but those who knew him were aware this was simply how Mr. Tate expressed himself. "Now, come on, you son of a gun – any words of wisdom for the adoring crowd?"

"Speech! Speech!" Frank Stephens yelled.

The group egged Darrin on. He took a hesitant step or two – but it was Tabitha who nudged him into the center of the circle. Darrin offered his daughter a gentle nod and took the full glass of bubbly handed to him by Larry. "You guys are too much. I don't really know what to say, except that I'm rarin' to go. I've often thought about what I would do as a full partner, and I want to thank Larry and Mr. McMann – where are Howard and Margaret, anyway?" Darrin's query was met with shrugs. "I'm very grateful for this chance – I have to admit I started thinking it would never happen. I half expect to go into work Monday with the company logo back the way it was," Darrin admitted, peering at a mock-aghast Larry.

"Not while I got somethin' to say about it," Keith interjected, triggering another series of guffaws.

"Other than that..." Darrin looked right at Phyllis and Frank. "Mom, Dad...thanks for always encouraging me to follow my dream, especially back in Missouri when I was a kid. I know you wanted me to become a doctor, Mom, but rest assured, in this business you see a lot of different ailments...the ones you get from the stress."

Darrin's parents smiled while the other guests tittered. Larry nodded knowingly.

"And Sam..." Darrin began. "You too, Tabitha...Adam...I know I've worked a lot of long hours. I've missed too many dinners and I haven't always been here for you the way I'd have liked to be. But you've always been with me, and every victory I've had is because of you. We've been through some crazy stuff, I don't have to tell you" – Samantha did her best not to react much in the mostly mortal crowd – "but I'd do it all over again, and I'm looking forward to starting this new chapter with the best family a man could have."

The ladies, especially, joined in a chorus of "Awww"s. Tabitha came forward and hugged her daddy, while Samantha, who was holding Adam, blew her husband a kiss with her free hand.

"All right, enough of this schmaltz," Larry jokingly reprimanded. "Do we or do we not have a party to start?"

"And I am just the man to make that presentation!" Keith made a beeline to the hi-fi, where he had stationed a hefty spool of 45s. He stacked several of the 7-inch discs on the record changer; as the first one dropped onto the turntable and the tone arm found its position,

Keith announced, "Get ready to groove, everybody. We're gonna start things off with The Politicians, featuring McKinley Jackson – *Funky Toes!*"

Samantha sidled up to Darrin as the sounds of a bass guitar and Clavinet filled their house. "Congratulations, sweetheart," she beamed, slipping her arms around him and giving him a kiss. Some partygoers started to dance while others mingled; still others stood uncomfortably. Samantha took a minute to absorb the music. She couldn't help a quick giggle. "Oh, Serena would love this."

"I'm just as well glad she's not here to submit a music critique," Darrin smirked. "Shall we?" The Stephenses ventured out to the makeshift dance floor Louise and Dorothy had created by merely opening the patio door.

"So you're my son's boss," Phyllis Stephens said to Larry Tate.

"Phyllis, you know we're here because Darrin made partner," Frank corrected, extending a hand to Larry.

"Nice to meet you both," Larry reciprocated warmly. "This is my wife, Louise."

"Hello! Now, if memory serves, Darrin said you're all from St. Louis?" Louise wanted to know.

"O'Fallon, actually," Frank noted. "'Bout a half hour out of St. Louie."

"Darrin wrote to us constantly about the agency when you first hired him," Phyllis relayed. "We've lived in the area for years now. It's hard to believe we've never been in a room together before."

"Well," came Louise's amiable response, "we are now."

Frank had to admit it to himself: Phyllis – his critical Phyllis – looked impressed.

Tabitha had initially approached her mother wanting to know if she'd really have to watch Adam. But Tabitha found herself stuck between Samantha and Mrs. Kravitz. She tried not to laugh at the memory of one-time houseguest Mrs. Kravitz standing in front of her with a face full of green goop.[7]

The sugar-borrowing neighbor was wearing a pale, slightly out-of-style dress with a borderline gaudy ostrich boa. "Don't you remember it, Mrs. Stephens? It's that dress they gave me when I got to model for that French designer your husband was representing[8]," Gladys half-boasted.

"Oh, yes," Samantha was slow to recall. "Monsieur...Aubert. Right?"

"Took me longer to squeeze into it than it did back then; on two days' notice I didn't have much time to reduce. Besides, with Abner I don't get a chance to wear this very often. Ever, really."

"I'm sure he liked the *kourabiedes* you brought," Samantha pivoted. "They seem to be the hit of the snack table."

"You know what Abner told me when I set the tray down on it? He hoped it was strong enough to hold up my cookies. At least when my nephew comes to visit next week I'll have a more appreciative mouth to feed."

"Nephew, Mrs. Kravitz?"

"Yes." Gladys seemed confused. "You've met him before."

"Which nephew, though?[9] I seem to recall there was Floyd[10]... and Edgar[11]...um, 'Flash'[12]..."

"And Tommy," Tabitha piped up.[13]

"And...Seymour," Samantha remembered.[14]

"And Sidney." Tabitha did her best to hide her lack of fondness for her cynical playmate. Having once gotten back at him for making fun of her belief in Santa Claus by turning him into a mushroom[15], it had taken everything in the young witch to not hex Sidney for disparaging Mary, the tooth-collecting Good Fairy, who had flown in the last time Sidney was here.[16]

"Well, of course it's Sidney," Gladys confirmed. "I know he'll be glad to see you again, Tabitha. Before I bring him by, Mrs. Stephens, I'll check him over. The past couple of visits he's had athlete's foot or some other kind of fungus."

Samantha gave Tabitha a stern look – Sidney's plight may or may not have been caused by Tabitha's lesson-teaching. Fortunately for Tabitha, the doorbell rang.

"Some late arrivals, eh, Mrs. Stephens? Go on and get that. I want to see where Abner got off to."

"Mother, I'm gonna go find Lisa," reported Tabitha, finally getting a chance to state her intention.

"Okay, sweetheart. You girls have fun!" Samantha opened her door and was pleasantly surprised to find the still gawky Adam Newlarkin[17] standing in front of her. "Adam! You made it! We haven't seen much of you since you moved back to Salem. We felt really bad about not calling when we were there[18]; we just got so busy on that trip. Thank you for making the drive down! Darrin will be thrilled to see you."

Adam gave Samantha a kiss on the cheek. "I can't believe it's been so long. Or that my ol' Army buddy has hit the big time."

"He's around here somewhere. Come on in and join the party!"

"At least it's not a costume party," Adam noted, remembering standing in this room in the '60s and being asked to put on a Paul Revere get-up so he could ride through the marketplace on a horse shouting, "Witches are good, witches are dear."

Mrs. Kravitz didn't have to look far for her husband. Abner was in a corner, surrounded by Bettys. "So you all worked with Mr. Stephens?" Abner asked the trio. "If I'd had co-workers like you at the plant, I'd never have retired!"

Blond Betty Wilson laughed good-naturedly. "Yes, we all met at the agency taking phone calls and dictation. I sat at that desk for three years."

The meeker Betty Moorehead brushed a hand through her short brunette 'do. "A little less than two for me."

Flame-haired Betty Ashmont grinned impishly. "I barely lasted three weeks. I guess I wasn't the secretarial type. Been Mr. Stephens' neighbor long, Mr. Kravitz?"

"Since '64, I believe. And call me Abner." The usually sardonic retiree was clearly loving the attention.

"Isn't he cute, Betty?" Ms. Ashmont asked of Ms. Moorehead.

"He sure is, Betty," Ms. Moorehead replied to Ms. Ashmont.

"Let me understand this now," Abner said, seeing the women in a new light. "You're all McMann and Tate secretaries...and you're all named Betty."[19]

"Uh huh," Moorehead and Ashmont affirmed in unison.

"There's a reason for that," Wilson offered energetically.

"Color me intrigued!" the playful Abner declared.

Abner suddenly found Gladys beside him, speaking in a loud whisper over the party's funk soundtrack. "In a minute I'm gonna color you black and blue." Gladys pulled back from Abner and tried to address the Bettys cordially. "Sorry to interrupt, but my husband said he...would dance with me. Didn't you, Abner?"

Abner made a face and raised his shoulders as Gladys towed him away. It was all the clerical trio could do to not to explode with laughter.

"Mr. Stephens has some interesting neighbors, doesn't he?" Betty Wilson asked the others.

"All of us being Bettys wasn't the only interesting thing about working at McMann and Tate," Betty Ashmont pointed out. "Once I walked into Mr. Stephens' office and it was raining on him. Right there in the room."[20]

"One Hallowe'en I thought I saw his regular hat change into a witch's hat[21]," Betty Moorehead volunteered. She and Ms. Ashmont looked inquisitively at Ms. Wilson. "You?"

Betty Wilson put an arm around each of her fellow desk jockeys. "Girls," she started, "how long do you have?"

Tabitha took Lisa into the den, away from the throng of adults who were acting a little sillier than they did when all this started. "Everybody seems to like your father's music collection," the witchlet remarked, unable to identify the sounds of *Ape is High* by Mandrill.

"I feel like every weekend I'm behind Mommy and Daddy in those big city record stores. They spend hours combing through them," Lisa eye-rolled.

"Hope Adam doesn't find us in here. Or that Jonathan Tate."

"How come, Tabs? Your little brother's nice. And Jonathan doesn't seem so bad."

"My parents and Mr. and Mrs. Tate always want Jonathan and me to play together because they're friends," Tabitha lamented. "But then my mother tells me to be careful around Jonathan 'cuz he's not supposed to know I'm a witch. It takes all the fun out of doing stuff with him."

"You mean you didn't have fun playing with me before I found out?"[22]

"I did, Lisa! But now that you do know I don't have to pretend anymore. Like I do with everyone else."

"I'm glad I spilled that paint on myself that first time I spent the night here, or I'd still be like your everyone else. Hey," Lisa murmured conspiratorially. "We're alone now. I wanna see you do something else with your powers. Can you make Michael Jackson appear in here? Maybe you could have him sing *Rockin' Robin* for us."

"Aw, I can't, Lisa," Tabitha said, disappointed. "I had to sit through a whole 'nother one of my parents' lectures about not doing any magic tonight. Besides, there are too many mortal grown-ups out there. But you know what – when you come over for your birthday, I'll ask Mother if I can bring Michael here for a special treat."

"I wish my birthday was tomorrow!" Lisa exclaimed.

The girls cut off their giggling, as they had learned to do when someone invaded their mortal/witch inner circle. The interloper was indeed Jonathan Tate, whose expression was pure glumness.

"How's it goin', Jon-boy?" came Lisa's perkier greeting.

"I really hate that *Waltons* movie," Jonathan pouted.

Tabitha's wall was up. "What are you doing in here?"

Jonathan's nose wrinkled. "I'm so bored. Mom and Dad are drinking that funny-smelling stuff and talking to everyone. Adam's the only boy here – he's just a kid and he barely says more than three words at a time. So that leaves you guys."

"Well," Tabitha relented somewhat. "What do you want to do, then?"

"I dunno. You got an Erector set?"

"No," Tabitha scoffed.

"Maybe some board games?"

"A few." Tabitha made her way to a chest of drawers, kneeling to get to the bottom one. "I think Mother keeps them in here."

"Didn't we play Candy Land the last time I was over?" Lisa said excitedly, joining her friend at the bureau.

"I wanna play Battleship," Jonathan moped.

"Here it is!" Tabitha announced, producing the pink-and-white Candy Land box from the drawer. "Unless you wanna try Monopoly..."

"Hey, what's this?" Lisa's attention went to the small stack of papers under the board games. "Did your brother draw these?"

Jonathan reached the girls as Tabitha pulled out several crayon-scrawled pieces of three-holed, lined paper. There were doggies and duckies and chickies and the occasional attempt at a stick figure. "Nuh-uh," was Jonathan's answer to Lisa. "They've got her name all over them."

"They sure do," Lisa nodded.

"Wow, I must have been really little when I did these," Tabitha said with wonder. "I didn't even know my parents kept them."

"Check this out." Lisa's tone had changed. "You spelled your name T-A-B-A-T-H-A on all of these. I've always seen you write it T-A-B-*I*-T-H-A."[23]

"Oh, my mother told me once it would be easier for mor – uh, grown-ups to remember. You know what I mean," Tabitha concentrated her gaze on Lisa.

"I don't," Jonathan said, stuffing his hands into his pockets, "but that's okay. You've got two names."

"I guess," was Tabitha's answer.

Jonathan hunched closer, yet didn't make eye contact with the girls. "I didn't even have a name until I was one years old[24]," he admitted.

"For real?" Lisa's mouth rounded.

"I heard my parents once. They said when I was born they couldn't agree on a name for me, so they...didn't give me one. I saw a card my aunt sent for my first birthday – it just says 'To Baby Tate.'"

Tabitha exchanged a glance with Lisa, then smiled. "Don't worry, Jonathan," she said, patting him on the back. "I promise we won't call you that."

"Wow, he's a beauty!" Adam Newlarkin declared. "When I was here, Samantha was expecting your first child. Now you have two."

Darrin held his son and ruffled his curls. "Yeah, the Terrible Twos already. Which makes him a very lucky boy to stay up for this party, doesn't it? Ah, he wouldn't be able to sleep through all this fuss, anyway. And now I finally get a chance to tell you...we named him after you."[25]

The elder Adam was genuinely shocked. "You...you did? Well, Darrin...that's...that's quite an honor."

"Bet you never figured on that when we were in Company D. And you might like this even better," Darrin added, showcasing the boy. "Adam Newlarkin Stephens."

"So you're where the Newlarkin comes from!" Frank grinned, happy for the confirmation. "You know, this little guy was originally going to be named after me. But I don't think Sam's dad was too keen on the idea."[26]

"Oh, you picked up on that, huh?" Darrin asked, eyeing the mirror his disapproving father-in-law had popped him into the fateful day of his son's naming. "Well, you could say it's better to placate Maurice than provoke him. He wanted the baby named after him, so Sam and I hatched a plot to scrap both namesakes and come up with a neutral alternative."

Frank gently pinched the delighted toddler's cheek. "He looks like an Adam anyway,"

"Your father-in-law sounds like a real character!" Mr. Newlarkin laughed.

While Frank was distracted by his grandson, Darrin leaned in to his old buddy. "There are times I'd rather take my chances with those grenades we had in basic training instead."

Luckily for Darrin, Adam Newlarkin didn't have time to fully process Darrin's comment, or didn't make time to, as Betty Moorehead crossed the foyer where the group was standing. The usually reserved Newlarkin raised an eyebrow almost imperceptibly, while Frank's powers of observation were a little more obvious. None the wiser, Darrin worked on defusing an early stage of Adam's fussiness.

"Well, Darrin, marriage has changed you!" Adam ribbed. "When we were serving, you had the biggest roving eye on the base."

"Then, too?" Frank snickered. "This boy couldn't keep his

eyeballs in his head all through high school. And college. I can't speak for after his move to the Big Apple."

"Where do you think I get that eye from?" Darrin said, looking pointedly at his pop. "I guess I did fancy myself a bit of a Casanova there for a while. Being stuck with a bunch of greasy guys in an Army barracks probably made it worse. Even marriage didn't cure me the first year or so.[27] But when you've got a girl like Samantha...well, she's one of a kind. You couldn't find anyone like her if you tried. Not on Earth, anyway." Darrin allowed himself a moment of private amusement with the literalness of his statement.

Little Adam was getting tired of being four feet off the ground and let his daddy know with an agitated yelp. Darrin had his own reasons for keeping the boy close tonight, and rolled with it. "Why don't we take this little fella on a tour of the room, gentlemen?" Darrin suggested. Winking at Adam Newlarkin, he added, "And maybe on the way we'll introduce you to Miss Betty Moorehead. At least I think she's still a Moorehead. Let's go find out!"

Adam followed three generations of Stephens boys nervously. "What? Now? But...but..."

"Great music, huh?" Louise commented to the Kravitzes just after the player dropped Manu Dibango's *Soul Makossa* onto the turntable.

"It's all right," Gladys said indifferently. "Abner and I aren't much into dancing."

"I'll say," Abner deadpanned. "Last time she was on a dance floor, they were doing the foxtrot instead of the funky chicken."

"*Feh*," Gladys muttered, turning her attention to Louise. Mrs. Kravitz was able to place Mrs. Tate now. She remembered she had taken her nephew Tommy trick-or-treating a few Hallowe'ens ago, and she could have sworn the boy had been turned into a goat.[28] Louise's husband even concurred for a minute before changing over to denying it. But there was no need to get into that particular detail, not with that *klumnik* Abner standing there. She hadn't appreciated the repeated lack of support from her husband whenever she reported witnessing unusual events[29], most of which had taken place in this very room. And she knew Abner had only gotten her out of town in that RV to spirit her away from the Stephenses. All the more reason Gladys decided to renew her quest for an ally. "Mrs. Tate, you've been to this house more than us over the years," she began coyly. "Have you ever noticed anything strange going on in here?"

Louise had. There was that time she caught Samantha talking to a cow just a few feet from here[30]. The time Louise found Samantha at home when she was supposed to be in Chicago[31]. The time she was sure she'd heard Darrin and Samantha's voices coming out of each other[32]. But there always seemed to be...well, if not plausible explanations, at least enough that anything extraordinary could be ruled out. "A few things," Louise found herself saying, the words trickling out with that sense of not being able to take them back once spoken.

"Oy, Gladys," Abner sighed. "Don't be such a *yente*. "This fine lady doesn't want to hear about – "

But Gladys was like a Rottweiler on the scent. "You know what, we've all known Mr. and Mrs. Stephens for a lotta years. There's no reason we shouldn't get to know each other. Maybe you and your husband would like to make a night of it with us sometime. We hardly ever have company."

Louise didn't know if she was accepting simply to be polite or not. "Oh...that sounds like fun! Do you play bridge?"[33]

"A little! I can brush up – and I'll make my casserole!"

Abner closed his eyes. "Speaking of funky chicken."

Betty Wilson had seen the Stephens and Tate children out of the corner of her eye, as well as young Lisa Wilson, and couldn't help thinking back to parties her own parents had thrown during her childhood in Canada – and how bored she'd been while the adults had a good time. So she struck up a conversation with Lisa, noticing with purposeful awe that they had the same last name and deciding what these kids needed was a turn on the dance floor. Betty was right – suddenly feeling like they belonged with the grown-ups, Tabitha and Lisa boogied on the patio, learning moves from each other. Jonathan spun around like a dervish possessed. Adam seemed to be enjoying himself the most; he stomped lustily, just slightly off-rhythm, giggling and shaking his head. Betty took the boy's hands at his level and proved a caring dance partner, while Lisa, Jonathan, and Tabitha locked arms and turned each other around. Dorothy and Keith, who had barely left the "floor" getting down to their music collection, happily waved at their daughter and soon joined in with the former secretary and the kiddie quartet.

Samantha and Phyllis perused the eatables spread out on the long table. Larry had been very thorough in the selection of food he'd had delivered; also, Lisa's parents had brought some Hoppin' John and sweet potato pie, which were some of the night's most popular selections. Then there were Gladys Kravitz's Greek sugar cookies.

"I think I've tried just about everything here, Samantha," Phyllis told her daughter-in-law. "But I could only take a few bites of that dessert your neighbor brought. Diabetes, or whatever it's called."

"*Kourabiedes*," Samantha corrected gently. "Mrs. Kravitz is experimenting with international cuisine."

"Given how overly sugary they are," Phyllis sniffed, "'diabetes' is closer."

Samantha reached for a champagne bottle dotted with condensation. "Maybe just one more of these," she promised herself as she happily filled her glass. "Don't worry, I'm not driving. And it's on a full stomach, Mrs. Stephens," she assured as she caught Phyllis' look.

"I've been meaning to mention, Samantha...you've been married to my son for eight years, yet you still call me 'Mrs. Stephens'."[34]

"Yes...I suppose you're right. At this point it's automatic."

"It's just so formal. How about, from now on, you just call me 'Phyllis'."

"All right," Samantha nodded, toasting Darrin's mom with a smile. "'Phyllis' it is. May take a little getting used to, though."

"Anything's better than when you were calling me 'Mother Stephens'.[35] Made me feel so old." Phyllis regarded the cookies. "Though Mrs. Kravitz can stay 'Mrs. Kravitz'."

Dorothy approached the table, just slightly out of breath. "Those kids of ours are dynamos, Samantha! Did you see them hoofin' it out there? I swear they're ready for *American Bandstand*."

"They're having a time, all right. And," Samantha said, more for her own benefit, "it's keeping them out of trouble."

"You sure you've got picking up after all of us, Sam?" Dorothy asked. "If I were hosting a get-together this big, I'd definitely need some help."

"Thanks, Dorothy, but I've got it under control," Samantha affirmed. "At least until the bubbly starts making people's heads bubbly."

"Talking of help, I'm surprised I haven't seen that fabulous Esmeralda on duty tonight," Phyllis remarked. "She's a little...quirky, but very efficient."

"Oh, she most certainly is." Samantha hoped Esmeralda wouldn't appear appreciatively like she did the last time Phyllis bestowed her with a compliment.[36] "I gave her the evening off. We have everything well in hand here – plus, with it being Saturday night, Esmeralda wanted to find some happening place she could wear those platform shoes Darrin gave her." Samantha left out the part where she had to tell Esmeralda it was better if only in-house witches were present at the party. All Samantha needed in a room full of mortals was the well-meaning maid sneezing one of them into another century. She was sure she had hurt Esmeralda's feelings and felt terrible about it, but she could smooth ruffled feathers tomorrow.

As Samantha leaned forward to serve herself a couple pieces of sliced lamb, something caught the light that caught Dorothy's attention as well. "Oh, Sam! Is that a new necklace?"

Samantha consciously brushed the golden "S" that lingered at her throat[37] above her bawdier, party-appropriate décolletage. "Newish. I found this in a jewelry store a couple of streets over from Madison Avenue. What else to do while Larry ties our husbands up in meetings," Samantha smirked, eliciting a chuckle from Dorothy.

"That reminds me, dear," Phyllis chimed in. "For the longest time you wore a beautiful little heart necklace – it had tiny diamonds all over. I never see you wear it anymore. How come?"[38]

Samantha noticeably inhaled. "Well?" she asked in her trademark, apologetic tone.[39] "Darrin bought it for me during our honeymoon in Manhattan. I had it on the day we first came to look at this house. And you're right – I hardly ever took it off. As far as I can remember, I wore it to a cocktail party[40] right before we had all the renovations done, but I never saw it again after that. It must have slipped off somewhere. Darrin was very understanding; I haven't quite forgiven myself, though." Samantha knew she could have cast a locator spell to trace it, or simply zapped up a duplicate, but the heart had been given in the spirit of agreeing to be a mortal housewife, so using magic to get it back would have seemed even more of a violation somehow.

"Maybe it'll turn up one day, Samantha," Phyllis offered. "You never know."

"That's right," Dorothy agreed. "And in a way you'd probably never expect."

Jonathan Tate was not a happy boy. He had lost his place on the patio dance floor because his mother decided to squire him around, introducing him to everyone. Why were parents so good at ruining anything fun?

"Did you ever think, when all this started, that we'd both have sons?" Louise asked Darrin proudly.

Darrin was carrying Adam again, still intent on heading off any magical mischief he might want to get into. Luckily, the sleepy kiddo was nodding off on Darrin's shoulder. "No, I never could have envisioned any of this," he marveled. "It's been quite the journey."

"Just be sure not to spend too much time climbing further up the ladder," Louise advised. "Larry's already missed enough of Jonathan's childhood doing that. Though," she went on in a quieter tone, "I suppose I'm as guilty as Larry. Jon's been under the care of so many nannies, governesses, babysitters[41]...it's easy to get caught up in being an ad man's wife, with all the client schmoozing and working to impress people. Maybe it's about time Mommy followed her own advice, huh?" Louise warmly squeezed Jonathan's hand. Then, seeing how the rest of her child was squirming, she told him, "Hey, why don't you go find Tabitha and Lisa if you want to."

Jonathan's first real smile of the night said it all. He scampered off the moment Louise let him go, running straight to Samantha, who was flanked by her daughter and her daughter's "sister."

Shifting Adam to his other shoulder, Darrin predicted, "Adam and Jonathan'll probably be running the agency one day."

"I wouldn't be at all surprised," Louise agreed. Trailing Jonathan with her motherly eye, she saw that he had found his grade-school contemporaries – and that Samantha was giggling right along with them. Louise let out a sigh of relief. "Well, I'm glad to see Samantha is her old self again. Seemed to me she was getting a little...I dunno... snippy there for a while. The last couple of months, anyway."

Darrin had noticed the change, too. It wasn't generally like Samantha to growl at him, make fun of the predicaments Endora zapped him into, or threaten to zap him during a disagreement.[42] As it turned out, Samantha had been under the influence of a low-grade witchy infection, something that Dr. Bombay hadn't caught when he'd diagnosed her with Bright Red Stripes disease two or three weeks ago.[43] After Bombay's usual bungling of his cure, he had popped back in to show Samantha what else his ultra-vascular self-denominating powered trichroscope (with of course the super-duper diagnostic predictor attachment) had turned up. Darrin thought the cosmic contraption just looked like the hexometers the quack usually brought[44], but what did he know. The important thing was, the magic microorganisms that had been affecting Samantha's personality had been dispensed with, and her demeanor was back to normal. All Darrin divulged to Louise was, "Naw, she was just going through something. But she's fine now."

The bing-bong of the doorbell cut through the opening bass line of Aretha Franklin's *Rock Steady*. "Here, let me take him," Louise said as she reached for Adam.

"Thanks. I'll get it, Sam!" Darrin called out, unprepared for who was standing at his front door. "Dave! You old rascal."

It was Darrin's lawyer pal from his early New York City days. The pal he barhopped with. The pal he downed bourbon with. And the pal he blithely tried to discuss his wife's witchhood with.[45] In this case, Darrin was thankful that Dave never seemed to listen. He engaged Dave in a robust handshake as he welcomed his friend in. "I had no idea you were gonna be here!"

The Cheshire cat had nothing on Dave's grin. "Sam tracked me down and invited me to your pow-wow – on the condition we didn't tell you."

"She deserves an award for keeping you a secret. Holy Hannah, I even missed you opening your own practice. When'd we last see each other, anyway?"

"Who knows. In '66, maybe?"[46]

"At least. Ah, for the simple, uncomplicated days, eh?"

"Yeah," Dave smiled nostalgically. "Everything was so black-and-white then. Hey, now that you're a partner at that big-shot ad agency, if you need representation, you know who to call. And by the way, when I drove up, I didn't see that traffic signal we fought to put in.[47] City Council take it out?"

"Morning Glory Circle isn't exactly the Connecticut Turnpike," Darrin said wryly.

"That's another thing!" Dave became somewhat incredulous. "I pulled out my old address book to remind myself where you lived and it said New York. Something about Patterson. But this is Westport?"[48]

Darrin found his voice rising above Aretha. "Hey, Mr. and Mrs. Kravitz! Look who's here! Your old stop light buddy!"

5 Getting to Know You

Mrs. Peabody's knees ached from hunching down between the bushes in front of the Stephenses' living room window. Since Tabitha hadn't mentioned what time their party began, Maudie had sat like a cop on a stakeout in her car across the street, ducking down when guests started arriving around 6:45. When dusk came, she risked detection and darted to her current position, only realizing later how chilly a Connecticut evening in April could be if not properly dressed. Mrs. Peabody had thought the gawky man was the only late arrival, but when the more confident one strutted up the walkway, she'd almost gotten caught. Not knowing if there would be any more stragglers, and not big on the idea of explaining herself to an arresting officer if one drove by and saw her trespassing, Maudie rose painfully, feeling the beginnings of pins and needless in her left foot and deciding to find a better snooping spot around the side of the house.

Luckily, no one seemed to be in the den; the big trick would be getting past the kitchen windows, since who knows what partygoers were congregating there.

Hearing that awful modern music thumping from the living room for the past hour, Maudie was grateful for the more muffled sound here, and that the stereo would draw people away from the kitchen and drown out her unfortunate choice of cloppy shoes. She was almost past the furthest edge of the window when Mrs. Stephens and a sophisticated redhead barged through the kitchen's slatted doors. Maudie stood stiff and straight against the highest hedge, barely allowing herself to breathe as these obvious long-time friends got out more ice for their company.

After what felt like hours, but probably was less than a minute, the phone rang, and the redhead marched out with an arsenal of frozen cubes. Mrs. Stephens unwittingly turned her back to Maudie in taking her call, so the teacher made a break for it. If one of her students were to behave like this, Mrs. Peabody reasoned, she'd send him or her to the principal.

Maudie scurried past the patio gate, the same one she had let herself in through when she'd seen Tabitha turn a crude toy castle into a glimmering fortress.[1] She ducked behind the adjoining fence, and – mercy of mercies – there was a hole in it just the right size for peeping. Granted, she could only see a portion of this side of the living room, and of course the flailing patio partiers, but more people were out here now than in, making fools of themselves. If something untoward were to happen, this could well be the place for it.

"Dave Blakely, I'd like you to meet two members of my agency family," Darrin told his one-time wingman. "This is Keith Wilson, my fellow account executive."

"Good to know you, Dave," Keith said, shaking the lawyer's hand firmly. "Fellow account executive? Darrin, you just got promoted over me, remember? I just hope you're not gonna crack the whip like this one," Keith added, jabbing a thumb toward Larry. "Remember, slavery ended 107 years ago."

Darrin was genuinely surprised when Larry enjoyed a jest at his own expense. "And this is Larry Tate, my...partner."

"Former boss," Larry informed Dave, also engaging him in a handshake, "and current best friend."

Unless Darrin misread him, Dave looked hurt. "I thought I was your best friend."[2]

Darrin was now 0 for 2 with the barfly. Mercifully, Keith threw the ball back to home plate. "Check it, Dave, my daughter's around here somewhere. I'll have to introduce you. Lisa's only ever seen attorneys on TV. She was a big fan of that show *The Young Lawyers*."

"The real thing's not nearly as exciting," Dave smiled, "but I won't burst her bubble. Say, any of you got a light?" he asked, producing a pack of unfiltered cigarettes from his sport coat.

"Sam might have one of my old lighters around here somewhere," Darrin relayed. "I don't know if there's any fluid in it, though. I haven't smoked in years."

"Really?" Dave said, surprised. "You were a regular chimney when we frequented barstools together."[3]

"Yeah, I quit some time ago, too," Larry revealed. "Don't really know why."

"They've had those Surgeon General's warnings on there for a while now," Keith reminded Dave. "I'm black, but I don't want my lungs to be."

"We sure did enough campaigns for cigarettes in our time, though, didn't we, Larry?" Darrin remembered.

"At least we stopped having to produce commercials for 'em last year," Keith added victoriously.

A far-away look played on Larry's mustachioed face. "I feel like we've done campaigns for everything at some point. This whole promotion thing of yours has gotten me thinking about some of the goodies you've churned out. For instance – "

The foursome of professionals was interrupted by Samantha, who glided across the living room carpet to their corner of the living room. "Hello, boys," she greeted. "Dave, I'm so glad you could make it."

Dave politely gave Samantha a kiss on both cheeks, European style. He'd already had a thing for her back when she was a demure '60s housewife[4], but the long, straight hair and Women's Lib influence in her look was really doing things for him. "I can't imagine where I'd rather be right now," he winked.

"Who was that on the phone, honey?" Darrin asked.

"Unfortunately, Margaret McMann," Samantha sighed. "She and Howard won't be able to make it. He had a little gastrointestinal something-or-other that required him to make a trip to the emergency room. Just a flare-up; she says he'll be fine."

"That's good to know," Larry said, feeling genuine sympathy for his sparring partner. "The McMann in 'McMann and Tate'...and 'Stephens'," he explained to Dave. "Sam, I was just steering us onto the subject of some of Darrin's greatest slogans."

"I know you've done some great work in my time," came Keith's compliment to Darrin, "but I've only been on the payroll since 1970. I'd love to hear some of these 'goodies'."

"Yeah, Darrin, let's see if I recognize any of them," Dave said gamely.

"Uh, well..." Darrin stammered, a little embarrassed.

"I still love that Caldwell Soup slogan," Samantha started. "'The only thing that will ever come between us.'[5] I mean, that was years ago, but it's always stood out to me. Maybe because it was the first slogan you created after we were married."

"'Inhale in health'[6] comes to mind," Larry recalled. "Though for the life of me I can't remember what product that was for."

"I've also always really liked that commercial for Beau Geste – you remember, Darrin," Samantha said, "the one with the young man who dabs on the cologne, ends up in the French Foreign Legion, and has to fight off girls?"[7]

"That was you, ol' buddy?" Dave said in awe. "I went out and bought a gallon of that stuff after that. Little bit of false advertising, though," he joked.

"Didn't your grandfather pitch that?" Larry wanted to know. "Grover Stephens? How is the Geritol Romeo, anyway? Ever hear from him?"

Darrin locked eyes with Samantha, thinking of the days he was her literal old man. "Oh, it's like he's always with me."

"He's back up in Montana now," Samantha volunteered, wanting to be done with that part of the conversation.

"Yes, Darrin, you've developed a lot of memorable campaigns. A lot of them here in this house. I'll never forget those fairy wings you wore under the Reducealator, Sam.[8] That Toothpaint stuff you guys came up with.[9] And that whole media sensation on *Hoho the Clown* to introduce the Tabatha doll[10]...I hear those still sell on occasion, even though the show bit the dust."

"I'm sure her namesake still has hers," Darrin reported.

"Pretty wacky, Dar," Dave decided, with Larry's expression indicating total agreement.

"You know us," Samantha grinned as Darrin curled an arm around her waist. "We don't do things in an ordinary way."

"Hallelujah," Larry declared, toasting Darrin.

Keith suddenly saw Lisa darting down the stairs with Tabitha. "There's my girl!" He quickly took Dave by the arm. "Let's have you meet her while we've got the chance. Who knows when we might see her again."

"Uh oh," Larry said after his eyes locked on his boy. "Jon's getting awfully close to the punchbowl. I'd better keep him from having any – I think Abner Kravitz spiked it."

"We'll mingle then," Darrin told his departing friends. "See you in a bit." The Stephenses watched Lisa excitedly shaking Dave's hand, then shared a knowing nuzzle. "Don't tell your relatives," Darrin began, "because if you do, I'll say you made it up, but...I may not be nearly as far along in my career if it wasn't for them and the magical messes we've had to scramble out of."

"Here's to convenient slogans."[11] Samantha raised her glass, and Darrin clinked his against hers lovingly.

"Ooh!" Dorothy Wilson squealed approvingly as the guitar licks of next record began to play. "*St. Louis Breakdown*! Oliver Sain is one of my favorites." Dorothy turned to Phyllis, who was standing between Louise and Gladys. "Darrin's from St. Louis, isn't he?"

"Not far from it," Phyllis replied, her gently tapping foot threatening to betray her matronly stance.

"Is that where you hail from?" Louise wanted to know.

"No, I grew up in Phoenix[12]," Phyllis clarified. "I had an older sister, Madge[13] – she hated the heat and wanted to move to a more temperate climate. So one day I was visiting her in St. Louis and she took me to see Chaplin in *The Gold Rush*. Met Frank at the theatre."

"*The Gold Rush*?" Dorothy gasped. "That must have been – "

"Let's just say it was when flapper chic was originally in fashion, not when it made its recent comeback."

The ladies laughed along with Phyllis and her self-deprecation. Inspired, Louise took the torch. "I can't remember when Larry wasn't in advertising. I mean, we met when television was just coming in. I had a job in this little music shop off Broadway and he'd stopped by to see how his campaign for the place was going. I'm still amazed he even looked at me, since I was wearing these horrible glasses at the time. Anyway, like I once told Samantha, he was taking forever to propose, so one night he blew a smoke ring; I stuck my finger through it and said 'I do!'[14] At least his cigarettes were good for something." Louise glowed at the memory.

"Keith and I met at the March on Washington in '63," Dorothy recalled. "Two, three hundred thousand people there and I like what I see on his protest sign and tell him so. And that was that! How 'bout you, Mrs. Kravitz?" Dorothy put to the lady festooned with feathers. "Where did you meet your fox?"

"Fox, huh?" Gladys said dryly. "I think you need those old glasses of Mrs. Tate's." Gladys was only half-kidding, but enjoyed the good-natured chortling this elicited from the ladies. "I sat next to Abner in college – Scandinavian Lit.[15] We never even talked until after his fraternity hayride...I fell off the truck. I'll never forget he proposed to me in a soda shop." She lifted her left hand to show a tiny diamond. "This is the engagement ring he gave me that day. We were too poor for him to get me a real wedding band so we just let this be it. But this" – Gladys showed off a larger setting above it on her finger – "this big honkin' one he bought for me after winning the Daily Double last year![16] I guess it was kind of his way of making up for it," she added, sentimentality overshadowing her bragging.

"Well, you and I know what it's like to be married to ad men, don't we?" Dorothy's statement earned a nod from Louise. "I'll bet Keith makes partner one day as well. Or opens his own agency. Good thing he's not so ambitious he doesn't make plenty of time for me and Lisa."

"I didn't see a whole lot of Larry in our early marriage," Louise differed. "He was relentless – until Howard McMann finally agreed to add Larry's name to the building. Not that going into partnership slowed him down all that much. I mean, we were married sixteen years before I became pregnant with Jonathan!"[17]

"Frank was fairly happy in his routine at the truck factory," Phyllis thought back. "Darrin may get his ambitious streak from me more than anyone. Unless you want to count Frank coming up with any number of cockamamie inventions after he retired. He's probably trying to balance out his years of monotony!"

Gladys had the most curious look on her face. "Only thing I've ever seen Abner ambitious about is that stupid flute he plays."[18]

"Really? I'm from Massachusetts, too!" Betty Moorehead told Adam Newlarkin. She found him lanky and awkward, but there was something real sweet about him, too. "Tewksbury."

Adam couldn't believe that less than an hour ago he was ready to kill Darrin for dragging him over to meet the former secretary. He'd wondered if his Army buddy was purposely trying to embarrass him because he had given passerby Betty the once-over. But it turned out Betty was demure and gamine at the same time. Not like those pushy, aggressive women who, as the kids would say, freaked him out. "Tewksbury's not far from my hometown at all! It's only about a half an hour drive from Salem," he gushed.

"I used to go to Salem all the time, before I moved down here," Betty remembered fondly. "I loved the wharves."

As for Dave, he had always thought himself a ladies' man. His claims to Darrin that he knew all about marriage because he was a bachelor[19] had been true, but the bravado in which he'd made those claims had been a smokescreen. In reality, Dave's continued bachelorhood came from worries that women found him unattractive. If he was, the spritely, spunky Betty Ashmont didn't seem to mind.

"A city attorney?" Betty asked.

"Yeah, out of my private practice on Long Island," came Dave's proud answer. "I represent the city and the mayor, but I also handle building codes, personal injury, civil rights cases..."

"Civil rights?" The auburn ingenue's ears pricked up. "I've been with the National Organization for Women since I left the agency. I was part of the Women's Strike for Equality – and you know the Senate just passed the Equal Rights Amendment. There's still so much that has to be done, for minorities as well as women. Maybe you know a way I could become more deeply involved?"

Normally Dave would be the first to infer an innuendo in a statement like that, but something about Betty kept him on the straight and narrow. "There's a lot I have left to accomplish in that arena, too. I'd love to brainstorm with you. Maybe over dinner sometime?"

Had Ms. Ashmont been in front of a mirror, she would have seen that her cheeks had suddenly come closer to matching her hair. A sly smile of approval played on her face, and she gave Dave a surprisingly bashful nod.

"Well, uh..." Adam fumbled, trying to keep his chat with Ms. Moorehead going and deciding on the music as a way of doing it, "'it's got a beat and you can dance to it.' Would you care to, um, get funky?"

The brunette Betty signaled for Adam to take her arm. "I would like that very much."

Dave was startled by Betty Ashmont's enthusiasm. "Yeah, so how 'bout it, Perry Mason? Shall we make a case on the dance floor?"

The former traffic light lobbyer happily let Ms. Ashmont lead the way. Maybe he'd steered Darrin wrong the whole time. Maybe there was something to this romance thing after all.

"Louise says you might be interested in coming over to play bridge sometime," Larry told Abner reservedly. He'd seen Abner's wife in court attempting to speak out against Samantha when "Benjamin Franklin" – or whoever he was – stood trial[20]; Larry remembered sitting next to Abner as a spectator, and that they were both befuddled by the experience. The few other times the smooth-talking ad exec had seen Gladys Kravitz had likewise left a bad taste in Larry's mouth.[21]

"We are?" Abner's eyebrows raised. "Well, we could give it a shot. Usually the only clubs Gladys and I refer to are the ones we want to use on each other."

"You'll fit right in with us," Larry groused. "There've only been a few bridge games I can remember where Louise and I didn't fight.[22] One was here, actually; she kept dragging out the evening 'til all hours even though I wanted to go home."[23]

"You sure we didn't buy our marriages in the same store, Mr. Tate?"

"It's Larry, please. How about you, Mrs. Stephens?"

"It's Phyllis, please," echoed Darrin's mother. "Card games make me think of rest homes. Long story.[24] But I want to thank you for giving my son this opportunity. I know he'll live up to your expectations."

"I keep thinking back to when Darrin first started with the firm," Larry recalled. "Louise has made quite the transformation since then. Maybe it's just us getting older, but she hasn't looked like herself the last several years – especially since she started dying her hair red."[25]

"Now that you mention it," Abner considered, "once Gladys became a redhead she never quite looked the same, either.[26] If she was gonna change herself, she could have at least come out looking like Sophia Loren."[27]

"You know what's funny?" Phyllis postulated. "Not long after Frank retired, it was like he became a whole other person. But now he seems like the same old Frank again.[28] Maybe it *is* just age."

The trio stood together like they collectively realized something, but didn't verbalize it.

"Speaking of age, Phyllis, how's Frank's pop getting along? Darrin and I were just talking about Grover earlier," Larry explained.[29]

"Who?"

Samantha and Keith were drifting through the living room with Frank and Gladys when they were nearly run over by Adam and Lisa, who were laughing their heads off being chased by Jonathan and Tabitha. Before Samantha could shout a reprimand over Timothy McNealy's *Sagittarius Black*, they were gone. "Those kids are gonna sleep tonight. Which means I may just be able to stay in bed past seven myself for a change," she tittered.

"Seems everything else around us changes, but kids always like to run through the house," Frank concurred. "Forty years ago, Darrin was doing the same thing."

Samantha couldn't help recalling the two times Mother had turned Darrin into a little boy[30], but it still might have been nice to see the genuine article, and at the proper time in history.

"Can you even remember what life was like before kids?" Keith opined. "I mean, Dottie and me had a full life, but once Lisa came along...well, it's just as if she's been with us the whole time."

"I'd thought about having children for cen – uh, forever, but I never met anyone that felt right with." Samantha hoped that Gladys, especially, wouldn't catch her witchy slip. "Not until Darrin, that is. We were both partial to having large families[31], but so far we're perfectly happy with just Tabitha and Adam. You never know, though. How about Lisa, Keith? You and Dorothy ever talk about giving her a brother or sister?"

"It would have to be a brother, because after all that sister stuff with Tabitha, I don't know if Lisa would take a biological sister seriously," Keith laughed.

"Abner and I just never ended up having kids," Gladys volunteered. Mrs. Kravitz was amazingly forthright considering her usual contentious tone regarding her husband. "You know how it is... something that big, you save for the right time...but somehow it doesn't come. And then you realize you waited too long. I'd hardly thought of children anymore until that year we brought orphans home for the holidays[32] – remember that, Mrs. Stephens?" Samantha nodded. "I at least tried to float the idea of adoption to Abner back then, but he didn't bite. It's just as well. With all my nephews stopping by in rotation, it's like having my own kids – once in a while, anyway."

Frank knew the others were waiting for him to weigh in on the subject. "When Darrin was three or four, we asked him if he wanted a baby brother or sister, and he said 'no.' We've never known if he actually meant it, but I guess we subconsciously took our cue from him. He seemed just fine with being an only child. And...I can't speak for my wife," the elder Stephens said in a way that made him seem like he was letting the cat out of the bag, "but I hadn't even planned on Darrin. Not until a rainy night Phyllis and I spent in Angel Falls."

Samantha thought of the day she and Endora helped to reunite Darrin's feuding parents at that locale.[33] She'd had no idea what part of the country the place was, really, but now Angel Falls had its own special meaning for her. It gave her Darrin.

"Hello, fine sirs," Dorothy said, greeting new acquaintances Dave Blakely and Adam Newlarkin, who seemed distinctively rudderless. "Where are those fine ladies you've been gettin' down with? Don't tell me you lost them already," she added jokingly.

"They're powdering their noses, or whatever you all do with that goop," came Dave's comical commentary.

Dorothy squared her eyes with a big smile on her face. "Hey, we perform feats of magic with that goop, and don't you forget it."

"It's just that Darrin and Samantha are mingling," Adam lamented, "and we don't really know anybody else."

"I feel ya on that one. I think we're all pretty much here because of Darrin."

"He's a great guy," Dave concurred. "Met him at the bar I where I hang out not long after he started at the agency. Put in a lot of time on those barstools, we did, at least 'til he and Sam got hitched. After that I kinda saw less and less of him. Tonight's the first time since *The*

Monkees premiered."[34]

"Same," said Adam. "We were virtually inseparable in the Army, but once we were discharged I only saw him the one time, when I'd attempted a move out here from Salem.[35] If Samantha hadn't called, I'd never have even known about the promotion."

"Huh. One time I represented this big honcho in advertising – Charlie Harper? Wouldn't you know, he was a college chum of Darrin's," Dave disclosed.[36] "Charlie said he and his wife came for a visit five, six years back – but hasn't heard from Darrin since."

"Yeah...that reminds me of a book signing I went to for this author, Bob Frazer.[37] We got to talking, and it turned out we both know Darrin. Bob said Darrin hasn't contacted him in years either."

"Hmm. Should I let Keith know there's fair weather in the forecast?"[38] Dorothy asked mostly in jest, eyeing Darrin talking to her husband from across the room.

The high energy beat of *Outa-Space* by Billy Preston pulled people onto the patio dance floor like it was metal and guests had magnets in their shoes. Gladys wandered among the few who had stayed behind in the living room, wondering where Abner had gotten off to now. Given the Stephenses were distracted, Gladys was tempted to also wander through the den, and maybe even upstairs, to see if there was anything that would confirm her suspicions there was something otherworldly going on in this house. She had conducted such a search once before, when she thought the Stephenses' baby daughter was picking winners in the stock market.[39] Gladys didn't know why she hadn't rifled through this place the several other times she'd had an opportunity.[40]

Drat, there were still too many people around. Probably time to collect Abner and go home –

Gladys about dropped her drink. There was Abner, on the dance floor...grooving with Darrin's mother!

Phyllis had been tempted all night, but she was sure Frank wouldn't go for it. A shame, too, since they used to cut quite a rug during the St. Louis jazz scene, later mastering the jitterbug. So she had tiptoed closer to the patio, deciding she would just dance by herself. She'd just barely gotten her nerve up when this song swept her into committing to her foot-tapping plan. And she loved it. This was up there with the time she had donned a wig and a tripped-out green ensemble trying to dress like "the woman of today."[41]

And Abner was as surprised as anybody. It seemed like he'd buried his youthful impishness under a mountain of cynicism over the years, but an impulse he couldn't control had him venturing out here. One foot in front of the other led to him feeling more alive than he had for decades. Abner Kravitz was having a grand old time.

As Phyllis lost herself in the music, she suddenly felt a nudge that threw her off the beat. It was as if something had bumped her right hip. Phyllis regained her balance and kept dancing, but she couldn't help looking around warily, as she had done during many of her visits here. Unlike those, she soon realized with relief, none of Samantha's kooky friends or family were around to shake things up.

6 I'm Dancing As Fast As I Can

Dave, Adam Newlarkin, and three Bettys stood by the open front door. "Well, we're gonna cut out early, Darrin," Dave said to his old drinking buddy. "This has been a great party, and we all wish you more success than you can handle. But uh...something's kinda come up."

"A double date," Betty Moorehead gushed, not quite as shy as she had been when the evening began.

"Congratulations, Mr. Ste – Darrin," Betty Ashmont said warmly, giving her former boss a peck on the cheek.

Mr. Newlarkin addressed Samantha. "Remember you were pregnant when I was here before and I asked you to practice on someone else?[1] Well, Tabitha and Adam are great kids. I'd say, in your case, practice made perfect."

After helping his Betty on with her overcoat, Dave reached into the pocket of his own, which still hung in the hall closet. Fumbling for a business card, he didn't notice his wallet falling onto the closet floor. "Don't be such a stranger, huh, Dar?" Dave said, handing Darrin the card and draping his coat over his arm.

"Yes, your friends would like to hear from you more often," came Adam's back-up.

"I promise I'll be better about that," Darrin swore. "It just can be very easy to get...distracted around here."

Distracted! Newlarkin looked at his empty arm. "Samantha, do you know what time it is?"

"Last I checked, it was just after nine."

"Dave, ladies – can you go on ahead to La Petite Maison?[2] It's just...well...I promised I'd let my parents know I got down here from Salem in one piece. I'll be right behind you. Just give me fifteen minutes or so."

"We could wait for you," Ms. Moorehead volunteered.

Dave wouldn't hear of it. "Hey, make your call, and we'll have a drink waiting for you when you get there. Shall we, Bettys?"

"You can use the phone in the kitchen," Darrin told Adam.

"I'll reverse the charges," Adam added hesitantly.

"You will not," Samantha reassured.

Betty Wilson touched the arms of her secretarial counterparts. "Now, don't you two have such a good time that you forget to come to my shower tomorrow afternoon."

Bettys Ashmont and Moorehead confirmed their attendance with "Oh, we won't" and "I can't wait", then allowed themselves to be escorted out the door by the eager Dave. While Adam hastened to the kitchen to placate his parents, Darrin and Samantha appraised Betty Wilson curiously as Larry approached.

"A shower?" Samantha finally asked. "Why, Betty, you aren't... you aren't..."

Betty let out a hearty laugh. "My *bridal* shower. Remember I said a few years ago that I was engaged, Mr. Stephens?[3] My fiancé and I finally set a date! Late summer."

"That's wonderful!" Samantha exclaimed as Larry and Darrin pat Betty's back in congratulations. "Any idea where you're going to honeymoon?"

Darrin jerked his head around when he saw his son practicing the 50-meter dash across the living room. "I'll go grab Adam, Sam. Before he trips Keith or Dorothy – or my mother."

"Sure, sweetheart. Maybe sit him on the couch with his Legos," Samantha called as Darrin left in pursuit.

"Well," Betty said, continuing the thread of the first conversation, "I've been thinking it might be fascinating to honeymoon in England."

"Really?" Samantha found a bout of mischief coming on. "Larry, why don't you see if you can arrange for Betty to stay at Whitsett Castle? You're good at making sudden accommodations there."[4] Samantha was remembering when Larry bludgeoned her and Darrin into spending a weekend at the fortress themselves, blocking their return home from Europe last year. But she immediately thought better of her playful pique – that oversexed ghost, Harry, who had bothered Samantha there, would probably harass Betty, too. Maybe by now the equally ethereal Duchess of Windermere had...ahem... spirited the philandering duke away.

Larry ignored or didn't catch on to Samantha's dig. "I'd have to say your party is a success so far, Sam. Two of my former employees finding potential beaux."

"I hope Betty and Betty have a great time," Betty Wilson beamed.

Samantha raised an eyebrow. "Maybe one of you can answer this, because I've always wondered. Betty Wilson, Betty Moorehead, Betty Ashmont...it seems like you can't go anywhere at the agency without running into a Betty. I've counted fourteen of you.[5] Why is that?"

Larry and Betty got very quiet. "Uh...well..." Larry relented sheepishly, "McMann has this weird quirk – he won't hire a secretary unless her name is Betty. I have no idea why."

"It's true, Mrs. Stephens," Betty piped up, shocking especially Larry. "Of course I knew, Mr. Tate! That tidbit has gone around the secretarial pool for years. Some of us even lied on our résumés so we'd be considered for the job."

Samantha wanted to laugh, but Larry still stood agape. "You mean not all of you are named Betty? Which ones aren't?"

Betty would only smirk coyly. "I'll never tell," she said, sweeping by Larry. Very quickly, Betty whispered into Samantha's ear. "Florence!" Samantha covered her mouth gleefully.

"All right, Larry; you think you're still steady enough on your feet to take another spin on the dance floor?" Samantha dared.

"I think I could manage it..."

Jonathan had joined Adam on the couch, where he'd been relocated by his father; the boys were building some kind of something-or-other out of Adam's Legos that only they could understand. Eight-year-old Jonathan wasn't thrilled about having to play with a baby, but there wasn't much else to do.

Darrin had found his daughter talking to "Aunt Louise" and retrieved her for a quick father-daughter moment. "You're being exceptionally good, Tabitha. Thank you. A grown-up party probably isn't very much fun for you kids – and I realize you could easily find other ways to entertain yourself."

Tabitha was pleased that her daddy noticed she wasn't using witchcraft. "I didn't even after Lisa asked me. And I like being downstairs. Usually when you and Mother have company, Adam and me have to go to our rooms."[6]

Tabitha's frankness took Darrin aback a bit. "I hope you know it was never because you weren't wanted."

"I know, Daddy. You just didn't want us doing no-nos in front of mortals. I'm really glad Lisa knows about us, at least. It's nice to be able to tell the truth to someone."

"I must admit, Tabitha," Darrin said confidentially, "it's kind of refreshing for me, too."

Lisa had spent the past ten minutes being toured around the room by her father, and her expression said that five had been enough. Keith was not unaware. "Ladies and gentlemen, this is the last stop on this train – Sofa Station, last stop." To Darrin, he added, "It's amazing how much heavier kids get when they're not into doing something."

"Listen, you guys have been mostly running around separately all night," Darrin pointed out, hoping to corral the young'uns. "How about something you can all four play together?"

"Well, the stuff we wanna do, the boys don't wanna do," Lisa sulked.

Jonathan pretended not to hear, snapping a blue Lego block onto a yellow one.

"And the stuff they wanna do, we don't wanna do," Tabitha confirmed.

Keith handily saved the day. "Hey, I know – you guys could play advertising agency. You all have pops who do up ads for a living – why don't you pick a product, or we can pick one for you, and then draw a layout of how you would sell it? It can be as silly or as serious as you want, and it'd give you an idea of what we do."

"That's novel," Darrin said. "I have an easel and paper and markers and crayons in the den you can use."

"I don't know that Adam's old enough to understand that game," Tabitha worried.

"Then he can help draw whatever product you decide on. He'll be your very own art director."

"We'll never all agree on the same thing," Jonathan finally offered.

"We all like cookies," Lisa realized.

"Okay! There you go," Keith smiled.

Darrin finalized the plan. "You kids can grab the box of cookies from the buffet table there, and knock yourselves out. Oh – and you can have some of them, too. Because a good ad man always has to know his product."

"A good ad woman, too," Lisa reminded him.

Darrin nodded. "That's right."

"Lisa, will you help me get the easel and stuff?" Tabitha requested.

"Me and Adam will get the cookies." Somehow the promise of baked goods made Adam seem less of a baby to Jonathan.

Keith watched the kids run off, trying not to laugh. "This should be interesting," he told Darrin. "Which one of us should play the dissatisfied client that breathes down their necks?"

"Hopefully Jonathan won't end up threatening to fire everyone every five seconds," Darrin hoped, remembering his experiences with Jon's father.[7] "Oh, that's right, Keith – you weren't there for that. Watch; the kids'll come up with a better cookie slogan than we can."

"Speaking of cookies," Keith announced, spotting Abner passing the sofa with a drink for his wife. "Hi again, Mr. Kravitz. Would you pass along my thanks to Mrs. Kravitz for the...unique dessert she made? They're from Greece, aren't they?"

Abner didn't miss a beat. "They're from grease, all right."

Maudie Peabody was getting frustrated as the introductory high hat, bass, and organ of The Staple Singers' *Respect Yourself* had the partygoers dropping whatever they were doing and hitting the patio dance floor. The teacher had been casing the Stephens house all night, and the only otherworldly thing she had witnessed was this godawful racket. Maybe snooping on the party had been a bad idea. Mrs. Stephens wasn't likely to do that strange gesture with her nose and produce feats of magic in this crowd, anyway. It was probably time to think about going home. If she could only get past the gate without being seen, she'd head out to her car right now.

Aside from celebrating having made partner, Darrin was doing something he'd never done before – dancing with his mother. Phyllis had some surprisingly good moves, and Darrin didn't know whether to marvel or laugh. He did know he just couldn't stop smiling inside.

Larry remembered when the agency hired Betty Wilson, and he never thought he'd be shimmying with her in a homemade discotheque one day. Joining them was Keith, who was enjoying his record collection to the utmost, more so because the party was really digging his personally selected tunes. His enthusiasm inspired Betty – and even Larry – to let go of any fears of looking silly they might usually give in to.

Given Frank's taste in music ran to the Andrews Sisters and the Dorsey Brothers, he found this newfangled sound rather easy to dance to. For her part, Gladys Kravitz tapped into a less uptight part of herself that rarely got a chance in the spotlight, which expressed through her suddenly lively hips.

Samantha, Louise, and Dorothy wordlessly got the idea to do a kind of circular march around Abner. Letting his feet shuffle appreciatively, Abner decided he may have to pick up this record

– and play his flute along to it.

Even though they were tucked away in the den, the good vibes emanating from the patio made their way in, making the mock ad agency activity that Lisa, Adam, Jonathan, and Tabitha were engaged in more fun. Lisa decided she would be the client the others could pitch to; Tabitha and Jonathan tried to explain their cookie concept to Adam, who was drawing an awkwardly irregular circle on the easel paper. When Jonathan decided to fix their layout and grabbed the marker out of Adam's hand, Tabitha gave Jonathan a look and handed her brother a fistful of crayons to work with instead.

Led by whatever muse communicates through music, the eleven adult revelers found themselves drifting toward their respective partners. Keith and Dorothy invented an intimate slow dance move that they sped up to sync to the drums. Frank and Phyllis joined hands and did a merry little hop as the horns did their thing. Gladys couldn't believe that was her Abner boogieing in front of her. Betty was the only solo act on the floor, but felt included as she happily weaved in and out between the couples.

Larry and Louise seemed like newlyweds, twirling each other to the rhythm. And Samantha and Darrin danced together with such love in their eyes, they might as well have been the only twosome on the floor.

As the "na na na na"s and spirited guitar riffs faded, it seemed only right to let loose with a hearty round of applause. The stereo's tone arm put itself away and the turntable stopped, triggering a barely discernible sense of disappointment among the group. Keith picked up on it. "That's it for that stack," he said as he headed back toward the living room. "But there's more where that came from!"

"No, no, no," Larry declared exuberantly. "I'm gonna take advantage of this moment of silence and say a few more words before the next round. Everybody back inside!"

"'Moment of silence'?" Darrin asked as Larry ushered the crowd into the living room. "What are we mourning?"

"My only having one partner," Larry shot back while everyone howled and formed a circle around him.

"Shouldn't we fill our glasses for a toast?" Dorothy wondered.

"And lose my momentum? There'll be plenty of time for drinking later."

"I never thought I'd hear *my* husband say that," Louise smirked, exchanging a knowing glance with Samantha.

"Har har. Ladies and gentlemen...and others," Larry announced, indicating Darrin. "We are gathered here today to join this man and this agency in...unholy matrimony."

"I'll get the rice," Samantha sassed. There wasn't one guest who wasn't laughing.

"All right, I need to sell this cookie," Lisa said severely, sitting up in her chair and doing her best brusque executive. Of course, it would have helped if she hadn't stuffed the product into her mouth right after saying it. "Convince me."

"The layout's almost done, Ms. Wilson, and we – " Tabitha's preliminary pitch was interrupted by the sound of her unhappy brother. "Jonathan, what are you doing?"

Jonathan Tate was tired and getting cranky. He had stopped writing the slogan he and Tabitha had agreed upon and pushed Adam away from his toddler masterpiece: a cookie with rainbow-colored chips. "That's stupid!" Jonathan wailed, grabbing the box of real-life cookies. "These chips are brown! He's ruining the whole thing!"

With everyone in the living room, Mrs. Peabody knew this was the perfect time to make a break for it. Yet, given the captive audience they seemed to have in the white-haired man with the mustache, she also knew she may not get another chance to have a closer look. She brazenly let herself in through the gate and snuck up to the bay window outside the dining room, which gave her an almost perfect view of the group. What she would do if any of them came back outside, she didn't know, but she could cross that bridge when or if she came to it.

"Darrin, you're not just my employee anymore; you're my equal," Larry said proudly. "And if you thought we did great things under the old arrangement, that's nothing compared to what we're going to accomplish now that we're a bona fide team. And McMann will still contribute what he always has to the agency – sitting on his boat drinking rum."[8]

Adam Newlarkin ventured out of the kitchen and made an apologetic approach during the chuckling. "I'm going to head out now, guys – thanks for letting me use the phone, Sam...Darrin. I was right; my mother wouldn't hang up until I swore and affirmed I had no bumps, no bruises, or inhaled more than my daily requirement of smog."

"Leave him alone, Jonathan!" Tabitha warned, tempted to cross her two fingers together[9] as tears rolled down Adam's red, cherubic face.

"You're such a baby, Adam – you do everything like one big baby!"

Lisa stood up and faced Jonathan. "This is only a game. What's your problem?"

Jonathan continued yelling at the boy. "That's the dumbest looking cookie I've ever seen! It looks like a unicorn threw up on it!"

Adam suddenly chucked his crayons at Jonathan, surprising Tabitha. The sobbing tyke ran out of the den before she could even make an attempt to catch him.

Dave was glad the front door was unlocked. He was scanning the floor of the foyer when he was nearly mowed down by a speeding two-year-old. Tabitha and Lisa followed briskly, while the sullen Jonathan trailed behind them.

"Personally," Larry grinned, rubbing his hands together, "I think we should start with the Saks account – "

"Hey, Lar, can we at least hold off on the plans for world domination until Monday?" Darrin saw his son running to Samantha but was interrupted by a touch on his shoulder. "Dave? I thought you left."

"Where are the Bettys?" Adam Newlarkin wanted to know.

"They're waiting at La Petite Maison. Have you seen my wallet, Dar? I went to pay for the first round of drinks, and lo and behold – "

"Adam, what's wrong?" Samantha instinctively swept her child up in her arms. As Tabitha and Lisa flanked her with hangdog expressions on their faces, the mother's tone became accusatory. "What have you kids been doing?"

"I thought it might be fun for them to play ad agency," Keith volunteered, feeling bad. "You wanna tell me what this is about, Lisa?"

Jonathan joined Larry in the center of the circle, looking as though he wanted to become a part of his father's leg.

"We were just working on a layout for the cookies," Tabitha tried to explain, "and then – "

Larry already knew where this was going. "Jon, you were told about causing trouble over here."

"I'm sure it wasn't that bad, Larry," Louise said as she gave Samantha an apologetic glance.

Samantha was doing her best to wipe Adam's tears away with her thumb. "Everything'll be all right, sweetheart – "

"No!"

Adam's volume came as even more of a surprise than his one-word rebuttal – especially since he still didn't talk much.

"Why don't I take you up to your room and get you nice and tucked in – "

"No!"

"All right, Adam, I think it's time for you to calm down – "

"No!" the boy cried, looking his mother right in the eye. "He's *mean*!"

Then it happened all at once.

Darrin took a step forward to help his wife. Louise took a step forward to help her son. And Adam waved his arm, with Samantha reacting a split-second too late.

In front of everyone, Jonathan Tate turned into a baby zebra.

Mrs. Peabody gasped from her spot outside the bay window.

Louise's eyes widened, and Larry looked down where his son used to be.

Keith and Dorothy's troubled gaze traveled from the zebra to Lisa, who looked at Tabitha with an expression of awe.

Betty Wilson, Adam Newlarkin, and Dave stared at each other in disbelief.

Phyllis and Gladys didn't know it, but they were both thinking the same thing – this was only one of many strange things they had seen in this house, and now their doubting Thomas husbands couldn't deny it. Not with this many witnesses.

Darrin nearly flew to Samantha's side. Samantha held Adam close, as if to protect him.

Mrs. Peabody watched Jonathan-as-zebra swishing his tail, confirmation starting to replace her astonishment. "Wait 'til Mr. Roland sees this," she told herself, wondering if she could get to a phone in time to summon the scoffing principal who had made her apologize for accusing the Stephenses of witchcraft.[10]

"Sam, what..." Larry began, his agitated tone finally breaking the silence in the room. "What is this? Where's my son?"

"Is that a...a zebra?" Betty asked in amazement.

"Oh, that's a zebra, all right," Gladys declared. She turned to Abner. "I dare you to tell me it's not!"

Louise looked at Samantha pleadingly. "Samantha...how is this possible?"

It was as if a million thoughts were transmitting between Samantha and Darrin in one helpless glance. Should they try to convince everyone they weren't really seeing what was obviously there? Should they laugh it off as some kind of sleight-of-hand party game they recruited Jonathan for? This time they couldn't even build an advertising campaign around it, since there were no clients in attendance.

Samantha mindlessly scanned the orange, gold, olive, and white squares of her living room curtains. She couldn't tell her mortal friends the truth. They would never understand. Worse, what would they do with such news? She thought back to the media frenzy that ensued when Endora zapped a few words in baby Tabitha's mouth and Gladys went public with it.[11] Later, when Darrin had hinted he wouldn't have married Samantha if he'd known she was a witch, Endora took them to an alternate reality where Larry was ready to cash in on Samantha's magic.[12] How far off would the actual reality be?

She should just do it. One twitch, one incantation, and she could put a spell on everybody to make them believe...whatever she wanted. Or she could just take Darrin and Tabitha and Adam and pop out with them. But that would be cheating Darrin out of his promotion, which he richly deserved.

What was the alternative, then? She'd temporarily lost her powers when she'd tried to tell Darrin's parents about herself, leaving her to scramble for a mortal explanation.[13] Mortals and witches...so much animosity between them these past eight years, all of which Samantha had been the flashpoint of. Maybe it truly would be better to keep them apart, to keep these very different groups segregated...

Samantha caught a glimpse of Dorothy and Keith. How many would still like to keep *them* segregated from mainstream society? The Christmas they had let Lisa sleep over with Tabitha, Samantha had twitched a racist client of Darrin's into seeing himself as African-American to teach him the ultimate lesson that skin color doesn't matter.[14] That everyone has a right to be who they are. Was Samantha being hypocritical now, backtracking into not letting herself be who she was?

There was the zebra, which a minute ago had been Jonathan Tate, its black and white stripes personifying the very unity Samantha had advocated for.

"Um..." Darrin offered, aware of his lack of originality and finding himself unable to utter other words. Samantha was far better at these spur-of-the-moment alibis than he was.

But it dawned on Darrin that his wife wasn't formulating one. He didn't recall Samantha ever looking more serene. They'd been together so long, knew each other so well, he could tell exactly how she wanted to handle this. He took a deep breath, and his countenance let her know he was behind her, all the way, no matter how things turned out.

"It's possible, Louise," Samantha started, "because Adam...and Tabitha...and I...are witches."

"Witches?" Dave asked, flabbergasted.

"That's right," Darrin verified, scanning his rattled guests.

"The three of us – me and the kids," Samantha went on, "we have supernatural powers...and Adam was a bad boy to use them in front of you." She squeezed his hand in a way that promised discipline was not far behind.

Lisa stared up at her parents as if she wanted to say something, but didn't.

"You're telling us...you're a witch." Abner shook his head rapidly, trying to understand.

The light bulb over Phyllis' head couldn't have been any brighter. "You mean...all along...you – "

Phyllis froze mid-sentence. Though most of the others had stood in stunned silence anyway, it now seemed to Samantha they were also completely immobile.

Darrin was, too.

Out of nowhere, thunder roared as if a tropical storm were moving through the house. Gusts of wind whipped up and lightning flashed wildly, and before Samantha could even try to shield her kids, every mortal in the room was gone.

Vanished.

Even the unseen, inanimate Mrs. Peabody outside the bay window disappeared into thin air.

As quickly as it had started, the gales and deafening rumbles died down, and the house was again lit normally.

"Adam? Tabitha? Did you..." But Samantha already knew the answer.

"Mother, where's Lisa?" Tabitha asked, the panic in the girl's voice rising. "*And Daddy?*"

"I don't know," Samantha replied, clutching Adam in one hand and the chain of her "S" necklace with the other, the breath nearly taken out of her. "Oh, my stars..."[15]

Part II
"Airdate": April 8, 1972
Episode #256
(60 minutes)

7 The Party's Over

Samantha rushed through the den into the kitchen, still carrying Adam and covering his head when she came barreling through the saloon doors. Taking one more glance at the patio, the frantic mother met her daughter in the foyer at the bottom of the steps.

"Anything?" Samantha asked Tabitha.

"There's nobody upstairs, either. They're all gone! What are we gonna do?"

"I'm – I'm thinking."

"What if you cast a spell? Maybe you can bring them back!"

"That's really not gonna do any – " Seeing Tabitha's desperation, Samantha set Adam down next to her and put her fingers to her temples, trying come up with a suitable incantation.

"Absence makes the heart grow fonder
Hear me now as first responder
Planets that twinkle, stars that burn
Those who vanished – at once return!"

Samantha zapped for all she was worth, with both hands...
Nothing.

"No, it's like I've always told you, Tabitha," Samantha said as her arms dropped. "Only the witch who cast a spell can undo it.[1] I mean, it wasn't always that way[2], but – ooh!"

"What's wrong, Mother?"

"There's sort of a...prickling in my fingers," the older witch explained. "Almost as if I were getting magical feedback. It's not just that I can't reverse this spell, it's like there's some kind of powerful block in place."

"But why would anyone do this?"

"It *has* happened twice before," Samantha recalled, "only then it was just your father who disappeared. There was this witch who was trying to force me to marry her son[3]...I'll explain that later. But another time your grandmother popped your daddy out to prove one of her points."[4]

"Call her, Mother! Maybe Grandmama knows where he is now!"

Endora materialized on the staircase landing, the pink cape of her green flying suit still billowing from her flight. "Grandmama most certainly does. Hello, Tabitha. Dear little Adam."

"So you did do something," Samantha frowned. "And you're going to tell me about it right now."

"And I came rushing back from Zambia for this! Oh, no, my darling," Endora declared as she descended the rest of the stairs to meet her family. "This time, the only one who's responsible for what's happening...is you."

Samantha felt her face pale. "What are you talking about?"

Endora looked upon her grandchildren lovingly. "Everything will be all right. But your mummy and I need to have a talk."

Samantha looked down at her children, finding she had to force her words out. "Tabitha, why don't you take Adam to your room, and I'll be up there in a few minutes to...let you know what's going on. If I know by then, that is."

"I'll give them a little assist – " Endora began to wave her hand.

"Mother, you know our rule," Samantha said, stopping her. "Besides, kids, it never hurts to get a little exercise." Samantha watched from the moment Tabitha took her brother's hand to the moment the child closed the door to her room. It was true Samantha was trying to honor Darrin's mortal wishes, even with him not there, but it was also true she was stalling.

"Sit down, Samantha," Endora ordered.

Samantha suddenly felt as if she were a girl witch again, about to be scolded for putting too much powder in King George II's wig. The feeling of dread contrasted sharply with the half-empty flutes of champagne on the coffee table, which were still bubbling.

Endora zapped up an ornate scroll and gave it to her daughter.

"I assume I'm not being summoned to Salem like I was the last time you handed me one of these."[5] Samantha was still stalling. But she couldn't deny the parallel to the official decree she once received to attend the Witches' Convention.

"Just read it." Endora was unusually stoic.

Samantha unrolled the gilt-laden document and could barely take in its calligraphy.

"That's right, Samantha. The High Priestess Hepzibah has demanded that you appear before her immediately. I've been dispatched to fetch you."

"Hepzibah? I haven't heard from her since she made herself a houseguest to observe my mortal marriage."[6]

"This goes far beyond that," Endora warned, standing. "And we're keeping Her Majesty waiting."

"But, Mother! This is all happening so fast! Can't you just take a minute and help me to – "

Endora softened, resting a hand on her daughter's shoulder. "Even I can't help you now."

Samantha swallowed, then sighed, realizing the gravity of the situation. "All right. I'd better let the kids know we're leaving, and see about finding them a sitter. And the faster, the better." Samantha snapped her fingers, surprising Endora by popping them out of the living room and into Tabitha's room upstairs.

Tabitha, who had gotten Adam to play with his Fisher-Price Little People, barely reacted when her mother appeared in her room instead of walking in. "Mother, what's going on?"

Samantha kneeled down to her daughter. "I'm not sure yet, sweetheart. Grandmama and I have to...go out for a while. I don't know when we'll be back. But I'll hurry home as soon as I can."

"This is about Daddy. I know it," Tabitha said, leaning in with the hope her little brother might not hear her. "I told Adam everybody's playing a game. But I don't know how long he's going to believe it."

"It's about more than Daddy, I'm afraid. Tabitha, you're old enough now to understand certain things, especially about the witchy part of our lives. I have to see Hepzibah. Remember her?"

"Yes. She zapped me into that frilly dress and let me try pickled eye of newt. Is she mad at you?"

"That's probably a safe bet."

"Why?"

"Because she told people she's a witch."

Three generations of witches followed the voice to the bed. It was Adam, looking up from his wooden toys intently.

Samantha rose to her feet. "I need you kids to hold down the fort. I'll see if I can get Esmeralda to sit with you. It's going to be tricky because we told everyone to stay away tonight. Maybe Aunt Hagatha – "

"If this has to do with Daddy," Tabitha said, her more adult tone catching Samantha off guard, "then I want to be there. I'm coming with you."

Endora shook her head gently. "No, my little witchlet. It's not a place for – "

"I'm coming along." Tabitha stood rigidly, her arms folded.

Samantha considered her very limited options. "We'll have to take Adam with us. And I want you both on your best behavior. This is very serious. So no horsing around. Understand?"

"Yes, Mommy," Adam nodded.

"Tabitha?"

The half-mortal, half-witch placed a "V" over her nose with her fingers. "Witches' honor."

"That's my granddaughter," Endora crowed. "We must start our journey, Samantha."

Without warning, the woman who had spent the better part of a decade cleaning floors and sewing buttons and roasting chicken like a mortal raised her arms up over her head in a grand gesture. The slinky cerulean sleeveless dress with the deep slit in the skirt she had chosen for the party turned into her flowing black flying suit with the translucent green gown. Likewise, Tabitha found her brown, short-sleeved button down dress with the orange sash replaced with a flying suit similar to her mother's, only with a gown of translucent purple. And Adam's cute little blue blazer and red, white, and blue striped pants became a junior-sized Victorian tuxedo. He looked like a mini-Maurice, *sans* red cape and top hat.

Samantha picked Adam up off the bed and placed him in Endora's arms. "You hang on to him, Mother – and Tabitha, take my hand. Everybody ready?"

With all in agreement, Samantha waved again with her free hand, this time even more majestically. As had happened not ten minutes ago when her husband and party guests disappeared, a strong gust and crackles of lightning accompanied a near sonic boom of thunder. Samantha couldn't remember if she had ever dematerialized with such fanfare, and she knew it wasn't necessary, but somehow the meteorological additions gave her some much-needed strength – and expressed a clearly communicated rebellion. Giant plumes of smoke mushroomed from the floor.

And a moment later, all that was left in Tabitha's room were her toys, clothes, and furniture.

8 Flying in the Face of Convention

Adam had fallen asleep in Endora's arms after a very active evening. Tabitha, however, was brimming over with wonder, clutching Samantha's hand tightly. Everything around them was a sea of ever-changing hues and sweeping suns and distant planets; it was like they were floating and zooming across the cosmos at impossible speeds yet remaining motionless at the same time. Tabitha couldn't be sure, but she thought, if she listened hard enough, she could hear soothing, humming choruses slowly panning back and forth. This must be what Grandmama was talking about when she lectured her mother about how their home had no boundaries beyond which they could not pass![1]

"I'd forgotten how long it takes to get to the Ancestral Grounds[2]," Samantha grumbled.

"We'll be there soon, Samantha," Endora said assuringly. "It's not much further now."

While lost for words, Tabitha could also barely contain them. "Mother, what's the difference between flying and popping?"[3]

Endora gave the hesitant Samantha a knowing glance. Tabitha had finally asked the witch equivalent of "Where do babies come from?"

"I mean, that time I fell and hurt my chin, you said I was too young to fly.[4] But popping into the *Steamboat Bill* show was cinchy[5] – and I don't remember it being anything like this. I was just in the den with Adam one moment and in the TV studio the next."

Samantha unconsciously tried to clear her eyes with her free hand. "I'm not really sure how to – okay. Flying and popping are pretty much the same thing; it just depends where you're doing it. In the mortal world, you're not traveling as far, so you disappear from one place and appear in the next almost instantly. Would you say that was accurate, Mother?"

"Yes," Endora nodded. "Although I would amend that to say what we're doing now is traveling into another realm, which requires us to move across the atmospheric continuum. If you were to put your room and Hepzibah's palace next to each other, it would seem to anyone watching that we were popping out of your room and into the palace. But the journey itself takes longer from our perspective."

Tabitha began to understand. "So it's kind of like beaming down from the *Enterprise* on *Star Trek*?"

"That's pretty close," Samantha smiled.

"*Star* what?" frowned Endora.

"Oh, right. You don't get good TV reception on Cloud 8."

"What about when I zapped myself into my *Jack and the Beanstalk*[6] and *Hansel and Gretel*[7] storybooks?" Tabitha also wanted to know. "Those seem like different realms. Yet I appeared and disappeared there very quickly, too."

"Those are creations of the mortal world," Samantha affirmed. "Going there is pretty much the same thing as popping. Make sense now?"

"Yeah, I guess. One more thing, though. How come mortals still think we travel by broom?"[8]

"You're my inquisitive little granddaughter tonight, aren't you?" Endora beamed.

"Why not? There's no in-flight movie," Samantha smirked. "You want to do the honors, Mother?"

Endora rolled her eyes. "You see, dear, mortals have always decried anything they don't understand. They did it when automobiles replaced the horse and buggy...when they drew lines on their land to say 'our country is better than your country and don't you come in here'..."

"How about we stick to the subject?"

"Very well. Several centuries ago, some humans discovered that if they mixed certain herbs together, it made them hallucinate."

"Do you know what that means, Tabitha?" Samantha put to her daughter.

"Sure! They went on a trip!"

"No more of Keith's records for you. Go on, Mother."

"These herbs couldn't be eaten, so those silly mortals used a broomstick to apply them. When other mortals saw them running around on brooms acting like idiots, they cried 'witch'."

"And the image stuck," Samantha added, hoping to wrap up the subject. "Presto – everyone thinks we need brooms to fly."

"I'm glad I told Lisa we don't ride brooms, then," Tabitha decided.[9] "But still, how did those mortals from centuries ago use the broomsticks to take the herbs? And how did that make other mortals think they were riding the brooms?"

Samantha inhaled quickly. "Oh, look down there! The Ancestral Grounds."

Endora pursed her lips in amusement at Samantha's sidestep. "That's a big palace, isn't it, Tabitha?"

"It sure is. Are we going inside?"

"Yes, we are, sweetheart," Samantha said, the knot in her stomach reminding her why they were there. "And remember what I told you. Your absolute best behavior. Okay?"

"Yes, Mother."

"Now hold tight. We're going in."

* * *

True to Samantha's explanation, the familial foursome materialized instantaneously in Hepzibah's cavernous throne room. Yet, to them, it was if they had flown through a sudden mass of clouds and found themselves standing on the golden marble floor.

Samantha had been to more baseball games[10] than football games, but, if she'd had to hazard a guess, she'd have said the throne room was as big as a football field – maybe two. For all the opulence of the walls and the ceiling which stood at least three stories above them, the space was unusually sparse – and Samantha, her mother, and her children were the only beings that inhabited it.

"No reception committee?" Samantha wondered. "I half expected to find a mob waving torches and pitchforks."

"Hearkening back to images of those mortal witch hunts isn't going to help anything, Samantha," Endora sighed.

"When you've been persecuted for marrying a mortal as long as I have, that image is not inappropriate." Samantha squinted as she looked around the cavernous chamber. "I haven't even been here since I was queen."[11]

"You were queen of the witches, Mother?" Tabitha's eyes grew wide.

"Only for a year – and not because I wanted to be," Samantha clarified. "You were pretty young then – plus I only took care of witch business after midnight, so I'm not surprised you don't remember.

Honestly, I think I can count on one hand the times I actually flew to this palace."

"I can hardly believe it," said the excited Tabitha. "Why only a year?"

Endora looked up helplessly at the ceiling's fancy patterns. "Why, indeed."

Samantha glowered at her mother. "I just wanted to live like a regular mortal housewife. But I found out I had been selected to rule at birth, and I was obligated to for a year. So the millisecond my year was up[12], I passed the crown on to Hepzibah. She'd been a High Priestess ever since I could remember; she seemed a logical choice. She prefers to be called 'empress,' mind you, which is essentially the same thing as a queen."

"She is now empress and High Priestess over us all," Endora declared.[13]

"Wait, she's both?" Tabitha asked, confused. "In my fairy tale books they always say a queen is above a high priestess. How can she be both?"

Samantha bent down to Tabitha, speaking in a half-joking, half-conspiratorial tone. "I think there must have been a bit of a power grab somewhere."

"But if you were queen..." Tabitha theorized, looking up at her brother and grandmother, "What does that make us?"[14]

Before Samantha could answer, a loud gong reverberated through the throne room, despite there being no one around to strike it, and an ensemble of trumpets blared, though no musicians played them. All of a sudden, four elegantly dressed attendants appeared, forming a square around Samantha and her relatives. "The High Priestess Hepzibah awaits," one of them proclaimed. A glittering throne instantly materialized at the head of the room in a huge puff of smoke.

The octad lifted effortlessly off the floor and floated toward the throne as if they were standing on an invisible platform, which, of course, they weren't. Samantha struggled to keep her disdain undetectable. *Cosmos knows I respected the crown*, she said to herself, *but I never would have gone for this inflated level of pomp and circumstance when I was queen.*

Tabitha couldn't help but swallow as the group gently set down in front of the throne. Then a light began emanating from it, becoming so bright it was as if the sun was housed within. A roar followed that would have been earth-shaking had they been on earth; seconds later the light died down and Hepzibah was seated where it had originated.

Samantha didn't think the High Priestess would still seem imposing after she had mellowed about Darrin coming to Salem while Samantha attended the Witches' Convention[15]; perhaps it was the throne's purposeful placement atop a set of golden steps, to which the attendants magically relocated. Hepzibah sat bone-straight, that much taller for her impossibly high pink hair that cascaded over her shoulder in large spiral curls. She held tight to her scepter, almost as if it were a weapon, and regarded her subjects stiffly. Astride the throne were her otherworldly black Dobermans, Caesar and Cleopatra. Samantha remembered their preference for zebra meat and was glad the newly transformed Jonathan Tate was nowhere near.

Endora set the just awakened Adam on his feet and taught him a quick bow while she leisurely arched to her sovereign. Tabitha executed a perfect, reverent curtsy. Samantha's curtsy beheld the anger and intimidation she was feeling in that moment.

The evident representative of the attendants spoke ceremoniously. "Former Queen Samantha, Lord High Chairman Endora[16], and the half-mortal children, Tabitha and Adam."

Tabitha's cheeks flushed. She had never been referred to that way by a witch before.

"This is no place for children!" Hepzibah bellowed. She glared at a cowering attendant. "Postlethwaite, have them taken to – "

"My children shall remain by my side," Samantha insisted, unable to believe this voice was coming out of her. "What affects me affects them. And I assume the reason for Her Majesty's summons does affect me."

"That it most assuredly does. Come forward!"

Samantha wordlessly tried to calm Tabitha's fearful look. "Stay with them, Mother," she quietly instructed Endora before cautiously advancing to the bottom of the steps. She looked up at Hepzibah, whose icy glare carried just the slightest hint of softness.

"It truly pains us that we should encounter you again under these circumstances," the High Priestess began. "When we last saw you, we decreed that we would study the mortal species further before making any major decision about your witch-to-commoner marriage. We warned your mortal husband that we would be watching him. More to the point, we have been watching you – and taken not only your present, but your history into account. The events of this evening disturb us greatly. Had this been the sole instance in which you laid bare your witchhood to mortals, we might have been able to overlook it as a lapse in judgment, or an ignorance of the ramifications of your actions."

Samantha allowed herself a brief moment to close her eyes, hoping the monarch wouldn't notice. She'd known the second she told her guests she was a witch that she was taking perhaps the greatest risk of her 300-year-old life, but she hadn't expected justice to be so swift.

Hepzibah continued. "Since you divorced yourself from our culture, you seem to have developed a peculiar penchant for revealing yourself to mortals – not only to the creature you married, but to dozens of others. No other witch has done so with such frequency, or with such blatant disregard to the perils of such confessions. We need not remind you of the persecution we barely escaped during the Salem witch hunts, despite the fact that none of us actually faced trial ourselves.[17] We need not remind you why, as a primitive species, mortals were then – as now – too gluttonous and xenophobic to consider coexisting with. And we need not remind you why it was ordained that witches would no longer move among mortals."

"So we're back to dissolving my marriage again," Samantha blurted out.

The High Priestess ignored the interruption. "Would that this only concerned your marriage, Samantha. You simply cannot be trusted to maintain secrecy about your witchhood in front of mortals. Therefore, you are hereby ordered to leave the mortal world at once. All memory of you will be purged from every mortal with whom you have ever come into contact. Including your Darrin Stephens."

Samantha was struck dumb. Yet she could also feel the rage boiling in her stomach. "You would do that?" she asked as quietly as possible, her voice trembling. "Purging Darrin's memory of me also means purging his memory of his children by me. You would take my children's father away from them – you would put them through the pain of losing their father? And you can be so cold, so unfeeling as to make this declaration as they stand in front of you?" Samantha seethed.

"We told you this was no place for children," Hepzibah asserted. "But we are not without mercy. Even though your offspring are only half-witch, they do possess powers, and they would be allowed to stay with you in our realm. If you prefer, we could simply purge their memories of mortals to spare them any distress; ergo, they would never remember this audience with us. We are indebted to our Lord High Chairman for suggesting this alternative."

Samantha looked back at Endora, unable to process the implications of her mother's involvement in this dire predicament. Her natural, instinctual focus was on her kids; Samantha was thankful only Tabitha was old enough to grasp what was happening. "Your Majesty," Samantha continued in a controlled tone, "when you debated dissolving my marriage prior to the 1970 Witches' Convention, I was ready to propose that my powers be removed and that I be released to live a fully mortal life. I would be willing to sacrifice my witchcraft now, and my heritage, if you would just –"

"Unacceptable," Hepzibah sniffed. "We removed your powers just months preceding said convention for unnecessarily revealing yourself to a mortal[18], and you certainly didn't learn from *that*! Our decision remains firm. The purge will take place immediately." The High Priestess prepared to stand.

"I'll tell you what's unacceptable," the livid Samantha declared. "You've arrested, tried, and convicted me without giving me a chance to plead my case. They don't even do that in the mortal world! Well, not in most countries, anyway."

"Let us make this clear, Samantha. If you were anyone but a former monarch, you would have been transformed into the object of your choice by now."

Samantha took an involuntary, hopeful breath. "That's right," she realized. "I used to possess that very throne you occupy. I believed in treating my subjects fairly, with due process. I will no longer tolerate being run roughshod over as if I were some kind of second-class citizen. I *am* a former queen. And as such, I insist upon having my say. I proclaim a hearing be held right now!"

Hepzibah could hardly believe her ears. "You what?"

"And I further stipulate that my husband be rematerialized to attend it."

"Absolutely out of the question! We told you once before that mortals are not allowed on hallowed ground," the High Priestess barked.[19]

"That pertained to a convention my husband had nothing to do with. This pertains to him directly, and I stand by his right to bear witness to it." Samantha couldn't be sure Hepzibah's pink hair wasn't getting pinker.

Endora had been largely horrified by her daughter's rebellion – yet, try as she might, she couldn't hold back a certain wave of pride as Samantha stared down the crown before her very eyes. Maybe the Samantha that had spent years rejecting her teachings had retained some of them after all. Or – could it be? – perhaps it was being part of the mortal world that had instilled this kind of gumption in her.

Hepzibah let out a long, exasperated sigh. "As you wish," she finally said. "But because it's you – and only because it's you. We shall convene the Witches' Council posthaste and hold a hearing. And the mortal you are so enamored of will be returned to you for the duration of it."

"Thank you, Your Majesty." Samantha's gratitude was respectful and genuine. She retreated to her children, happy for the chance to fight for them, and for what would be an all-too-brief respite before that fight began. Because convincing Hepzibah not to deliver an instant ruling had been the easy part.

Now came the hard part.

9 Goin' Courtin'

Hepzibah swung her scepter so vigorously that Samantha unconsciously took a step back. The next thing Samantha knew, she, Endora, and the children were standing alone together in a great hall that might have resembled the United States Congressional hearing rooms Samantha had seen on the evening news had it not been for the expanses of pink and purple that billowed among sparkling constellations above them. A constant, light fog floated along the floor.

What seemed like a raised courtroom counsel table or judge's bench loomed overhead at least six feet, sprawling in front of the group in a massive semi-circle that was home to several chairs. At its center, at eye level, there was a platform that looked like it could be used for display. Tallest of all, splitting the bench and giving the entire structure the impression of a pyramid, there imperiously sat another mighty throne, from which its occupant could survey all activity from nearly two stories up. Clearly, Hepzibah had appointed herself magical magistrate.

The sheer pageantry of the bench's gold-trimmed lines, intricately patterned planking and gleaming chandeliers that levitated above it made the small, plain table that awaited Samantha come across as almost flea market by comparison. The same held true for the railing behind the table and the gallery behind that – which, to the naked eye, had no discernible end. Apparently all the thought had gone into the legislative *accoutrements*, but not so much into anyone being legislated.

"Perhaps some on the Council will show leniency," Endora said flatly, to no one in particular.

Samantha eyed Endora contentiously. "Leniency? 'We are indebted to our Lord High Chairman for suggesting this alternative.' You were in on this! You didn't stick up for me with Hepzibah; you merely tried to find a way to feel less guilty about the impact of Darrin being out of our lives. Then again, an end to my marriage is what you've wanted from the beginning – never mind that the grandchildren you claim to love wouldn't be here without it. You couldn't cajole me into leaving the mortal world on my own; now Hepzibah's trying to force me out, and you advise her? Nice work, Madame Lord High Chairman."

Endora opened her mouth to offer some kind of reply, but couldn't seem to get a word out.

Tabitha hated it when her grown-ups fought, and, because of the heightened tensions, there was the sense that everyone, including Adam, would just as soon leave this battleground. The tone changed significantly when Darrin suddenly popped in next to the hearing table.

"Daddy!" Tabitha threw her arms around her surprised father's waist, and Adam ran over to hug Darrin's right leg.

"Oh, sweetheart, thank the universe you're all right!" Samantha glided to Darrin and held him close, completing an interesting family portrait.

"Sam, where am I? What is this?" Darrin's head moved back and forth rapidly, trying to take things in. "A second ago I was standing next to you in the living room awaiting everyone's reaction after you told them – " It only took Darrin one more moment to add it all up. "Ah. The Witches' Council."[1]

"Yes," Samantha admitted soberly. "And Hepzibah. At least she honored her promise to bring you back. Darrin, they want to – "

"They want to take us away from you and make you forget all about us!" Tabitha bewailed.

Darrin's scowl could have frozen the desert. "And how much of this, Endora, as if I didn't know, are you responsible for?"

Endora made a concerted effort to avoid her son-in-law's gaze. "There's something I have to take care of before the hearing," the formidable witch announced cryptically. "Don't start without me." With that, Endora was gone.

Brilliant light flashed across the "sky." Samantha recognized its signal and knelt down to Tabitha and Adam. "Okay, kids, now you stay with Daddy," she bade her children as a cool wind began blowing their hair. "And remember – whatever happens – I'm right here." Rising, Samantha gave Darrin the shortest, most meaningful kiss she'd ever given him. "I have to seat you in the gallery."

Darrin's eyes were full of love and carried the full weight of the moment. "Good luck."

Samantha waved her arm, dematerializing her loved ones and situating them in the first row behind the railing. Darrin sat Adam on his lap with one hand and held Tabitha's with the other, awed and fearful to see Hepzibah appearing in front of her seat of power.

The High Priestess pointed her scepter straight up, then rotated it clockwise in ever-increasing circles, making the opposite motion with her free arm.

> *"Scales of justice that weigh unseen*
> *The Witches' Council I now convene!"*

Thick clouds formed over the bench just below Hepzibah, glowing colors bouncing among them. Samantha stood behind the sole chair at her table, looking up as shadowy figures came into view, four to the left of the High Priestess, four to her right.

"The Noble Eight," Samantha whispered to herself.[2]

One by one, Council members stepped through the ethereal mist.

In a sequined black and maroon gown, dark hair teased high upon her head, the witch Malvina became clear.

Samantha was aghast.

"Your Majesty, she's biased!" Samantha called to Hepzibah. "If my husband hadn't rescued me, I would have been next in line for beheading by King Henry VIII thanks to her!"[3]

Malvina stood imperially. "Zap anyone out of a painting lately, Samantha?"

Things did not look good, not if Malvina's presence was this early a sign. Samantha only hoped that Herbie, the warlock she'd released from Malvina's pictorial prison in the Tower of London, fared better than she had when Malvina blanked her memory and arranged for her to meet the Lion of England, nearly becoming his sixth wife in the process.

Next was Grimalda, all lace and cameo and huge Victorian hat. Her friendly wave was intended for a recipient who sat beyond Samantha. "Hello, warlock Adam," she cooed.

"Great," Samantha said *sotto voce*, leaning back so Darrin could hear. "Another one who was willing to dissolve our marriage. I can't believe she almost stole our son away into the bargain."[4]

"I could have abided her if she'd just helped test Adam's powers and been done with it," Darrin agreed.

Perhaps the tallest member of the group came forward: George the warlock.[5] He was still as rakish and handsome as he'd ever been in the perfect lines of his suit. "We meet again, wild heart," he said, grinning mischievously at Samantha, who frowned as she regarded her one-time beau.

"So this is where you've been hiding the past several years. Quite a step up from your usual homewrecker role."

"Hey!" Darrin's mouth gaped in recognition. "Isn't that the guy who turned me into a penguin?"

In a flash, Endora and the ever-Victorian Maurice popped into the gallery on either side of Darrin and the children. "I told you a penguin had already been done," Endora reminded her open-marriage husband.

"At least I don't dress like one," Darrin snarked in response to his father-in-law's style. "I'm not surprised Endora brought you here to round out the anti-mortal cheering section."

"As always, Darby," Maurice replied, "your ability to underestimate astounds. For where but at the side of one's daughter should a father be in times of tribulation?"

"How come you've never been around the other times Sam's had tribulations with this bunch?"

Maurice gave Darrin a look. "Typical mortal nitpickery. Did you really think the momentousness of these proceedings would escape me? '*Please it your majesty, this is the day appointed for the combat,*'" came Maurice's customary Shakespeare quote[6], "'*and ready are the appellant and defendant –* '"

"Daddy, shh," Samantha warned. She could tell who the next adjudicator was just by her silhouette. It was fellow former queen Ticheba, who had abdicated her throne to Samantha five years earlier.[7] Samantha thought back to her own rule and began to wonder if she didn't know why all this was happening. Filing her suspicions away, Samantha addressed the erstwhile sovereign. "I'd have thought becoming one of the Noble Eight after stepping down from the throne would have been a...step down," she commented, not sarcastically.

"Some of us continue in service," the elderly Ticheba replied, her hair still in regal red ringlets. "Some of us do not."

Samantha didn't dare speak to the next arrival. Judge Bean stoically strode through the haze to take his place on the bench to Hepzibah's adjacent left. His scrunched expression had never left his face; Samantha wondered if he had ever smiled once in his unnatural life.

"I didn't know he was still on the Council," Endora whispered.

Samantha kept her back to her mother. "You mean you didn't keep in touch after you lobbied to have him declare Aunt Clara earthbound?"[8]

"Where's Clara been, anyway?" Darrin asked as Adam began squirming on his knee. "It's been forever since we've seen her."[9]

Samantha sighed the sigh of someone who'd had a tender spot touched in their heart. "I'm not sure."

The Contessa Piranha[10] somehow managed to slink forward to her seat while maintaining an air of complete disinterest. The sight of the socialite sorceress, who still wore her pearl choker against a satiny black gown that made Samantha think of widow's weeds, put the slightest hint of a smile on Samantha's face. "However, I *am* sure nepotism is alive and well in the atmospheric continuum."

"When you've got it, flaunt it," the Contessa smirked coyly.

"Nepotism?" Maurice, the usually collected warlock, seemed confused.

"Piranha is Hepzibah's niece," Endora explained.

"I thought I'd seen her in my circles," remarked Maurice.

There were only two Council members left to be accounted for. Rubenesque in stature, surrounded by all manner of fluff and feathers, Samantha recognized the approaching woman as Carlotta, who had nearly replaced Phyllis as her mother-in-law due to the medieval arranged marriage Endora and Carlotta had casually agreed upon between Samantha and Carlotta's son, Juke.[11]

"I wonder how Juke is these days," Endora said, trying and failing to get Samantha's attention.

Darrin looked quizzical. "For some reason...I don't know why... that woman makes me think of lions and tigers and bears."

"Oh, my," Endora sniggered, finishing the *Wizard of Oz* quote and keeping the memory of Darrin running from Carlotta's animal sounds to herself.

Samantha couldn't believe who rounded out the Witches' Council. If he had been mortal, he'd have been a kid in his early, maybe mid-20s, with cheeks you'd want to pinch and slap at the same time.

Rodney.[12]

The callow boy warlock Samantha had once babysat now played a part in deciding her fate – a fact she would have railed against had she not had to resist mocking laughter from remembering him with chocolate on his face after he changed back from being a cake-eating canine determined to destroy her marriage.

"I see the Council has gone to the dogs," Darrin sniffed. Had he really almost given that warlock a home?

The Noble Eight turned to Hepzibah. This action prompted Maurice and Endora to rise; Endora likewise brought Tabitha to her feet, then smacked Darrin on the arm to get him to stand. Darrin bewilderedly complied, setting Adam in front of him and doing his best to hang on to the increasingly wriggly boy. As if responding to an inaudible cue, Samantha, her parents, and the Witches' Council all bowed to Hepzibah in tandem, with Endora guiding Tabitha. Darrin was hard pressed to show that kind of respect to any entity who wanted to purge his memory of his wife and kids, but he did so, realizing the importance of not making waves at this moment.

As the cosmic contingent began to seat themselves, Maurice gestured to Adam, who had begun making noise and was trying to crawl out of Darrin's grasp. "Give me the boy," the theatrical warlock told his mortal son-in-law. Darrin was genuinely surprised when Maurice tenderly cradled Adam and affected a gentle gesture over his head that caused the toddler to nod off.

"There's no reason my grandson should be witness to this," Maurice insisted.

"Thank you, sir," Darrin heard himself say. "Though at two-and-a-half, there's probably very little he'd remember."

"He's half warlock," Maurice noted both proudly and uneasily. "One never knows *what* he might remember."

Sitting alone at her modest table, Samantha turned around and reached for Darrin's hand. "Well, sweetheart...here we go."

"Even if they end up making me forget everything about you," Darrin swore, "every moment of us has been worth it. By the way... where are Larry and Louise and the others?"

"Pick a place in the cosmos. The only thing I'm sure of is that they haven't been harmed."

"Samantha – " Endora entreated, extending her bejeweled hand to her daughter. But Samantha faced forward wordlessly.

Judge Bean zapped up a gavel and banged it hard on the bench before him. "I hereby call this hearing of the Witches' Council to order," he declared before officiously tossing the gavel up in the air, where it disappeared.

Hepzibah stiffened in her throne. "Witch Samantha," she called, her voice echoing through the witchy chamber. "As our one-time sovereign, you know that the Witches' Council was created millennia ago, not only to serve as a legislative body, but to act as a watchdog of sorts as mortals began developing their primitive societies. The latter was more a formality, as our world was generally kept free of contamination by humans. Nevertheless, as the first witches moved amongst them in the Middle Ages, it became necessary to protect ourselves from their ultimate ignorance and barbarity.

"The mission of the Council remains clear: to create regulations that preserve our witchly society, and to assure compliance to them. Interacting with mortals has time and again proven to be disastrous; their mere knowledge of us has led to centuries of misconceptions that have impelled them to abuse, imprison, and even murder each other in our name. While we realize you have not violated our covenants out of malice or any conscious attempt to be willful, your continual failure to abide by our meticulously crafted directives can no longer be tolerated.

"Because we realize the severity of the punitive actions determined – and because of our respect for your place in our hierarchy – we have allowed you this opportunity to speak on your own behalf. We, of course, know you to be a witch of great integrity, and we look forward to your candor in these proceedings. Speaking before this Council requires that you do so under oath. Witch Samantha, please rise."

Nervously but nobly, Samantha stood – then actually rose six feet off the ground to face the Noble Eight at eye level, the cape of her flying suit fluttering in the unceasing breeze. Judge Bean waved his hand, and a second later faced Samantha in mid-air. "Place your index and middle fingers on either side of your nose," he instructed. Assured by the sight of Samantha forming the V in front of her face, the Judge continued. "Do you solemnly swear to tell the truth, the whole truth, and nothing but the truth, so help you, Cosmos?"

"Witches' honor," Samantha replied dutifully.

"You may be seated."

As Judge Bean popped back to the bench, Samantha effortlessly drifted back down to her chair. Tabitha watched her mother with sheer fascination, and Endora and Maurice exchanged a prideful glance. Darrin forced a neutral expression, not wanting his in-laws to see he was equally impressed.

"Witch Samantha, you are now under oath," Hepzibah proclaimed. "This hearing before the Witches' Council may therefore commence."

Squeezing her hand into a fist ever so slightly for courage, Samantha began. "Thank you. High Priestess Hepzibah, esteemed members of the Council, I very much appreciate this opportunity to explain myself and my actions. I would like to start by addressing – "

"You have not been recognized," Hepzibah interrupted.

Samantha's face reddened. "I'm sorry...it is my understanding that I am here to speak on my own behalf."

"It was not specified that you would be allowed to do so at the commencement of these proceedings." The High Priestess trained her gaze down to a bench seat on her right, at the end of the semicircle. "The floor recognizes the witch Malvina."

Even from Samantha's vantage point at floor level, it seemed as if Malvina was looking down her nose at her.

"Witch Samantha, before you engage in these flagrantly incessant reveals to mortals, do you consider the effect they may have?"

Samantha wanted to protest Hepzibah's pivot around what she thought were the established parameters of the hearing, but she felt as though she had no choice but to flow in this new direction. "The short answer is 'yes'," Samantha told Malvina, "but I would note that each case comes with its own circumstances."

"Would you clarify to us the nature of these 'circumstances'?"

"There were instances in which finding another way to explain away witchcraft to mortals wasn't viable, like tonight; in other cases, I disclosed my magical identity for the purposes of education."

"Would you say a certain Mr. Brinkman was one such case?"

Samantha struggled. "Could you refresh my memory as to who that is?"

"Certainly." Malvina aimed a zap toward the middle of the bench's arc, reaching over to point at the floor below Hepzibah. On the platform appeared what seemed like the inanimate projection of a man; he was a skinny, plain man in a pin-striped suit, his close-cropped gray hair not adding anything aesthetically.

Samantha shook her head. "He's still not ringing any bells."

"Hallowe'en 1964," Malvina hinted.

"Hallowe'en 19 – oh, the first year I was married to Darrin!" Samantha exclaimed. "Right. Mr. Brinkman was a client who wanted to advertise his candies using a picture of a stereotype witch... blacked-out teeth, warts, et cetera."[13] Appraising Brinkman's frozen form, Samantha felt his own nose rather resembled the old crone he wanted to depict. "But we formed a protest group to convince him to abandon that image and teach him that real witches were unlike his misconception."

"We?"

"My friends Bertha and Mary, and my Aunt Clara. We briefly turned him into a crone so he might comprehend the way he planned to represent us." Samantha couldn't help a weak smile. Like her beloved aunt, Samantha hadn't seen Mary nor Bertha in ages.

"What about this man?" Malvina waved, and a somewhat portly fellow in a silken paisley robe and pajamas replaced Mr. Brinkman. In one hand, he held a pot of gold. In the other, a gun.

"Um..." Samantha reached. "Daniel...Donald..."

"James Dennis Robinson. Another client of your mortal husband's – this one in possession of a treasure belonging to a renegade leprechaun."[14]

"Brian O' Brian," Samantha remembered.

"Correct. You used witchcraft to subdue this man, didn't you?"

"I had to. As you can see, he had us at gunpoint."

Another zap produced a shifty, homely gentleman in a bow tie and houndstooth fedora.

"Him you don't have to name," Samantha said, cringing. "That's Charlie Leach."[15]

"A private detective who stumbled onto your witchhood and threatened to go public with it – not once, but twice."[16]

"Yes. Wonder of wonders he never came back."

"What do you suppose would have happened had any of these mortals gone public about your witchhood?"

"Well, if I remember correctly, Mr. Brinkman wouldn't have. He told us he'd come to believe in witches, but later seemed to think our entire encounter was a dream," Samantha reported.

"And Mr. Robinson?" Malvina inquired. "He was armed and dangerous by mortal standards – he could easily have come away from that entire encounter spreading the word you were a witch."

"I never actually told him I'm a witch. I only moved a chair and a phone to stop him. Though, admittedly...that wasn't the most effective thing I could have done."

"Charlie Leach was probably the most dangerous of the triad," Malvina insisted vigorously. "You sent him to Mexico as a deterrent – yet, after he doggedly came back and threatened you again, all you did was turn him into a mouse for a minute and produce a fake money tree as ransom for a mortal woman who had been changed into a cat. Is that accurate?"

Samantha got a little flustered. "Yes – it is...my mother had transformed Darrin's client, and we needed to get her back from Mr. Leach – "

"Did it occur to you that Mr. Leach could have gone to mortal newspapers or a television station with the truth of your witchly identity when he ultimately didn't get what he wanted? And that, by allowing him to roam free with knowledge of that identity, you were not only endangering yourself, but potentially endangering us all?"

"We were just trying to deal with the situation at hand first before..."

Malvina made the Leach projection disappear. "Thank you, witch Samantha. I now turn the floor over to the warlock George."

Darrin stared at the Witches' Council in confusion. "How could they possibly know all that?" he asked rhetorically. "It's not like they were there for any of it."

"I assume you recall when we made ourselves invisible," Maurice prompted Darrin, patting Adam's head and calling up the time he bestowed his son-in-law with powers of his own, which they'd used to spy on a McMann and Tate competitor.[17] "The Council could have been monitoring Samantha the same way."

"Also, Durwood, every witch gives off molecules unique to the individual," Endora expounded. "With the right spell, it is not inconceivable to collect those molecules and extract memories from them. And, there's always good old fashioned surveillance via the atmospheric continuum."

"Big Brother *is* watching," Darrin scoffed, referring to *1984*, the dystopian George Orwell classic he'd once read in college. "Man, it must suck to be a witch."

Endora raised an eyebrow thoughtfully.

10 On A Trial Basis

Samantha watched George straighten his fancy suit jacket. She hadn't seen him since her newlywed days with Darrin; George had turned himself into a raven as part of his plan to lure Samantha back to the witchy life, only to be lured himself by the charms of then next door neighbor Danger O'Riley. Hmm...Danger...

Somehow, George made even his inquiry toward his former flame sound suggestive. "Samantha – is it true that you once put a dream spell on your husband to warn him of the dangers inherent in telling the world you're a witch?"[1]

Samantha hesitated, feeling Darrin's gaze behind her. "Yes...it is."

Darrin's voice was barely above a whisper. "That was you?"

"Would you explain to the Council what led you induce such a dream in him?" George posed.

"As I recall," Samantha began, "we'd had an argument after I used my powers to subdue a drunk who'd been pestering me. In his upset, Darrin suggested we go public with my identity."

"I see."

"But he was just angry! I knew that, so I thought if I showed him what could happen if mortals found out I was a witch, he would go soft on the idea. And soft he went."

"Crisis averted," George commented, hinting at neither sarcasm nor sympathy. "Are you able to call to mind the warnings your dream spell entailed?"

"Let's see," Samantha said as she fiddled with her "S" necklace. "I depicted some mortals as scared – and others as greedy and wanting to take advantage of my witchcraft." Samantha often wondered how the Kravitzes, and Larry Tate, respectively, would react in the waking world; if she ever got back to 1164 Morning Glory Circle, she might find out. "I projected a public craze and had the United States military taking us into custody so I would magically protect the country."

"Did you also project the truth of your witchhood onto a group of mortals at one Burning Oak Country Club?"[2]

Samantha had completely forgotten about that. "Yes," she admitted, wishing she could shrink down in her seat. "Darrin's agency had a client who wanted us to join. The members were snobs claiming they were purebred Americans...so I dug into their pasts to show them they were just like the immigrants they were trying to screen out."

"Did you have help obtaining this information?" George wanted to know.

"Um, yes, from my Aunt Hagatha and my mother."

Maurice gave his wife a sideways glance. Endora shrugged.

"Was it necessary to reveal yourself as a witch to prove your point?"

"No," Samantha answered sheepishly. "I was trying to promote equality for minorities, which is something I feel very strongly about – and I guess, in my pique, I cited us as the ultimate minority."

"Cited to six mortals directly, with nearly another dozen standing by listening."

"I...don't think any of them believed me."

"Could you have scared them, or inspired greed in them? Perhaps created a public craze, or been taken into custody to magically protect the United States? The events at Burning Oak came very close to realizing the cautionary tale you told via dream spell."

Samantha stared up at Hepzibah, aghast. "Is this a hearing or a trial?"

"Let's move on to individuals," George continued. "Two years ago, your powers were removed by the Council for exposing your witchcraft to this woman."[3] George stretched his hand out flat in front of him, and Phyllis appeared, motionless, on the platform facing Samantha. Darrin bolted up in his seat between Endora and Maurice, half horrified to see his mother on display by witches, half relieved he could see for himself she was okay.

"She had witnessed my mother and me zapping furniture back and forth," Samantha explained, resisting the urge to fire a blaming glance at Endora. "So, yes, I told Mrs. Ste – Phyllis – that I'm a witch. She was perfectly fine with it. Though afterwards, I worked to convince her she had only hallucinated things."

"Had it not occurred to you that having your powers cut off was meant to serve as an overall warning?"

"Honestly, no; I thought it only applied to the situation regarding Phyllis Stephens."

"And just five weeks later, you revealed yourself yet again, this time to a mortal toy salesman called Irving Bates!"[4]

"How else was I supposed to explain Tabitha turning him into a little boy?"

George turned his palm straight up again, causing Phyllis to pop out and Mrs. Peabody to pop in.

"How about this mortal?"[5] George had become much less flirtatious by this point.

"That's my teacher!" Tabitha exclaimed. Endora gently shushed her granddaughter; Darrin helped by holding the girl's hand.

Samantha felt as if someone had thrown a burlap sack over her head and taken to her with a stick. "Yes...I told her as well."

"What were the circumstances of *this* reveal?"

"I caught Mrs. Peabody snooping on Tabitha. You see, my mother had endowed Tabitha with knowledge befitting a genius; naturally, that drew the attention of her mortal elementary school teacher. She saw Tabitha levitating a ball in the backyard and wanted to tell the authorities we were from outer space. I felt that telling her the truth instead was the lesser of several evils."

George cocked his head. "To you, what does this mortal's posture indicate?"

Samantha examined the woman with the bun tightly wound on top of her head. Mrs. Peabody stood with her hands framing her eyes, her mouth agape. "It looks...as if she's trying to see in someplace."

"Into your house. Tonight. She watched you confide your identity to your party guests," George announced.

"What?"

"She never bought your story that you're a family of retired vaudeville magicians. You yourself heard her say she still believes you're a witch. If we send you back to the mortal world, what do you think she will do with the knowledge she just gained?"

Letting out a slow breath, Samantha quietly replied, "I have no idea."

"Thank you, Samantha." Did George's tone reflect just a little regret for his hard line with a witch he once adored? George waved, and Mrs. Peabody disappeared. "The floor now recognizes Judge Bean."

"Daddy, it's not fair," Tabitha told Darrin as Mrs. Peabody faded from view. "They're not letting Mother tell her side of things."

Samantha turned to acknowledge her daughter. "It's like that sometimes, sweetheart. In both the mortal world and the witch world."

"Are you going to let them get away with it?"

"Samantha!" Judge Bean's shrill bark was unmistakable, nearly causing Samantha to jump. "Your mortal abode has been graced by several visitors from the past, has it not?"

"By 'from the past,'" Samantha asked, wanting clarification, "I assume you mean visitors from history?"

"I do."

"Our...abode...has, Judge – though usually by accident and never from the use of my own powers." Samantha suddenly remembered she'd once conjured up Cleopatra to entice Julius Caesar into going back to B.C.[6]; she hoped Judge Bean wouldn't read the realization on her face as her having lied under oath.

"What, if anything, do the following historical figures you encountered have in common?" The Judge zapped five imposing figures into the display area; they looked like a humanized table of contents from a history book. "Sigmund Freud[7], Queen Victoria[8], Napoléon Bonaparte[9], Paul Revere[10], George Washington[11]."

Samantha felt like she was back at one of her witches' finishing schools trying to answer a stumper put to her by one of the professors. "Um...they all hail from the eighteenth and nineteenth centuries?"

"They were all told you're a witch," Judge Bean snorted. "By you."

"Now, wait a minute!" Samantha's head swam in her attempt to sort out long-ago details. "If I remember right, it was Uncle Arthur who squealed to Napoléon about us, not me. And I only made the point to Queen Victoria so Aunt Clara would send her back, since she had implied the queen would object to her being a witch." Looking up at Hepzibah, Samantha asked the High Priestess, "Actually, has anyone ever told you that you bear a striking resemblance to Queen Victoria, Your Majesty?"[12]

Darrin quietly leaned toward Samantha's left ear. "When was Queen Victoria at our house? You've never mentioned that."

"Well? You were out of town at the time – "

"I still have the floor," Judge Bean reminded the hall. "Witch Samantha, do you understand what you risked in letting these lesser evolved mortals return to their own times with knowledge of your being a witch, let alone the knowledge that witches exist at all?"

"I appreciate the potential for risk, but how do we know visitors from the past even retain memories from the present?"

The judge folded his arms. "George Washington did. When your maid, Esmeralda, rematerialized him, he had told his wife, Martha Washington, about the wonders of the 20th century.[13] One has to assume he also informed her about your supernatural status. Thank you." The quintet of notable mortals vanished.

"Carlotta?" came Hepzibah's invitation to speak. Samantha had to keep from laughing as the Contessa Piranha not-so-subtly waved away the bright pink ostrich plumes that drifted from Carlotta's cuffs while Rodney tried not to sneeze.

"I would like to delve further into the subject of Samantha's impact on historical figures." Carlotta spoke imperiously, with almost a musical cadence; as had been the case when Samantha last experienced Carlotta, Samantha detected a slight hint of a European accent. "When the witch Clara brought Benjamin Franklin out of the past, did you also inform him he was in the 20th century?"[14]

"That's correct; like General Washington, I thought it would be easier to tell Mr. Franklin the truth rather than jump through hoops denying it. Especially when he could see for himself he wasn't in his own time period."

"And did you share this same kind of calendric information with the visiting Queen Victoria?"

"Yes."

"Julius Caesar?"

"Yes..."

"Paul Revere?"

"Yes!"

"And one would presume all of them returned to their time with knowledge of the present," Carlotta asserted. "You showed Benjamin Franklin the significance of his inventions – you gave Paul Revere foreknowledge of other inventions. And you allowed Julius Caesar access to information about his own assassination! How might history have changed if the emperor did not die in 44 B.C. as he was fated to?"[15]

Samantha planted her hands flat on the table to stay grounded as she stared determinedly at Hepzibah. "I will concede that I haven't always exercised the most responsibility when it comes to sharing details of the present with visiting figures from history," Samantha told the High Priestess, "but this entire line of questioning is irrelevant! At issue here are the ramifications of my telling mortals I'm a witch. Present-day mortals. And that is the only issue."

Hepzibah considered this. "True," she said after a period of silence. "That these mortals from history obtained information about their own futures from Samantha is cause for concern, but has no bearing on this hearing. The Council will strike Carlotta's inquiry."

"Fine," Carlotta huffed, crossing her arms and making her feathers fly. "I thereby surrender the floor."

"We will move on to the witch Grimalda," Hepzibah instructed. "And Samantha – in case you were wondering how it is history remained unchanged after you were so careless...the visitors' memories were purged by the Council."

"An experience you are about to share," Maurice pointed out, looking straight ahead and not at Darrin. The great warlock's tone didn't give away whether he was for or against that actuality.

As Grimalda began to speak, Samantha could barely believe this was the same witch who had sat on her couch thrilled that little Adam had finally displayed powers of his own. "I should like for you to outline, Samantha, how it was you came to be Queen of the Witches."

Samantha gently indicated Ticheba. "Her former majesty made a surprise visit to my home one day. She told me she was abdicating and that I was to assume the crown from her. None of us in our family knew at the time I was chosen at birth for queendom – I must admit I've never quite understood our form of monarchy. In the mortal world, the throne is passed down through royal families."[16]

Endora and Maurice traded an uncomfortable glance. When Darrin noticed it, Endora softly murmured to her husband, "Here, I'll take Adam for a while." And with that, her snoozing grandson was suddenly in her arms, freeing Maurice to stretch his.

"While that's a fascinating perspective on witches' royalty," Grimalda went on flatly, "what I'd like to know is, do you remember the Oath of Office you took during your 1967 coronation – specifically, its final two lines?"

"Certainly," Samantha assured. "'To preserve, protect, and to defend/The Laws of Witchdom to the end.'"

Grimalda became somber. "When you turned yourself into a stereotypical old crone to deter an amorous magazine salesman[17], were you defending the Laws of Witchdom to the end?"

"I..." Samantha found she had no defense for this one.

"Conceivably the time you changed into a crone on a skating rink in front of more than a dozen mortals and made a spectacle of yourself on the ice[18] was your way of 'accepting the crown' and 'holding it dear,'" Grimalda rebuked, referring to the earlier part of the Oath.

Samantha willed her voice back into action. "In a way...yes. Our skating instructor was disparaging witches. And he made passes at me with Tabitha a few feet away; I felt he needed to be taught a lesson. I might add that I was no longer queen during either of these instances."

"Oh, do let me understand. To correct a mortal's misconception about witches, you presented yourself as our single most hated image, then restored yourself – which basically confirmed your witchhood to an entire rink of mortal skaters. And it is the height of contradiction that this was the exact same image you denounced the mortal Mr. Brinkman for perpetuating when you revealed yourself to him campaigning against it."[19] Grimalda kept going though she saw Samantha open her mouth to speak. "I have nothing more for this witch, Your Majesty," she called up to Hepzibah.

"Then the floor recognizes our former queen Ticheba," the High Priestess declared, nodding toward the chair to her immediate right.

In the entire eight years of Samantha's marriage, she'd never once given a thought to the idea of being separated from Darrin, at least not outside his eventual mortality. This despite all the spells her mother had cast on him, the times her father had threatened him, the constant pressure from witchy friends, family – and indeed, the very Council before her. But, at this moment, a life with no Darrin Stephens – a life in which Darrin Stephens would not know of her existence or that of their children – was realer than it had been since she told Darrin "I do" at that justice of the peace in Manhattan.

"During your brief reign," Ticheba commenced, as royally as if she were still perched upon the throne herself, "did you reveal yourself as a witch to a mortal called Jesse Mortimer?"

"Was he...the grumpy old man I took to the North Pole to meet Santa Claus?"[20]

"He was. How did you transport that grumpy old man to the North Pole?"

"On a – " Samantha knew finishing the sentence would be like throwing herself into quicksand. "On a broom."

"You flew Mr. Jesse Mortimer to the workshop of Santa Claus on a broom," Ticheba frowned, "while ruler presiding over all of us – as the witch in whom rested the highest responsibility toward speaking for us and representing us fairly and accurately. Rather than use the opportunity to debunk one of our greatest stereotypes, you, a sitting monarch, perpetuated it."

Samantha finally allowed herself to look back at her parents. Her eyes were imploring, fraught – and yet she knew there was nothing they could do.

"This is reminiscent of a similar situation three years earlier, in which you presented yourself to a human boy, displaying to him the broom and witches' hat he expected before flying *him* to the North Pole[21]," Ticheba added. "Granted, you weren't queen then, but it must be noted that you willfully eschewed educating a mortal child about who and what witches really are, instead cementing his misconception about us."[22] Ticheba exhaled sharply. "I take no pleasure in saying this, Samantha, but I have my doubts as to whether or not you have a place in our witches' world, let alone the mortal world."

"This is ridiculous," Samantha told Hepzibah, cutting in before the remaining two Council members could be called. "I lobbied for this hearing to get a chance to speak!"

"You *have* been granted a chance to speak," Hepzibah replied, "by answering the inquiries of the Noble Eight. The floor recognizes the Contessa Piranha."

The High Priestess' niece twirled one of her spiral curls. "Someone needs to say that we have gotten rather off-topic. The only reason we gathered into this emergency session and dropped whatever other interesting thing we might have been doing is because, just this evening, Samantha unmasked herself as a witch to a dozen mortals. Discussing her actions while living in the mortal world establishes a pattern, yes, but it is only tonight's events that bring this judgment against her, and therefore tonight's events should be our focus. Witch Samantha, what possessed you to disclose your witchly identity to your party guests?"

"You already know," Samantha stated. "You saw that disclosure play out over the atmospheric continuum, didn't you?"

"I would like to hear it from your lips," Piranha permitted.

"All right." Samantha shifted in her chair. "My son turned one of the mortal children into a zebra in view of my aforementioned guests. I knew they wanted answers and that there was no way of explaining that transformation without telling the truth. It was a risk, of course – but, in my opinion, a calculated one."

Piranha's diamond choker glittered in the light of the levitating chandeliers. "Like the historical figures that became privy to your witchhood – and 20th century information – you could have simply made those mortals forget what they saw."

"I pondered that," Samantha conceded. "However, after doing so, I felt I had no reason not to trust this particular group of people."

"Trust, eh?" The Contessa waved her perfect French manicure, and the frozen forms of the Wilsons appeared in the display area below Hepzibah.

"Keith and Dorothy?" the perplexed Samantha asked. "Like they can't empathize with being part of a marginalized group?"

"You haven't known them all that long," Piranha pointed out, "and just because they're a fellow minority doesn't automatically insure empathy. Remember, no matter what, they're still mortal."

Darrin had to keep Tabitha from rushing forward from her chair.

Piranha zapped again and the Wilsons were replaced by Larry Tate. "Do you, honestly and in all sincerity, trust *this* mortal after the many times he's fired your husband and demonstrated greed over personal loyalty? I'm sure I don't have to remind you he was ready to cash in on our much-talked-about historical figures – Benjamin Franklin, Napoléon, and George Washington most specifically." The next mortal the Contessa materialized for display actually elicited soft groans among the Council.

Gladys Kravitz. Her ample, red-headed presence made Piranha's next words carry extra weight for Samantha. "'No reason not to trust this particular group of people,' you said. No reason not to trust this woman who thought you were an alien[23], who attempted to expose you in a mortal court of law[24], who threatened to go to the authorities after those creatures from Tabitha's Hallowe'en book transformed her bratty nephew[25]," Piranha scoffed. "You've spent enough time among humans now to know that they're all the same. For centuries, they killed each other in the Crusades because some didn't pray to the same deity. Your own chosen country waged war on itself because enough of its citizens felt it was right to enslave those of a different skin color. How many wars are going on right now here in 1972 because mortals simply can't resist forcing dominion over one another? Face it, Samantha – they are constitutionally incapable of existing without persecuting those who are different. And your party guests are no exception." Piranha popped Gladys out in a huff.

"Darrin's not like that," Samantha insisted. "And I know him better than any other mortal."

"Let's talk about your Darrin, shall we?"

All heads turned toward Rodney, who was cockily observing his fingernails.

"The Contessa Piranha still has the floor," Hepzibah reprimanded.

"It's all right, Auntie," Piranha pooh-poohed. "I've said my bit. Go ahead, Rodney." The young sorcerer, who was obviously trying to present himself as older in his snazzy suit, cleared his throat. "Oh. I mean, Warlock Rodney now has the floor."

Rodney looked as smug and haughty as Samantha had always remembered him to be. "At what point did you tell Darrin Stephens you're a witch – the day you met?"

"No," Samantha replied stiffly, already sensing where Rodney was headed.

"Then it must have been when he proposed to you."

"No."

"Really? Then when exactly did you tell him?"

Samantha parted with her answer reluctantly and irately. "On our wedding night."[26]

"On your wedding night!" Rodney repeated in mock horror. "Most brides surprise their new husbands with lingerie. Why did you wait so long to tell the human what you are? Could it be you were afraid he would reject you if he found out sooner?"

Samantha's face was stone. "There was...that factor."

"Maybe that wasn't an unfounded fear. In deciding whether or not to continue his days-old marriage to you, this Darrin immediately ran to his doctor and his friend Dave about your witchy identity. So much for trust."

The words came out before Darrin could attempt to keep them in. "Yeah, but they thought I was full of it! So what difference does it make now?"

"The mortal will remain silent," the High Priestess bellowed, "or we will have it removed from these proceedings."

"'It'?" Samantha flared.

"You know, Samantha, the Council has been observing your mortal husband from the beginning. Long before I came to visit you in my clever canine form that time," Rodney continued. "Tell me, wasn't he concerned that the mother-in-law he was about to meet had five eyes?"[27]

"All right, yes, but that came from me baiting him because – "

" – he was worried she would have a pointy hat to go along with a pointy nose. Then there was the case of your friend Gertrude. Your husband dissuaded his mortal pal from marrying Gertrude because he thought she was a witch – while freshly married to you, also a witch. A bit hypocritical, *n'est-ce pas*?[28] Moving on, do you happen to remember a Machiavellian mortal named Gideon Whitsett?"

Samantha was getting so tired her memory failed her. "Not off hand."

"Gideon Whitsett was the ordinary human your husband blamed for sabotaging his – what do you call it? Job? He claimed witches would take over his agency. Its building. The street. The world![29] On top of that, he referred to a member of this very Council as 'a big spook' – the warlock George."[30]

George pushed up his cuff like he was contemplating using

magic. "Did he now?"

"What do the actions of my husband have to do with my telling our mortal party guests I'm a witch?" Samantha railed. "It's plain as day you're trying to punish him and my children alongside me, but this hearing is about my conduct and my conduct only. What's next – prosecuting Adam for creating this situation?"

"He did inform your Mrs. Peabody of his mother's supernatural designation[31], but I guess we can let that one slide," Rodney offered.

"Oh, then allow me to commend you on your generosity."

"The respondent will refrain from editorializing," ordered the High Priestess. "Continue, warlock Rodney."

"Samantha, how did your husband feel about the idea of having a child by a witch?"

"Once Tabitha and Adam were born, he loved them as much as I've seen any mortal father love his children."

Rodney tsk-tsked. "'Once Tabitha and Adam were born.' How about...before they were born?"

"I...don't understand the question."

"Isn't it true that before your first pregnancy, that mortal" – Rodney pointed directly at Darrin – "that very mortal wondered *what* his child would be, as if you would one day give birth to some horrible creature?"[32]

Samantha instinctively whirled around to face Tabitha, silently entreating. But Tabitha was staring at her father in horror, slowly pulling away from him.

"Tabitha," Darrin said desperately. "I know how that must sound to you, but I can explain it as soon as we – "

Without a word, Tabitha crossed her index fingers three times and disappeared.

Samantha was on her feet a second later. "I'll be right back. I have to go after my daughter."

"We have not given anyone permission to leave," Hepzibah droned.

Samantha was livid. "You're all right with a little girl – a minor even by witch standards – wandering around unsupervised who knows where?"

"Relax, Samantha," Rodney said nonchalantly. "I'm almost done. Then you can go find her."

Samantha could swear the room was spinning as she again took her seat.

"I'd like you to please tell the Council what happened some seven years ago when you allowed your mortal access to your powers."

Darrin's brow furrowed in confusion.

"Come on, Rodney," Samantha implored. "Enough is enough."

"Then I'll tell the Council. He – "

"He'd sprained his ankle and was bedridden. I decided to infuse the house with magic to fill small requests – food, comfort, things like that – while he recuperated."[33]

"And wasn't he almost immediately seduced by said powers to the point he wanted to tour the world living by witchcraft?"

Samantha was at the end of her rope. "You mean the Council didn't unanimously approve that decision? I would have thought there'd be a celebration rivaling the V-J Day parades at the end of World War II."

"If this is how the mortal closest to you behaves," Rodney said, leaning forward as sternness took the place of his smugness, "then how can the other mortals in your circle that learned you're a witch tonight be expected to behave any differently?" Rodney turned to gaze up at Hepzibah. "I surrender the floor, Your Majesty."

For several seconds there was an inadvertent void it seemed no one wanted to fill. Samantha watched the fog eddying over the floor, feeling as though she was going to burst out of her skin. Finally, Hepzibah rose from her throne and spoke.

"We believe we have heard sufficient testimony," she began, resting the tip of her scepter on her left palm. "While we grant there were often mitigating circumstances behind many of the instances in which mortals gained knowledge of the witch Samantha's true identity, that is not enough to inspire rendering a different decision. Therefore, from this moment forward, the mortal known as Darrin will have his memory purged of anything having to do with Samantha, who shall remain within the witches' realm and be barred from ever returning to the mortal world." The High Priestess raised her scepter. The purples and pinks above began getting darker.

> *"With the Noble Eight the throne contends*
> *This mortal's mind, I hereby cleanse! – "*

"No!"

Hepzibah stopped mid-zap, incredulously brandishing the scepter behind her head. "What?"

Samantha stood slowly. "I...said...*no*."

The High Priestess' eyes widened. "How dare you obstruct the carrying out of a royal decree!"

"No, Your Majesty. How dare *you*." No one among the Noble

Eight escaped Samantha's glare. "How dare all of you. When I requested this hearing, it was for the purpose of having my say!"

"You have had it," Hepzibah fumed, now pointing her scepter at Samantha. "And we might add, you have done a most thorough job of incriminating yourself."

"How easy that was, only being allowed to answer questions from the Council that were engineered to have me incriminate myself! You know what this is? It's a...kangaroo court!"

Samantha vigorously waved with both hands, and suddenly about a dozen of the marsupials were hopping around the great hall.

"Samantha, really," Malvina said, rolling her eyes. "Such histrionics."

Rodney smirked. "I dunno. I think they're kind of fun."

"I hope the janitorial staff knows the right spell to clean up after these beasts," Piranha sniffed.

"I hate to think what we'd have before us if she'd zapped up a hung jury," George snickered.

"Silence! All of you!" Hepzibah was not fooling around. She scowled at Samantha. "Remove the creatures at once!"

"I'm just illustrating a point...Hepzibah." On one level Samantha realized she was taking her existence into her hands merely referring to the empress by her given name, but she was so furious that she decided to "go for the gusto," as that TV beer commercial's slogan suggested.

"We fail to see what possible point wildlife could make."

"We're right back where we started – only instead of just you trying and convicting me, we've got the whole lot of you trying and convicting me! I am not leaving this hearing room unless I am given the floor and not interrupted until I surrender it."

"You do realize," Hepzibah said ominously, "that you could be forced to comply with our ruling."

"You know what? Do what you want, Hepzibah. But *I demand to be heard!*"

Ten witches and one mortal collectively held their breath in that moment, not counting one young half-warlock who was mercifully still in a state of supernatural slumber in Endora's arms. Samantha decided if it all ended now, she'd at least go out being true to herself.

The High Priestess raised her head. "This Council shall reconvene in one hour. At which time, the witch Samantha...shall be heard."

Saying no more, Hepzibah made a sweeping gesture with scepter and vanished, taking the entire Witches' Council with her. As Samantha stood there looking at her husband, her son, and her parents, the cavernous chamber was eerily silent – except for the sound of bouncing kangaroos.

11 Daughters of the Revolution

Samantha seemed as though she were in a fog, undoubtedly coming down from the adrenaline surge she'd needed to face Hepzibah and the Council.

"Um, Sam?" Darrin said, trying to get his wife's attention. "The kangaroos?"

"What?" Like someone trying not to fall asleep, Samantha shook her head animatedly. "Oh! Sorry." Samantha took a moment to focus, then twitched her nose – and the animals were gone.

"'Kangaroo court,'" Darrin remarked as he stood up, which prompted his in-laws to do the same. "I'll never be able to hear that term again without seeing this in my head."

Samantha reached over the railing that separated the hearing table from the gallery and collected sleeping Adam from Endora. "Oh, what a mess you've gotten me into, huh?" Samantha half chuckled, kissing the boy's forehead affectionately. "I suppose it was only a matter of time. Sweetheart," she asked of Darrin, "I need you to watch Adam while I look for Tabitha."

"Samantha! You have less than an hour to craft a defense against the Witches' Council!" Endora reminded her daughter.

"I don't care. I've got to go after Tabitha!"

Maurice tried to calm Samantha. "Don't you worry about that. I'll find my granddaughter and bring her back to you."

The mighty warlock placed his top hat on his head and was making ready to pop out when he heard an unexpected voice say something unexpected.

"Take me with you, Maurice."

It was Darrin.

"I hardly need a mortal along to track down a young witch," was

Maurice's reply.

Darrin was uncharacteristically calm with his father-in-law considering their long-standing volatile relationship. "Listen, Maurice...what Tabitha heard was about my attitude before she was born. She's upset with *me*. So if we're going to make this right, it has to come from me. We can fly from Maryland to Madrid to the moon if that's what it takes. But I'm the only one who can fix this."

Maurice studied Darrin carefully, cracking just the hint of a smile. "All right, Dolphin[1]. Just don't foul this up."

"I guess you're on Adam duty then, Sam," Darrin confirmed. "By the way, is Adam all right like that, knocked out by witchcraft? I mean, what if he has to go to the bathroom or something..."

"There's no need for concern in that regard," Maurice said reassuringly. "In fact, why don't we make the boy more comfortable?" Samantha's father made a grand zap toward the Council's display area, where an impossibly large bed came from nowhere. Another zap and Adam popped out of Samantha's arms, materializing on the giant mattress where the peaceful toddler was dwarfed by pillows the size of couches.

"While they go in search of Tabitha, I'll help you build your case," Endora informed Samantha.

"I don't want your help," Samantha spat. "Maybe if you had protested Hepzibah's ruling instead of encouraging it, I wouldn't have been grilled eight times over by witches who don't care any more about my marriage than you do. Siccing that seductress Sarah Baker on Darrin weeks after our wedding[2] – Ophelia, the kitty-turned-human a few months ago![3] I'll build my own case, thank you very much." Samantha turned on her heel and headed toward the mammoth bed to check on Adam. But Maurice appeared in front of her, blocking her path.

"Don't speak to your mother like that!" Maurice scolded. "We are still your parents. And...we've simply wanted what's best for you, that's all."

"You mean what you thought was best for me."

Endora popped in next to her husband. "Samantha – it's true we've never supported your marriage." She called out to Darrin, who was still in the first row of the gallery behind the railing. "Durwood, you know that better than anybody." Endora placed her hands on Samantha's upper arms. "Darling, I am violating an edict by telling you this – but much of my meddling has been...under the directive of Hepzibah.[4] I promised her right from the beginning that your marriage wouldn't last, back when Ticheba was still on the throne.

Even in those days, Hepzibah held an impressive rank of her own as High Priestess; she gave me carte blanche to interfere any way I wanted. And I cannot tell a lie – a lot of it I did for kicks. Maybe I'm more like your Uncle Arthur than I thought." Endora grimaced as she spoke of her practical-joking brother.[5]

"There have been times I've wondered," Darrin divulged.

"You're angry because I didn't stand up to Hepzibah," Endora continued. "You know as well as I do that once she gets a notion in her head, she generally cannot be moved – and she's worse than Ticheba in terms of transforming those who don't share her viewpoints."[6]

Samantha was rigid. "So you were more afraid for yourself than you were for me."

"I suggested wiping my grandchildren's memories in an attempt to protect them from the repercussions of Hepzibah ending your marriage! I tried to help in the only way that seemed possible, and that is the truth. I'm sorry you took that to mean I was aiding and abetting her judgment against you. Of course I've spent these years working to break up you and Dennis – but I never thought it would happen to this extreme. And I admit I never really took into consideration how it would affect Tabitha and Adam.[7] Until tonight."

Samantha kept a wall up, but seemed to have removed a brick or two from which to peek through. "So your helping me defend myself against the Council would make some kind of difference."

"I'd use the full force of my powers in the endeavor. To...well, to make up for my part in this."

"I don't know – " Samantha was surprised to see a receptiveness in Darrin's eyes, a look that actually suggested reconciliation. "Though I suppose together, we could come up with something more substantial than if I worked alone."

Maurice patted his wife on the arm, taking the opportunity to step in. "There's something else. It's not so that none of us knew you had been chosen to be queen. Your mother and I were told when we were expecting you. It was a life we tried to prepare you for – it's why we raised you the way we did, with every finery and the highest education, even by witch standards. But then you married a mortal, abandoning the destiny you didn't even know about. It would be safe to say there was a lot of resentment on all sides. From us," Maurice acknowledged, indicating Endora, "from much of the family. But especially from the Witches' Council."

Samantha's face became awash in confirmation. "I knew it. That's why they only started harassing me *after* I abdicated the throne!"[8]

"That move fueled their fire, yes," Maurice added. "And I would be lying if I said we did anything to extinguish it. But if the mortal life is truly what you want, Samantha...then it's time to let your parents come to your aid." The warlock instantly posed as if he were on a stage in London's West End. "'*Renowned prince, how shall poor Henry live, unless thou rescue him from full despair! –* '"

"Maurice, just track down Tabitha, would you?" Endora interrupted. "We have work to do."

"Yeah, who knows where she could be by now," Darrin worried.

"It's my feeling," Maurice confided, "that she isn't far at all."

Samantha, who had softened, gave her father a peck on the cheek. "Daddy, you even do Shakespeare's female roles with panache. Queen Margaret, right?"

"From *Henry VI – Part 3*, naturally. I taught you well." Maurice offered his arm to his son-in-law. "Hang on, Dustbin. I hope you don't get airsick." A second after Darrin grabbed Maurice's elbow, they were gone – with a surprising lack of fanfare.

Samantha stared up at Hepzibah's empty throne. "All right, we've got a lot of ground to cover," she told her mother. "I already have a few ideas – inspired by the very words of our own Witches' Council – but I don't know if it's going to be enough."

Endora zapped the dapper, dozing Adam off the massive bed and back into Samantha's arms. "Hold your child and follow me to Cloud 8. We have some molecules to collect."

"But the way they can monitor us – "

"Wait 'til you see the protection spell I'm going to cast over my house," Endora whispered into her daughter's ear. "You did once say I have the most powerful one-two punch in the cosmos.[9] Come along, dear!" Endora put one arm around Samantha and waved the other grandly. As the three generations of supernaturals popped out, Samantha couldn't decide whether to envy Adam or pity him for missing all of this.

*   *   *

After literally flying through the seeming endlessness of the witches' realm on the arm of a man who had literally disintegrated him – twice[10] – Darrin couldn't have been more surprised to suddenly find himself in his own living room. Drinks were still strewn around the coffee table, the end tables, on top of the TV; the ice in them had long since melted. The food – including Mrs. Kravitz's *kourabiedes* – waited patiently for consumption, though Darrin thought that some of the offerings were starting to look a little long in the tooth.

"Are you serious, Maurice?" Darrin said, chiding his father-in-law. "The potentially millions of places my daughter could zap herself to and you bring us here? When Sam was pregnant with Adam, Tabitha ran away by popping herself into her *Jack and the Beanstalk* book.[11] And one time I was at work, Tabitha turned herself into a cookie to make a break for it..."[12]

"Shh, Dobbin!" Maurice warned in a hushed tone. "Don't you understand that this is the perfect place for her to take refuge? What better sanctuary than home – when she thinks no one else is here?"

Darrin unconsciously covered his mouth. "I guess that does make a certain amount of sense."

"And if she hears you..." Maurice began.

"...she could just disappear again," Darrin finished. "Well, that rules out my calling for her – if she is, in fact, home."

"Only one way to know for certain. I'll race you upstairs – your mortal slowness might just work in our favor." After Maurice waved and popped out, Darrin gave himself a few extra seconds before making his way to Tabitha's room. He had a feeling Maurice's insult wasn't just an insult this time.

Tabitha had found one of her parents' suitcases and was gloomily attempting to fill it with as many clothes as she could, barely noticing the flowery multi-colored curtain next to her light green dresser. After her socks and separates were packed into her luggage, she then plodded to her closet and picked a pair of shoes up from its blue carpet, stopping at the shelf near her bed to retrieve a few favorite stuffed animals. Pitching her items on the bed, it occurred to her that she could have just zapped the suitcase full, or skipped the house completely and conjured up whatever she needed wherever she was going. Maybe she was too used to her parents telling her not to use witchcraft. Or maybe she just wanted to see her beloved room one more time.

The young witch nearly jumped when her grandpapa magically arrived with his loud, booming voice. "Tabitha!" Maurice exclaimed a little too chipperly, but not so much that Tabitha noticed. "What a great big girl you've become. Flying all the way back from the Witches' Council – and solo at that. Here just a few months back your mother had said you hadn't flown at all.[13] Impressive!"

"I guess," Tabitha shrugged. She wasn't in the mood for talking – or being talked out of leaving.

"We ought to spend more time together," Maurice told the child. "How about sometime soon we go someplace special, just you and me. Anywhere in the world – or another world! Just name it."

"I dunno. We'll see."

Maurice was getting that sinking feeling that came upon him when an audience didn't love one of his performances, which only happened once every few centuries. "So, your mother tells me you've started in a mortal school.[14] That must be fascinating. I don't know if you recall I experienced life as a mortal recently, when I came down with perimeridictimitis..."[15] *Come on, Durbin; tomatoes are about to fly in here...*

Darrin gently padded into his daughter's room. When Tabitha caught sight of him, she tried to cross her index fingers together and perform her special magical gesture, but Maurice gently stopped her. "Why don't you give him a chance, my darling." Looking Darrin right in the eye, Maurice told his son-in-law, "The curtain just went up. You're on."

"I don't wanna talk to you," the crestfallen Tabitha insisted. "That man said that you thought I was gonna be a...a..."

"A 'what'," Darrin nodded. "I'm sorry you had to hear that. Even more, I'm sorry to have to admit it's true – before you were born, I did worry what a child of mine and your mom's would be like." Darrin knelt in front of his daughter, whose retreat was foiled by Maurice standing behind her. "See, when I was growing up, I was taught that witches didn't exist. And if they did, they were ugly old crones – just like the kind you've seen in pictures and costumes every Hallowe'en. I'd gone my entire life with that image in my head – because that's what everyone around me believed, and I had no reason to believe otherwise...until I met your mother. Out of nowhere, things I'd always known to be impossible became possible. And it was amazing. But I did have trouble adjusting at first.[16] I mean, you go from being told witches are evil to the prospect of having a child with a witch – that's not an easy jump to make. Can you...understand what I mean?"

"Maybe." Tabitha was still mostly unmoved.

"The day your mom first told me we were having you...it was right after she had changed me back from Aunt Clara turning me into a monkey[17] – well, I'll tell you about that later. Anyway, you've never seen two people more excited to learn they were going to be parents. And the day you were born – I wish you could have seen it. Your Grandma Endora and I hugged, if you can believe that."[18]

"I think I'd have to see a picture to prove it."

"You didn't exhibit any powers your whole first year.[19] Did it throw me when suddenly you were floating pots and pans around the house every chance you got?"[20] The recollection got a smile out of

Tabitha. "Sure it did. But I never wanted you any less because of it. In fact, there have been times I've found myself in awe of what you're able to do. Maybe more in awe of how you've worked so hard at *not* using your witchcraft because you knew that's what I wanted."

"Well, we have a rule – " Tabitha started.

"No witchcraft," father and daughter said in unison.[21]

Darrin lovingly stroked Tabitha's hair. "I'm sorry you were hurt hearing what a bonehead I used to be. There's still a lot I don't understand about witches and witchcraft – and that's after just about seeing it all. But I do know one thing. I know how much I love you, and your mother and your brother, and I wouldn't want you guys any other way."

Tabitha looked up at her grandfather, then her father. A moment later, Darrin found Tabitha clinging to him tightly. He embraced her and rubbed her back reassuringly.

Maurice's comment was delivered with soft, extempore warmth. "Now that's what I call a standing ovation."

Darrin pulled away and took his daughter's hands, lovingly observing the girl. "Look at you, so grown-up in your flying suit...I love the purple...my little princess..."

"Princess?" The light in Tabitha's eyes could have illuminated a night game at Shea Stadium. "Princess! Daddy, can we go back to the Witches' Council now?"

Darrin had mixed feelings about subjecting his daughter to the Noble Eight again. "I don't know, sweetheart...I mean, they're letting your mom speak finally, but it is getting kinda late, and – "

"If that's where my granddaughter wants to go, then go there we shall!" Maurice proclaimed, his resounding theatricality back in full blossom. Darrin stood and prepared to again take Maurice's elbow, but instead, Tabitha offered her own hand. As Darrin squeezed it, Maurice hunched down. "All right, Tabitha, are you ready? Do you think you can lead the way?"

Tabitha nodded and closed her eyes for a moment, deeply concentrating. Then the trio vanished.

12 Geese and Ganders

At Cloud 8, the sleek little cat Shadow finished cleaning herself and popped in a dish piled high with tuna, not particularly paying attention to Endora's imperceptibly slow rotation. The commanding witch's hands were spread toward the sky as if they were great receptors of some untold power. Her eyes were closed and her head was thrown back; her mouth just slightly gaped open, adding to the trance-like effect. Had Samantha's own eyes been open, she might have found humor in her mother's revolving position, but she was absorbed as well; her fingers were at her temples and she gently moved her head back and forth, giving the impression she was speed-reading or desperately trying to memorize something.

Samantha inhaled deeply, then let it out over what could have been a whole minute. With that, she seemed to come back into her body, shielding her eyes as she opened them to the celestial bodies beyond.

Endora's breath was heavy and her arms flopped at her sides; she was grateful to find a chair to support herself near the floating bed where the slumbering Adam was still under his grandfather's spell.

"Mother, are you all right?"

"Yes, dear," Endora replied quietly. "It's just that molecule extraction was a lot less of a strain a millennium or two ago. Did you get what you needed?"

"And more. My face is tingling from it all. I can't believe how much of that I didn't remember."

"Good. Just let me collect myself and we'll get back to the Witches' Council. There's only about two minutes left to the recess."

"Let me at 'em," Samantha said, energized. "After defending

George Washington a few weeks ago[1], I should be able to come to my own defense handily. Wow, what was *in* those molecules? I feel like I'm ready to go ten rounds with Muhammed Ali."

"Muhammed – um, boating, isn't it?"

"Boxing," Samantha corrected. "Big mortal men put giant gloves on their hands and lots of padding in their mouths, then punch each other out in a square called a 'ring'. And I thought baseball was complicated."[2]

"Oh, boxing!" Endora exclaimed. "Were you there with your Uncle Arthur and me when Max Schmeling defeated Joe Louis in the '30s? Nineteen thirties, of course. Never could understand why that brother of mine dragged me with him to watch two perspiring men prancing around in shorts."

"That, Mother, is a discussion for another time."

* * *

Maurice's hands fidgeted behind his back, where neither his mortal son-in-law nor his half-mortal granddaughter could see them. Darrin was far more obvious, pacing so vociferously he cut a path in the endless fog at his feet. Tabitha collectedly stared at both of them.

"Darby, keep pacing that way and you'll wear a hole in the atmospheric continuum," Maurice said to Darrin, not looking at him.

"You might find this hard to understand," Darrin pointed out, "but given what we're facing, I'd just as soon get it over with. I didn't start feeling panicky until we got back here. The suspense of whether I lose all memories of my wife and kids is almost more unbearable than if I actually lose them. Selfish, maybe...but it's the human in me."

After a few more of Darrin's back-and-forths, Maurice reached out and stopped him. "Can you recall the time I presented to you a watch infused with my own witchcraft – and I turned you into a dog for refusing to accept it?"[3]

"Give my mortal memory some credit," Darrin frowned. "I still get cravings for Gaines-Burgers."

"Samantha was so compelling in convincing me to change you back that I told her she should have been a lawyer. If anyone can move the Witches' Council on your behalf...it's her. '*Oh, ye of little faith.*'"

"I thought witches didn't go in for Biblical stuff."

"Many witches were *there* for Biblical...stuff. One day, if I can be in a room with you long enough for you not to annoy me, I'll tell you about the instance in which I encountered John the Baptist – "

Suddenly it felt like all the oxygen – assuming oxygen was available to breathe in this unearthly locale – was being sucked out of the hall. Again, intense light ricocheted above, and this time even Darrin knew what it meant.

"Right on the dot," Maurice observed sardonically.

"Where's Samantha?" Darrin fretted.

"She'll be here...she'll be here."

All eight Council members popped in along with the High Priestess Hepzibah, who gravely clutched her scepter in both hands. "We now reconvene this session of the Witches' Council..." She was distracted by a large object in her display area. "What in the name of all that's witchly is that bed doing here?"

Maurice looked the closest to sheepish Darrin had ever seen him. "Oh! Terribly sorry." He hurriedly zapped the giant four-poster he'd created for Adam off the platform and out of existence.

"As we were saying," Hepzibah reiterated crossly, "the Witches' Council is once again in session, this time to hear the witch Samantha." Then the High Priestess became aware that only Darrin, Maurice, and Tabitha stood before her. "Mortal!" she roared, singling Darrin out. "Where is the witch Samantha? Surely you are privy to her whereabouts. We will nullify her forum to speak in ten seconds! Ten...nine...eight..."

Darrin found himself uncontrollably shuffling behind Maurice to avoid Hepzibah's scowl, now knowing how the Cowardly Lion must have felt facing the Great and Powerful Oz.

Samantha and Endora saved Darrin from further ire, appearing next to Samantha's assigned table, where the rest of the family had congregated. Adam was once more in his mother's arms. "I'm here, Your Majesty," Samantha said respectfully, but not particularly reverently.

"Do not waste this opportunity to speak, witch Samantha, and do not waste our time. Our clemency is not inexhaustible."

"One last indulgence, if it please." Samantha handed Adam over to Darrin, then turned to Maurice. "Daddy, as much as I hate to interrupt Adam's extended slumber, this is something I'd like him to be awake for."

Maurice obligingly waved his hand over the boy's forehead, and Adam sleepily stirred and yawned, unfazed by his non-human surroundings.

"Adam, sweetie," Samantha said lovingly. "I want you to be real good and real quiet while Mommy takes care of a few things."

She kissed him on the cheek, then bent down to give her daughter a quick peck. "You, too, Tabitha." Samantha popped everyone into the gallery, but couldn't be sure she didn't see an unusual glint in Tabitha's eye as she did.

Samantha turned to face Malvina, Grimalda, George, Ticheba, Judge Bean, the Contessa Piranha, Rodney – and especially, Hepzibah.

"We remind you that you are still under oath," Hepzibah ordained. Samantha nodded, and the entire legislative body took their seats. "The floor now recognizes the witch Samantha."

"Thank you, Your Majesty." Samantha ventured out from behind her table and strode back and forth along the semi-circle of the six-foot-tall judge's bench, scrutinizing each of the Council members. "You know, I was a little girl during the Salem witch hunts of the 1690s[4], but you've revived it in a way I wouldn't have thought possible in the 20th century. Bravo!" Samantha accentuated the mock accolade with slow applause that reverberated through the vast chamber.

"This is not the place for – " Hepzibah started to say.

"I have the floor." Tabitha had never seen her mother so furious, so forceful. "I stand here before you because I have committed the unforgivable sin of telling mortals that I'm a witch. If you only knew in how many ways Darrin and I tried to keep my identity a secret – just how many extremes we were willing to go to, and did. It's comical, really. Mortals could make a television show out of it.

"When I last stood in this very hearing room, I appealed to you to restore my powers, which you had removed to coerce me into leaving my mortal husband[5]. To restore the powers of my cousin, Serena, and of my Uncle Arthur, because they dared to side with me. To restore Tabitha's powers, because she was guilty only of being my daughter. The clouds were so conveniently thick that day when I accused you of condemning me for being different, I couldn't see any of you. I'm grateful to this time look you all in the face as I say I have never known such a group of self-righteous and spiteful hypocrites in my three centuries on this plane."

"That is enough, Samantha!" Hepzibah bellowed. "We shall not permit you to – "

"I...have...the...floor!" Samantha barked back, making each word a sentence. "And now, I am ready to call as witness the – "

"What?" "Witness?" The Noble Eight's astonished murmurs clearly voiced their opposition.

Judge Bean rematerialized his gavel and pounded it. Once the hall was again quiet, he squinted at Samantha. "This is highly improper. And unprecedented!"

"And being willing to excise my husband's memories of his family isn't?" Samantha retorted. "I shall use my time as I see fit. And it was agreed upon that I would speak without these interruptions. While I get the feeling I ruffled more than a few feathers giving up the throne" – Samantha hoped Hepzibah wouldn't catch on that her father had squealed – "I remind you all that I am a former monarch, and I insist upon the respect that title demands." Getting no more argument, Samantha said in a calmer tone, "I now call as witness... the witch Endora...the former queen mother."

There was another collective gasp in the room, but no vocal objection. Even Maurice looked surprised as his sometime wife zapped herself off her gallery seat and appeared in mid-air in front of Judge Bean, who grudgingly fulfilled his duty, staying in his seat as a silent protest. "Do you solemnly swear to tell the truth, the whole truth, and nothing but the truth, so help you, Cosmos?"

"Witches' honor," Endora swore, flashing the familiar "V" in front of her face.

"You may be seated."

Instantly, Endora was perched on the chair Samantha had occupied during the earlier session. Samantha gave her mother a worried, almost apologetic look. But Endora returned it with a highly subtle nod and the hint of a smile. Buoyed, Samantha began.

"Witch Endora, have you ever revealed your supernatural identity to mortals? At any time?"

Endora had often asked Samantha what a mother was for if she couldn't help her daughter in her hour of need.[6] Raising her head slightly, she answered, "On occasion."

"Are there particular occasions you can recall for us now?"

"I...once told a trio of mortal boys about being a witch."[7]

"When that would have been?"

"If I recall, a month or so after you were married."

"Were there any other occasions where mortal children were made aware of your witchcraft?"

"One I can think of. The next Hallowe'en, a different trio of youths participated in that bizarre ritual they have of collecting confections; these ruffians approached and tried to extort said items from me."[8]

Samantha rubbed her chin. "How and why did you expose your powers to them?"

Endora looked impish. "I turned myself into a tree. Why? To shoo them away. And...because it was diverting."

Samantha turned toward the Council. "Quite a different rationale than defending minorities or offering explanations to mortals who witnessed magical transformations." Samantha stepped up on the display platform. "Much has been made of my unfortunate decisions to perpetuate mortals' misconceptions about our kind. Witch Endora, did you not publicize that erroneous witch image yourself on All Hallows Eve, 1969?"

"Not intentionally," Endora rationalized, "but ultimately...yes."

"What led to this publicity?"

"I was incensed with your husband for encouraging activities that would further solidify the way mortals perceive us," Endora explained. "So I turned him into an old crone; at the time, I was sure that was how *he* still perceived us. And...he was photographed."[9]

"Didn't that photograph end up in the newspaper because, as a crone, he had broken a record collecting money for UNICEF – the United Nations Children's Fund, in case the Council was wondering – which only served to put that image in front of hundreds, if not thousands of mortals?"

"It did."

Samantha now approached her mother, hating what she had to say next. "Finally...we share something else besides genes, I believe. You yourself have been romantically involved with mortals – haven't you?" Sensing the Council's discomfort despite having her back to their bench, Samantha knew she had gotten to them. She then glanced at Maurice, trying to gauge his reaction. Was her parents' "informal marriage" really as open as they'd always claimed?

A borderline devilish expression played on Endora's face. "There's been a dalliance or two," she said. Samantha was still watching Maurice...who almost seemed as if he approved. Samantha had never understood the relationship between her mother and father, but she'd long ago realized it was not for her to understand.

"Why don't we just hit the highlights," Samantha suggested, stuffing down an ill-timed urge to giggle. "There was an author who was the victim of mistaken identity, correct?"

"Oh! Dear Bobby." Endora smiled at the recollection of Darrin's old friend, Bob Frazer.[10] "I met him posing as you – while taking your place at a dress fitting."

"Was it a casual, hello-and-goodbye meeting?"

"Galaxies, no. We – how do the mortals say it? – painted the town red. Several towns, actually, over the course of several days. As expected, the entire time, he thought I was you."

"And did he ever find out you're a witch?"

Endora shook her head. "No. I saw no reason to bring it up."

"But you did bring it up with a different mortal – a Bo Callahan?"

"Bo...Calla-who?" asked Endora, squaring her eyes.

Samantha licked her lip. "I'll give you a two-word refresher. 'Love potion'."[11]

"Love potion...love po – well, of course. Rollo! One of your incredibly attractive ex-beaux!" Endora's recognition was short-lived. "I never thought of it before...but Bob Frazer and Rollo looked an awful lot alike..."[12]

"Let's not confuse the Council. Would you please explain to them the link between the warlock Rollo and Bo Callahan?"

"Certainly. I brought Rollo to see you, hoping he would lure you away from your mortal existence."

George muttered under his breath. "Not very original, considering you recruited me to do the same thing."[13]

"Rollo had a supply of love potion," recalled Endora, "so when his charms didn't work on you, I felt the potion might."

"And what happened instead?"

"I accidentally took a sip of your drink, which Rollo had spiked. I confess I don't remember too much after that."

Samantha again faced the Council. "I do know what happened after that – but in an effort to avoid admitting hearsay, allow me to present the events as they happened, as absorbed by the atmospheric continuum." Samantha twitched her nose, and a projection of a colorfully dressed Endora on the arm of a businessman with gray, curly hair faded in; they were standing in front of a plain, older mortal woman. The woman assured Endora and the man that the judge would be out soon and that getting married didn't hurt none. The man seemed bewildered, not understanding how they'd gotten to the justice of the peace – Endora replied it was witchcraft; when you were in love, the whole world was witchcraft. The man concluded that it was all a crazy dream, anyway, and after that short presentation, the figures dissolved into nothingness.

In the gallery, Tabitha looked up at her father. "How come I'm always asleep during the good stuff?"

"Rollo told me afterwards what I'd done under the influence of his potion," Endora professed. "It's a little horrifying seeing it."

Samantha put her hands on the table and faced Endora directly. "So you did tell Mr. Callahan about your being a witch."

"The atmospheric continuum doesn't lie. It seems as though he didn't believe me."

"Just like the members of Burning Oak Country Club didn't

believe me[14]," Samantha noted. "I thank you, witch Endora; I have no more questions." Out of the line of sight of Hepzibah and the others, Samantha gave her mother a quick wink. Endora popped herself back into the gallery.

"I'd also like to draw attention to the fact that Rollo was using his love potion on mortal women," Samantha told her semi-circle of accusers. "And if you do further molecular extractions as I have, you will see that my mother and I are hardly the only witches to have romantic encounters with humans. My own father," Samantha said, indicating Maurice with a long sweep of her arm, "has been seen in cute little Parisian bistros with mortal morsels. Remember Yvette and Angelique, Daddy? Your 'karate instructors?'"[15]

Maurice looked as hungry as he had when Samantha and Endora had found him in the café flanked by French *femmes*. "How could I forget," he leered. "Such form."

"I would also submit – and all this can be verified – that my friend and maid Esmeralda accepted the attentions of Italy's very mortal Bonanno Pisano, and Darrin's client, Count Bracini, also of Pisa.[16] Aunt Clara briefly dated one Kensu Mishimoto on the rebound from her sometime beau, Ocky.[17] My cousin, Serena, purposely searched for a mortal mate through computerized matchmaking services[18], not to mention carried on with my husband's ancestor, Darrin the Bold[19], which could have changed history.[20] And, let's not forget, there was Serena's intense fling with a certain...Harrison Woolcott."

Piranha tried to maintain an uneasy poise.

"Harrison Woolcott," Samantha repeated, "a billionaire mortal who was stolen away from my cousin – by the Contessa Piranha."[21] Mouths fell open in the semi-circle, none wider than the mouth of Piranha's aunt, Hepzibah. "Piranha should be disqualified – if not from the Council itself, then certainly these proceedings, as she has a clear-cut conflict of interest." Samantha then pointed to a well-dressed warlock on her left. "And you, warlock George! You, who castigated me for informing humans of my witchly heritage... when you did the exact same thing during your involvement with Miss Dora 'Danger' O'Riley![22] Your Majesty, George should also be barred from this hearing!"

"Ah, yes, 'Danger'..." George recalled, whistling. "Is she still in my harem? It's gotten so big, I can't keep track."

"I hope her sister 'Pleasure'[23] hasn't had to put out a missing persons report on her," Darrin mused, to the confusion of Maurice, Endora, and Tabitha, but not Adam, who zapped up a floating ball to entertain himself.

Samantha looked up and put her hands on her waist. "Noble Eight, what I'm trying to say here is that if you're going to punish me, then you're going to have to punish everybody. My parents... some among you...and Her Majesty!"

Even Maurice sat up upon hearing his daughter's assertion. The Council members made quite the commotion amongst themselves. Hepzibah fumed silently.

"I now call as witness...the High Priestess Hepzibah!"

Hepzibah stood erect and threw her scepter on her throne. "You have the utter gall to propose to question us!"

"Reclaiming my time!" Samantha declared. "Oh – and I'm afraid this will require Her Majesty to be under oath."

Judge Bean's eyes had widened so much, it may have been the first time in his multi-millennium life his face wasn't scrunched. He apprehensively zapped himself out of his seat on the bench and appeared at his sovereign's side, knowing he could wind up an amphibian at any moment. "Your...Your Majesty...if you would?"

Nearly snorting, Hepzibah turned to face the trembling judge. Before he could even speak, the High Priestess merely placed two fingers astride her nose. "Witches' Honor," she seethed.

"Um...you...you may be seated."

Hepzibah grabbed her scepter, which made Judge Bean jump. She pointed it at the defendant's table, and instantly she sat in its chair, while Judge Bean found himself back at his post with nary a gill in sight.

"I'll be brief, Your Majesty," Samantha promised in a less confrontational tone. "Preceding the Witches' Convention of 1970, did you meet a mortal named Ernest Hitchcock?"[24]

Hepzibah actually swallowed, exhibiting something Samantha had never seen in the monarch before: guilt. "We did."

"What were the circumstances behind this meeting?"

"We had determined we would observe the mortal species in an effort to understand your witch-to-commoner union," Hepzibah reported. "Encountering Mr. Hitchcock was part of that decree."

"You accepted his invitation to lunch and returned to my home wearing a corsage one would assume he bought for you," recalled Samantha. "Would it be safe to say that encounter turned romantic?"

Hepzibah stared at Samantha almost helplessly. Samantha stared right back.

"And the two of you had made arrangements to see each other while in Salem. Did you?"

After several moments, Hepzibah finally spoke. "We refuse to answer on the grounds that it may incriminate us."

Samantha smiled. "All right, Your Majesty, we'll skip that part."

"Of course, we only took an interest in Mr. Hitchcock after you placed that silly love spell on him. Don't think we didn't see you twitch him into an arduous state while in your husband's office," the High Priestess insisted.[25] "And, unlike you, we never told him that we're a witch."

Samantha pursed her lips. "Actually...you kind of did. As you were leaving the office with Mr. Hitchcock, he asked if you'd ever been to Crete, and you told him you hadn't been there for centuries. Not a blatant reveal, no – but certainly something outside a mortal's usual frame of reference. Thank you, Your Majesty, no more questions. But again I say, if I have broken a law that states witches are not to move among mortals – let alone reveal ourselves to them – then many of us here tonight are guilty of the same violation, and therefore *all* subject to punishment."

Hepzibah popped out of the chair and returned to her throne, unable to bear what she suspected were eight pairs of Council eyes boring through her.

13 Let's Hear It for Mortals

There was a sense in the hall that Samantha was done presenting her case – but she wasn't. "Before I surrender the floor, there are a few more people I think we should hear from. People who were specifically mentioned during my questioning by this Council... people who have received no representation *from* this Council. In other words...mortals."

Samantha thought she'd have to zap up a supply of smelling salts for the occult octet. Even the unflappable Rodney seemed decidedly flapped. "You can't bring mortals in here!"

"Hasn't there been one in here all along?" Samantha gestured toward Darrin. "By permission of the High Priestess herself, no less. This entire trial – and make no mistake, that's what this has turned into – has been centered around mortals. You are all ready to hand down punishment that would permanently alter the life of a mortal – but you only want to hear from witches? Surely you're not willing to make your bias that obvious."

Silence.

"I'd like to start by introducing to you the human child – now a young man – to whom I defamed witches by taking him to the North Pole.[1] High Priestess Hepzibah, Noble Eight...the mortal Michael Johnson." Samantha waved the cape of her flying suit, and suddenly a tall, lanky teenager in a striped henley and flared jeans appeared. He had reddish brown hair that fell long around his shoulders and an impish grin that was obvious even when he wasn't smiling. Noticing after a brief moment that he wasn't where he'd been a second ago, Michael whipped his head around, trying to make sense of the imposing figures and ethereal pastels not native to his world.

"What the – what is this place? Where – "

Then he saw an old friend.

"Mrs. Stephens?" Michael gravitated to her out of an unconscious desire to feel safe. "I almost didn't recognize you! You look so different."

"You look pretty different yourself," Samantha smiled. "Head a foot taller...hair a foot longer!"

"Aw, I guess I'm just doin' my thing," Michael said bashfully, turning away for a moment. "Hey, where am I? Why did you bring me here?"

"Have a seat, Michael," Samantha sighed, giving him her chair. "I don't have time to explain in detail, but it's important that you and I have a chat about that Christmas we spent together. All right?"

"Well, yeah, Mrs. Stephens, anything for you. Only I have to get back soon – I was studying for my Algebra final."

"On a Saturday night?"

"It's a pretty important exam," the teen shrugged. "Well, whatever this is, it's nice to take a break from those coefficients and polynomials."

"Can we please proceed and dispense with this banal blathering?" Grimalda groused.

"He cannot possibly be allowed to speak," Carlotta protested. "As a mortal, he is ineligible to take the Witches' Honor oath!"

"Then he can speak under the umbrella of my own oath," Samantha offered. "I will take responsibility for his words." Turning to Michael, she asked him, "You're still that bluntly honest kid I remember, aren't you?"

"Bluntly honest man now. I just turned eighteen!"

Samantha raised a friendly eyebrow. "Michael, would you please tell everyone where we met, and when?"

"Sure. At the Westridge Orphanage. I was sent there not long after my dad died, so it had to have been...at least seven years ago."

"Do you remember the circumstances?"

Michael nodded. "You and Mr. Stephens were part of a program to take us orphan kids home for the holidays so we'd have some kind of Christmas. I was pretty angry with the world back then. I'd started a fistfight with this other kid because he believed in Santa Claus. The orphanage considered me a problem child and I was sure no one wanted me...then you sat down. For some reason you were the only person I felt comfortable enough even talking to."

"So Darrin and I brought you to the house."

"Yeah, and you both kept trying to get me to open up. I remember

Mr. Stephens put this dorky Santa suit on, but I thought Christmas was a bunch of bunk...until..."

"Until what?" Samantha asked gently.

"Until you told me you knew there was a Santa Claus – and you knew because you were a witch."

Several Council members exchanged self-satisfied glances.

"Did you think Christmas was bunk after that?"

"Not once you and Mr. Stephens and me got to the North Pole and met Santa." Darrin's ears perked up. "I'll never forget the actual St. Nick telling me it didn't matter what we looked like on the outside, because it's what we feel on the inside that counts."

"That was real?" Darrin said to himself.

"'It's what we feel on the inside that counts'," Samantha reiterated, giving Hepzibah a look. "Michael, did you believe me right away when I said I was a witch?"

"No. I made you prove it. There was this big puff of smoke and suddenly you were wearing a dress kinda like what you have on now, except plainer. And then you conjured up this big pointy hat and flew us away on a broom."

Samantha folded her arms. "Michael, there's something you really ought to know. Witches don't actually ride brooms, nor do we wear pointy hats. By complying with your requests to materialize them, I let you believe a myth about us that isn't true, and I was wrong to." Samantha hoped this correction would placate Hepzibah and the Council somewhat. "One last thing, Michael. How did you feel about me being a witch? Threatened? Scared?"

"Naw, all I knew was that you were a very nice lady who actually cared and went the extra mile to make my life a little brighter, which I have to admit was pretty dark at the time."

"I should like to make an inquiry of the boy." It was Ticheba, who could barely hide her disdain.

Feeling protective, Samantha approached the teen with a look of motherly reassurance. "Would that be all right, Michael?"

"Yeah, why not?"

Ah, the bravado of youth.

"Young Michael," Ticheba began, "when you learned that Samantha was a witch, what did you do with the information?"

"I'm sorry," came Michael's respectful apology. "Do?"

"With whom did you share the knowledge?"

"You mean did I tell anybody? No, not all through the rest of elementary school, nor junior high, or – " Michael held his breath for a moment. "Oh, wait – that Christmas, after we came back from the

North Pole, there was this other kid Tommy from the orphanage... the kid I punched out. He was staying across the street with these people, the Kravitzes. I brought Tommy a present and mentioned Mrs. Stephens had taken me to see Santa on her broom. I swore him to secrecy, but I guess Mrs. Kravitz must have overheard because later Tommy said she'd been asking him all these questions about it."

"*Gladys* Kravitz," Ticheba reminded the Council.

"But Tommy didn't fink on me," Michael insisted. He then did something Samantha hadn't expected – he looked straight up at the Noble Eight, his gaze not missing Hepzibah. "Listen, I hope this isn't out of line or nothin', but I get the feeling Mrs. Stephens is in some kind of trouble. Call it instinct; I spent enough time in trouble myself.

"I just wanna say that I'd be lost in space right now if it wasn't for her. I would probably have kept rejecting the couple who wanted to adopt me, and I never would have known what it was like to be part of a family again[2]. I'm sure I'd have run away from Westridge eventually and ended up on the streets – and I was angry enough that it's not a stretch I could have started stealing and stuff. I could be in jail today, or who knows where. I meant to stay in touch with Mrs. Stephens over the years but I thank her all the time, privately, for saving me from myself. She gave me something positive to believe in when I needed it most. And that never would have happened if she hadn't told me she's a witch."

Michael turned his attention to Samantha. "Can you send me back now? I really wanna get an 'A' on this Algebra exam."

"You got it, and no broom this time. Don't stay up too late studying. We miss you – come see us soon, okay?"

"You're welcome any time, Mike," Darrin concurred.

"That'd be outta sight. I have so much to tell you, especially about my life with the Johnsons...Bill and his wife Jeannie. Wow – these your kids? Hi, guys!" the former orphan said to Tabitha and Adam. "You don't know me, but I'd love to hang out – and if you guys ever need it, I don't make a bad babysitter." Michael took one last look at the Witches' Council. "Um...nice meeting everybody? All right. I'm ready, Mrs. Stephens."

"Samantha."

Michael flashed his endearing, toothy grin. "Samantha."

Samantha blew Michael a kiss in between her zap and his disappearance.

Hepzibah remained stoic. "The Council will purge the mortal boy's memory of having been here."

"You are really hung up on this memory-purging thing, aren't you?" Samantha scoffed. "No, I'm sorry – 'the mortal boy' will retain memories of his visit. This is still my time, and it will only reinforce Michael's positive impression of witches to remember this event." Samantha again paced the bench's semi-circle. "Speaking of positive impressions, here's an adult who full well understood he was in contact with the supernatural. Witches and warlocks – straight from Queens, New York – Mr. Irving Bates."[3]

Samantha fanned out both hands, and an unorthodoxly handsome man with dark hair popped into the hall. He was in his mid-30s and wore an orange shirt with giant lapels and a cream-colored pair of impossibly wide bell bottom pants. He danced vigorously...but stopped when he realized there was no music compared to the space he had just occupied.

The man seemed flustered until he saw Samantha; in seconds he relaxed into casualness. "This another one of your non-scheduled flights?" he asked her.

"Sorry about the lack of warning, Irving," Samantha apologized self-consciously, "but it became necessary to zonk you across – "

" – the atmospheric continuum," they finished together.

"That's okay, Samantha. I was just groovin' to some James Brown – you know, one of his latest: *Talkin' Loud and Saying Nothing*."

"I can't think of a more personal dedication," Darrin said to himself, glaring at the Noble Eight.

"Hey, I knew witches couldn't just live in the suburbs of Westport, Connecticut; this place is righteous!" Irving's panoramic glance stopped on the source of his second childhood, prompting a happy sprint to the railing of the gallery. "Hi, Tabitha! Look at how much you've grown in a year. And hello – Dad," came Irving's greeting to Darrin, only Samantha getting their private joke. "Well, well," Irving added upon seeing Adam. "Nobody told me I had a 'little brother'."

"It's nice to see you again, Irving, but I've brought you here for a rather serious reason," Samantha explained. "You see before you our Witches' Council – they're sort of like Congress or the Senate – and up there is the High Priestess Hepzibah. She's...well, I can't say she's our version of President Nixon, given his circumstances; she's probably closer to England's Queen Elizabeth."

"Yow. Why do I think I'm going to like Carol Burnett's version better?" the observant Irving picked up from scanning the witchy group. He let Samantha guide him to the chair facing Hepzibah and the Noble Eight, getting that uncomfortable feeling that always came over him around figures of authority.

"All right," Samantha started. "How do you know me?"

Irving's eyebrows arched in reflection. "Uh, you and Tabitha came into the toy store where I worked to buy a present for a birthday party. You were at the register paying, and I started talking to Tabitha about how nice it would be to be a little boy again. Suddenly I was one. So I looked up your address on our copy of your receipt and knocked on your door."

"Do you remember how you reacted when I told you I was a witch – and that you had become a 9-year-old again because of witchcraft?"

Irving chuckled. "I told you I wouldn't hold it against you because I'm a liberal. Not in the political sense per se; I just think everybody should be free to be who they are."

Carlotta gestured wildly, causing more feathers to fly from her cuffs. "And yet, you picked up the phone to call the police once Samantha revealed herself to you. After telling her there are no such things as witches!"

Looking both amused and perturbed, Irving eagerly accepted Carlotta's challenge. "I put the phone down seconds later, since I knew the cops sure weren't gonna believe me. No such things as witches? Long hooked noses, big ol' warts, right? Here's the thing... you look at someone like Samantha – and especially Tabitha – and you realize that isn't true. Nice sleeves, by the way."

Samantha had to suppress a giggle. So did Rodney.

"So, did you tell anyone about me being a witch?" Irving's one-time hostess asked.

"It's not for me to tell," Irving shrugged. "Besides, I seem to recall commenting that I'd get put into a straitjacket if I told anyone – and Darrin nodding like he knew what I was talking about."[4]

Darrin smiled again, but Malvina wasn't convinced. "You expect us to presume you weren't in the least bit tempted to take advantage of Samantha's witchcraft to procure things for yourself?"

Irving looked just this side of incredulous. "Honestly? That never occurred to me. What, I should have wanted Samantha to grant wishes or something? She's not a genie."

Samantha moved toward Irving, a sly grin on her face. "Yeah, we don't talk about genies. Before I send you back to wherever you were dancing, do you have anything else to say about your experience meeting witches?"

Enthusiastic as ever, Irving jumped in. "Just now, you zapped me out of a discotheque – I was boogieing down with the new lady in my life. See, that was one of the things I learned from getting turned into a 9-year-old. When you're a kid it's all about dreams and flights of fancy and lack of limitations. Then you grow up and suddenly, dreams are bad! You're too old for childlike wonder! You've got to be practical! And you fall into this trap of settling for less and squashing down every dream you ever had because you're supposed to.

"Being a kid again for a day reminded me of who I was before I let society tell me how to live my life. When I got back to Ruthie – you remember, Samantha; she was my girlfriend at the time – I could see she was too perfunctory; she'd fallen into that trap as much as I had. I guess I always knew me and Ruthie were a bad fit – that's why I was always standing her up. A few months ago, though, I met a woman who appreciates my childlike streak, and check this out: I find myself wanting to marry her. Wild, considering I'd always had nightmares about marriage before!

"I sold toys so I could be a big kid, but I hated that job. After I got fired for going AWOL because of Tabitha shrinking me, I realized I felt relief, not regret. Now I have a job *testing* toys – I've never been happier. And ironically, it's taught me more about responsibility. I know now that you do have to embrace being an adult – the mistake is not keeping the child inside of you alive."

"You know, Endora," Darrin quietly said to his mother-in-law, "somehow none of that crossed my mind – and you turned me into a kid twice."[5]

Irving addressed his youthful benefactor. "Tabitha, it took you to get that through my thick skull. And Samantha, if that's what witches do, then you're pretty cool as far as I'm concerned. Meeting you two is probably the best thing that could have happened to me."

"I think the evidence here literally speaks for itself," Samantha told the Council. "Irving, I also think we'd better get you back to that disco."

"D'ya suppose you can return me to exact same moment you plucked me off the dance floor? That way no one'll be freaked out by my sudden reappearance. Let me know how this all goes – and I'll have to bring Rebecca by Westport to meet you guys. I can tell she's gonna like it there a lot. Okay, Samantha...I'm second in line for take-off!"

"'Bye, Mr. Bates!" Tabitha said to her old young friend.

"See you soon, Tab." Irving started dancing in place, so Samantha incanted:

"Back up time and take a chance for
The moment Irving left the dance floor!"

Getting down to the beat in his head, Irving waved to the Stephenses. Then he was gone.

Judge Bean let out a weary breath. "Are we done with this parade of mortals?"

Samantha realized the moment had come. There really wasn't much else to submit, and she could tell that both Hepzibah and the Council were itchy to render a "verdict" and be done with things. How simple it seemed for them to cavalierly decide the fate of an entire family. "Yes...however, before a judgment is rendered – "

"Uh, Sam..."

Samantha spun around. Darrin had stood up, to Maurice and Endora's surprise.

"Actually, there is one more mortal we haven't heard from."

"Oh? Who?"

"Me."

14 You and Me Against the World

Darrin looked more resolute than Samantha could recall seeing him. "I'd like to bring up the rear of this parade, if that's permissible."

Samantha looked to the Noble Eight for objection, instead sussing out a lingering ennui. She should have known better than not to include Darrin in this. He'd always had an opinion to express before – and he deserved to express one now more than ever.

Darrin tried to climb over the gallery railing, as it didn't seem there was another way to enter the hearing area. From the corner of his eye, Darrin saw a flash of pale green – it was Endora waving her arm at him. The next thing he knew, he was sitting in the hot seat. Perhaps the hottest seat of his life.

"Sweetheart," Samantha said, wondering if it would be the last time she'd be able to use that term of endearment toward her husband, "the floor is yours."

"Thank you, Sam. And actually...thank you, too, Witches' Council. I know I'm the last person you want to hear from. But if there's any mortal who knows more about what it's like to be in the presence of witches, I'd like to meet him.

"I'm not going to deny that I've locked horns with most witches I've met. Just ask my in-laws behind me. I feel like, ever since the beginning, I've had a target on my back because so many of you deemed me not good enough for Samantha – that doesn't inspire a guy to be the most friendly. I've long since lost track of how many spells have altered my personality, how many animals I've been turned into, how many insults I've endured...simply because I don't have powers and a nearly unlimited life span.

"I knew pretty much right away Samantha was the girl I wanted to marry. Then to exchange vows, only to find out on your wedding night that your new wife isn't human...I don't know if you can fathom something like that, or how ingrained mortal beliefs about the supernatural are. My mother was always a little quirky, so maybe I was more open than most of my kind; maybe not.

"Rodney, you're right – I did worry Endora would have five eyes, and I did discourage friends from getting involved with women I thought were witches, which *was* hypocritical. And you bet I called witchcraft 'nonsense.' I mean, it might as well have been New Math. Maybe I'd have clashed just as much with adversarial in-laws if they were human...and maybe I fought back harder because you were all going to be more powerful than me no matter what. It's like a typical mortal power struggle, only with impossibly unfair odds.

"Did I rail against Samantha's witchcraft and forbid her to use it? Yes. As a mortal male, I'm expected to be the breadwinner – how am I supposed to provide for someone who can zap up whatever she needs or wants for herself?[1] I admit I got pretty bull-headed about it, especially in the early years, and I think I still owe Sam more than a few apologies. But I loved her *more* for going along with my rule of no witchcraft. Not because she wasn't using her powers – which I can imagine must have been difficult to suppress – but because she cared so much about me she was willing to suppress that part of herself. Now, it might be mundane to this Council, but to us, our marriage is extra special because of what we each bring to it. Not to mention these two kids here, who, even knowing what may happen before we're done tonight, I can't picture living without.

"Sam's always held that the only thing stronger than witchcraft is love.[2] Do you really think if you send me back to my house having purged my memories of my wife and kids that they'll forever be out of my heart, out of my soul? On some level I'll know they're missing; maybe one day I'll even remember them despite your spell. And I don't really believe, despite your deep disapproval of me, you'd be so cruel as to make Tabitha and Adam grow up without their father."

"Hepzibah said their memories could be purged as well," Samantha reiterated weakly, having come to accept Endora's attempt at grandmotherly aid. "To spare them."

Darrin eyed the High Priestess carefully. "I'm sure you think that course of action is the most humane, Your Majesty, if I can use that term here. But it's not. What's supposed to happen in this witchy environment when they start asking why they don't have a father? Sure, you could make them believe a warlock is their dad, but no matter what you do to me, Tabitha and Adam are as much half-mortal as they are half-witch. I'd be willing to bet that there isn't a spell strong enough to make them forget that part of themselves.

"This must be a crowning moment for you – pardon the pun. The moment witches are finally rid of me. Rodney, Carlotta, George – you all tried to separate me and Sam.[3] Malvina, you sent Sam to the 16th century without a second thought to how that would affect me or our kids."[4]

Malvina rolled her eyes. "You got her back, didn't you? With the help of that stool pigeon, Endora."[5]

Endora looked as if she were ready to hex the warlock Herbie's ex-/current wife, but Darrin went on. "Judge Bean, Contessa – I've never had any direct beef with you, but you sit on this Council in agreement with the others. And Ticheba, you surprise me perhaps most of all. When Samantha became queen, I wasn't even invited to her coronation. Yeah, I probably wouldn't have gone. Yet I'll bet none of you stopped to think that Sam taking the throne made *me* part of the royal family.[6] That's how the monarchy works in the mortal world, anyway; I'm sure I wasn't the king, but I must've been a consort or a duke or something, and most of you witches still looked down your noses at me. Except for Esmeralda...sometimes Uncle Arthur, I guess...and Aunt Clara. Man, I miss her.

"In the end, I realize the issue here is mortals having knowledge of witches. Well, I've had that knowledge for eight years, and I've rarely tried to benefit from Samantha's witchcraft – usually when I did, it was magic forcing me to do so. Now that my friends, parents, and neighbors know about Sam, I'm the mortal that's got enough experience to keep them from using her, blabbing about her, or falling prey to that whole crone misconception. You know what? In terms of fair representation of witches, you've got no stronger advocate than Samantha herself. When Clara stranded us at the first Thanksgiving and settlers in Plymouth accused me of witchcraft, it was Sam who implored them to accept all differences.[7] And the time I had to rescue her from Old Salem – "[8]

"Where you told an entire group of witch hysterics about your wife's witchcraft," Grimalda spat.

"Yeah, because it was the only way I could think of to restore Samantha's memory and get us home," Darrin insisted. "But she did inform *those* mortals that they were only persecuting themselves, since there was no way they could try an actual witch. It seems to me Samantha traded her power of witchcraft for the power of speaking out against prejudice and bigotry – something she's taught me a lot about. You should be proud of her, not determined to punish her."

Adam, who had been sitting mesmerized, watched his parents embrace and dematerialized his forgotten ball.

"Thank you, Darrin. Time to play musical chairs again – "

Darrin gently stopped Samantha's hand. "Oh, no. At this point, the seat I've got is ringside. And if I know what's coming next, I'm not giving it up for anybody."

Samantha gave a single nod and smiled. "Noble Eight – Your Majesty – this has been a long ordeal, at least for me, my husband, and my children, especially in light of what its end result could be. And while I am glad to have finally been given a chance to make a case for myself, I have a few closing words.

"I keep thinking back to telling Tabitha one Christmas that everyone is entitled to believe in what they want – and if they don't want to believe, that's all right, too.[9] For the purposes of this hearing, I'll amend that to say, 'Everyone is entitled to believe in what they want as long as they don't impose those beliefs on others.' My entire marriage, almost everyone in the witch world – from my parents to this Council and our sitting monarch – has tried to tell me how to live my own life. I say, as long as I live that life in a way that doesn't hurt anyone else, or myself, that's all that matters.

"'But!' you say. 'Mortals knowing about witches *does* hurt us!' Yes, the Salem witch hunts were recurring examples of paranoia, superstition, and unfounded fear. But how long are you going to penalize the mortal world for something that happened in the 17th century? I'd like to think that, despite their three-steps-forward-two-steps-back tendencies, humans consistently show a capacity to evolve. To grow. To move past their closed-mindedness and intolerance a little more with each passing generation.

"I've lived among mortals. You haven't. Oh, I know, there are still far too many who are hateful and bigoted. But to say all mortals are like that is generalizing. It's like saying all Arabs are terrorists, or all black people are poor. That all gay men are promiscuous...or all witches are evil.

"I'm not saying mortals don't have an 'us versus them' mentality. They do. 'We're right and you're wrong and you have to do it our way.' That came to perhaps the biggest boiling point in their history just three decades ago in Europe, when one man deemed a single group chosen and everyone else disposable. Remember how even we were afraid to pop into Paris, Warsaw, Amsterdam, Vienna – for starters – because of the oppression and extremism that had taken over there? Mortals know they have to keep an eye on themselves to avoid creating that again. Next time it could even happen in the

United States – twenty, thirty, forty-five years from now. I won't go so far as to say what you're doing is a similar authoritarian abuse of power – but the way you want to control my life sure skirts the line. Think about it: if you're willing to strip Darrin and Tabitha and Adam of their memories in an effort to punish me, how much further would you be willing to go?

"Mortals definitely need to learn that there is no such thing as 'us versus them'. But witches need to learn it in tandem. There is no 'them'. There is only 'us'. We are all '*us*'.

"When Darrin and I were newlyweds, my friend Mary said she didn't know why we didn't tell everyone we were witches, because then they'd find out what wonderful, nice people we really are.[10] It couldn't have surprised me more when Tabitha later came to the same conclusion on her own.[11] If we keep our identities secret, don't we run the risk of letting mortals maintain their misconceptions about us? And, I would argue, whether or not I choose to share some or all of the truth about myself with anyone is my choice. Ultimately, what we're talking about isn't one ideology having supremacy over another – it's about being a decent being...human and otherwise."

Over the whoosh of the never-ending breeze and the cascading mist that lingered at her feet, Samantha softly added, "I now surrender the floor."

Then Hepzibah stood.

"Witch Samantha," the High Priestess said, an unexpected gentleness in her voice. "We will reiterate that you are not the only witch to violate our realm's long-standing edict against making mortals privy to our supernatural identities. Indeed, this dictate was established centuries before even former queen Ticheba's rule. And, as you are all aware, we ourselves created the office of the Resident Witch of Salem in 1692 to protect the witch image and assure no more persecution by mortals.[12]

"Somehow, in more recent times, enforcement of this edict has become sporadic at best – to the point lines between witches and mortals have significantly blurred. To the point the edict itself has been forgotten almost completely. And yes," Hepzibah added, looking directly at Samantha, "we ourselves have violated this decree via our experimentation with the mortal Ernest Hitchcock. Perhaps these proceedings were necessary to remind us all how lax witches have become, ourselves included."

The High Priestess extended her indicative gesture to include Darrin. "Yours is the last existing witch-to-mortal marriage. There were others[13] – as you know, Samantha – but they have either dissolved of their own accord, owing to the ultimate irreconcilable differences inherent in a union between two species, or they have dissolved by considerable persuasion from this Council. That is, in large part, why your marriage and constant exposure to mortals is particularly conspicuous to us. And, it should be mentioned, no other witch-to-mortal couplings resulted in offspring, which present numerous potential and unknowable complications in and of itself.

"It is time for all witches to rededicate themselves to preserving and protecting the magical way of life. The soft spot we once said we have in our royal heart for you[14] has in no way diminished," Hepzibah admitted to Samantha, "but we must henceforth ordain, with no delay, that mortals cannot have knowledge of witches, despite your very compelling arguments. Nearly a dozen more humans would otherwise come away with an awareness of our true nature because of your reveal tonight. Therefore, the judgment of this Council, and ourselves, stands: no one in the mortal world will retain memory of the witch Samantha – "

"Stop!"

Before Samantha even finished turning around out of her mother's instinct to recognize distress in her child, Tabitha waved her arms and disappeared. The next thing anyone knew, young Miss Tabitha Stephens was floating in mid-air with the Witches' Council just below her and the High Priestess Hepzibah just above her. Reaction was immediate and overlapping.

"Oh, this is ridiculous," Malvina grumbled.

"Are we ever going to be finished here?" the Contessa Piranha sighed.

Rodney folded his arms in exasperation. "We'll have to hear from the little boy next."

Judge Bean became unusually animated. "Someone remove the child from – "

"No," Tabitha said calmly. "My mother used to be queen – that makes me a princess.[15] And *I demand to be heard!*"

Darrin had never thought of his daughter as royalty, but suddenly it seemed she had always been – especially since not a single witch protested Tabitha's assertion.

Tabitha hovered along the semi-circle, looking all eight members of the Witches' Council in the eye. "Ever since before I was born you've been trying to make my daddy leave me," she pointed out forcefully, in a way her relatives had never heard the 7-year-old speak. "My grandmama and grandpapa, too. Nobody thinks I notice this stuff. Even when my powers were tested, Grandmama and my great-aunt Hagatha and my great-aunt Enchantra wanted to send me to a special witch school, but what they really wanted was to take my daddy away from me."[16]

"You could not possibly remember that," Carlotta barked dismissively. "You were barely a toddler by mortal standards."

"I remember everything," Tabitha revealed, shocking everyone. "I can remember all the way back to when my mother was carrying me."

Samantha was hearing this for the first time; she found her breathing had become ragged. "It must be because of her half-witch, half-mortal metabolism," she muttered to no one in particular.

"Your Majesty, you even threatened to dissolve my father right in front of me at the dinner table when you visited[17]," Tabitha scolded, her youth keeping her oblivious to her brazenness. "Well, he is a good person and I love him and it's not right that witches keep saying nasty things about him and wanting to make him go away from me. *Leave my daddy alone!*"[18]

A few Council members looked as if they wanted to oppose, but couldn't find the words to. Darrin was overcome with pride; not being able to see behind him, he couldn't notice that Endora and Maurice were sharing in it.

"Everyone's making a big deal about how bad it is for mortals to know about witches," Tabitha continued. "I wanna talk to a mortal who knows about *me*. Please bring my friend Lisa Wilson here from wherever you sent her."

Ticheba gave Hepzibah a stern look. "Your Majesty, it is highly irregular to even entertain – "

"What's the harm in letting the girl talk for a minute?" Grimalda interrupted. "After all, there was a time she was considered a prodigy[19], despite her lineage."

"And last time I checked," Tabitha reminded those in attendance, "even a former princess ranks higher than most of you."

Samantha looked on in awestruck disbelief. All the years she'd had to go up against the Council, and it only took her little daughter – who once adorably floated her pretty pony across the room[20] – to wipe the floor with them.

Hepzibah, still standing, produced her scepter. "As you wish," the High Priestess told Tabitha. "But do not take advantage of our generosity."

"I won't," Tabitha promised. "First let me take the oath."

"It's hardly a requirement in this case – "

"But I want to."

Tabitha flew over to Judge Bean. He arose, albeit reluctantly. "Do you solemnly swear to tell the truth, the whole truth, and nothing but the truth, so help you, Cosmos?"

Tabitha flashed the "V" astride her nose. "Witches' honor." The Stephens girl then drifted down to the fog-covered floor, alighting next to Samantha. "I wanna talk to Lisa the way you've been talking to people, Mother."

"All right, Tabitha. Your father and I will be right over here," Samantha said assuredly, gesturing at the gallery. She snapped her finger, popping her and Darrin in behind the railing, where Adam was happy to finally get some cuddles from his mother.

Hepzibah cut the air with her scepter, causing an inanimate Lisa to pop into the display area. Suddenly the mortal girl unfroze; to her she'd just been standing in the Stephenses' living room. Confused and afraid, Lisa looked around feverishly.

"Where's my mommy and daddy? I was just with them a second ago!" Lisa seemed as if she might burst into tears...

Until she saw her "sister."

"Tabitha!" Lisa ran to her friend and threw her arms around her. "What happened? What is this pla – " Lisa got her first real glimpse of the magical environs she found herself in. "Oh, wow...and here I thought that whole thing with our polka dots was better than Disneyland.[21] But where are my parents?"

"They're okay; I promise you'll see them soon. Lisa, would you take the stand at that table for a few minutes? I want you to testify about some stuff."

Lisa finally saw the Witches' Council as she climbed into the chair. "Why am I here, Tabs? We're not gonna play a game, are we..."

"Sorta," Tabitha replied. "It's kinda like that TV show you like, *The Young Lawyers*. Only witch style. How long have we been friends?"

"Shouldn't I swear on a Bible or something?"

"It's not nice to swear. Anyway, when did we meet? Do you remember?"

"For sure," Lisa pshawed. "It was back when I was in first grade. I'm almost done with second now."

Tabitha not only felt very grown-up, she seemed it, too. "And you didn't know I was a witch at first."

"Nuh-uh. Not until I got to spend the night at your house and spilled paint on myself. You cleaned it up with witchcraft."

"Did you feel any differently about me once you found out I wasn't a mortal?"

Lisa knitted her brows. "Should I have? It already felt like you were my sister; after that you were still like my sister, only with something extra and cool."

Tabitha smiled. "Thanks, Lisa! Now I've just gotta ask you something else. What did you learn about witches that day?"

"Let's see...well, I remember I asked if you rode a broom and you said you didn't do that or wear pointy hats or have warts on your nose," Lisa answered thoughtfully. "Anyone can see that from looking at you. Right?"

"Can you tell the jury one last thing?" Tabitha wanted to know.

"Just one? This is kinda fun – even if those people up there are kinda scary."

Samantha and Darrin seemed to be sharing the same amused thought: *Out of the mouths of babes...*

"I told our queen I wouldn't take too long asking questions," explained Tabitha.

"You guys have a queen?"

"Lisa, please. Has our friendship changed at all because I'm a witch? Have you ever been afraid of me or wanted to make me zap up stuff for you just because I could?"

"Afraid of you?" Lisa looked as though someone had suggested she was a boy. "I can't believe anyone would be. And I can't believe some people would want to have you cast spells for them or something. I mean, that wouldn't be right. Okay, sometimes I've asked to see you do stuff on account of it's groovy and all, but you always tell me your mommy and daddy won't let you. That's okay. I think I like you more since finding out you're a witch – we're both a little different than a lot of the world, aren't we?"

"Yeah, uh-huh!" came Tabitha's enthusiastic response. She then looked up at Hepzibah and the Council. "And if Lisa can accept witches...maybe the other mortals can, too."

Samantha leaned over the railing tenderly. "But sweetheart, kids have a much easier time accepting what's different than grown-ups do."

"Have we given them a chance?" Tabitha was adamant. "Uncle Larry and Aunt Louise and the others didn't even have time to say anything after you told them you're a witch. The Witches' Council just made them disappear. We look like mortals; they look like us. I think that means there's some mortal in every witch, and that all mortals have magic in them, even if most of them don't see it."

"When you gave us the black-and-white polka dots because we wanted to be sisters," Lisa recalled, "Mrs. Stephens told us that all men are brothers, even if they're girls. That makes – what do you call us? Mortals? It means mortals and witches are brothers, too."

"Plus I'm half-witch," Tabitha reiterated to the Noble Eight, taking Lisa's hand. "So's Adam. You guys talk about that like it's something bad, but we're the only ones who know what it's like to be both. Maybe we can help Lisa's parents and everybody understand. Shouldn't you wait and see what they say first instead of acting like they're going to be mad or scared or make us zap up money and stuff for them?"

Hepzibah felt herself drawn to the girls' clasped hands. Black and white – witch and mortal.

"We must admit...we'd only ever considered the witch Samantha's children to be less than perfect due to their 'contaminated' lineage," the High Priestess confessed. "It only now occurs to us that Tabitha and Adam are actually the blending of two cultures. That it's possible – however remotely – they could be symbols of unity between witches and mortals. We now recall we once remarked on the mortal Darrin's love for Samantha[22]; perhaps it has escaped our notice that love may be the one thing all creatures have in common."

"I say we call for a vote," George said suddenly, surprising everybody.

The High Priestess was firm. "No vote is necessary. We will rescind, temporarily, our previous judgment – and allow Samantha and her family to return to the moment we removed the contested mortals. If said mortals demonstrate some sort of development and accept Samantha as a witch, as young princess Tabitha has suggested," Hepzibah nodded at the very appreciative girl, "we shall move forward and declare this matter closed. However – if those mortals fulfill our prophecy and conduct themselves in a way that is perilous to any or all witches...then, Samantha, we will have no other alternative but to remove you and your children from the mortal world and purge all mortals' memories of your existence. Is this satisfactory?"

Samantha rose, not sure how she was keeping her balance. "It is, Your Majesty."

"Then prepare for your journey to...1164 Morning Glory Circle." Hepzibah continued as Darrin also got to his feet and propped Adam up on the bench while Tabitha led Lisa to the railing separating the gallery from the hearing area. "We have one more royal proclamation: there is to be no interference with the outcome of these events. And we mean by *any of you*." Malvina, Grimalda, George, Ticheba, Judge Bean, the Contessa Piranha, Carlotta, and Rodney all wore expressions that indicated they did not miss the meaning of their sovereign's command. Not even Maurice and the ever-meddling Endora were excluded from Hepzibah's notice-giving glower.

"'Bye, Lisa," Tabitha said, hugging her best friend. "I'll see you and your mom and dad in a few minutes. And *thank you*." She found herself lifted over the railing by Darrin and held close to her own parents.

Hepzibah waved her scepter mightily; the ensuing gale almost drowned out Judge Bean's closing gavel-banging and the High Priestess' final words:

"Remember, as always – Hepzibah will be watching!"

A second later, Samantha, Darrin, Tabitha, and Adam were all standing on the tan shag carpet in their own living room.

 **Proof and Pudding**

Samantha took in the abode she had inhabited for nearly a decade as if she were seeing it for the first time. "We're actually back," she said with more than a hint of disbelief. "You know, for a while there I didn't think it would happen. Though we're not out of the woods yet. What time is it?"

Darrin checked his watch. "It's late. It's 9:30."

"9:30? Late?"[1] Samantha did a double take. "You're looking at me awfully funny all of a sudden."

"Don't you feel like we've had that exchange before? When was that, when was that...oh, yeah. The time Larry berated me for turning down membership at Burning Oak and jeopardizing that account."

"Why would something so minor have you so puzzled?"

"It's probably nothing..." Darrin supposed. "It's just that I've been noticing things like that a lot more lately. Like we repeat situations, sometimes word for word.[2] You don't think Arthur has us going through some kind of running gag, do you?"

"Your guess is as good as mine, sweetheart."

"Anyway, what I meant was, it may be 9:30 here, but for us it's like the middle of the night." Darrin studied Adam and Tabitha. "You guys must be exhausted, huh."

"It's certainly been a big night for you both," Samantha told her children. "And Tabitha, I have never been prouder of you than I was watching you go toe-to-toe with the almighty Witches' Council. I will never forget how you stood up for your father and me."

Darrin pulled his daughter into a hug. "You're one fighter I want on my side, that's for sure."

"I just did what's right," Tabitha said earnestly. "That's what you've been teaching me and Adam to do from the beginning. Where is everybody? Lisa and the others should have been here by now."

"I'm going to guess Hepzibah gave us a little lead time," Samantha concluded, "but there's no way of knowing how much, so we'd better match our positions as closely as we can. We don't want anybody sensing the difference when they pop back in." Samantha twitched her nose, replacing her and her kids' goin'-to-meetin' witches' clothes with their contemporary party wear. "Let's see... Darrin, you were over there...Tabitha, I believe you were next to me on this side. And Adam, honey" – Samantha took her child up in her arms – "you were right about here. After we're done with all this, you two are going straight to bed...and I will not be far behind."

"Double ditto," Darrin agreed. "Hepzibah and the Noble Eight really take it out of a guy."

Just then a kind of whistling sound cut through the air, almost in a Doppler effect, as if something was up in the air and gliding downward. Samantha thought it sounded similar to the one-time arrival of Brunhilde, the witch who mistook her for Serena and banished her to the Old South for fooling around with Brunhilde's husband.[3]

"I think we're about to catch up with the normal flow of time. The mortals should be here any second – and hopefully the witches will obey Hepzibah's non-interference command." Samantha gave Darrin a last private glance. "You ready, sweetheart?"

Darrin kissed his wife quickly. "Let's find out what our friends and family are made of."

There was what felt like an electrical buzzing in the room, and everything seemed to slow down...

Then all the missing mortals – Frank, Phyllis, Abner, Gladys, Betty Wilson, Dave, Adam Newlarkin, Larry and Louise Tate, Dorothy and Keith Wilson, and their daughter Lisa – returned to their original spots. Plus one baby zebra that had previously been Jonathan Tate.

"You're telling us...you're a witch." Abner shook his head rapidly, trying to understand.

The light bulb over Phyllis' head couldn't have been any brighter. "You mean...all along...you...were right?"

"Are we drunk?" Larry asked Louise.

"Phyllis, what in tarnation are you talking about?" Frank boomed.

"The first day we met, you and your funny Aunt Clara said you were witches[4]," Phyllis reminded Samantha. "Don't you remember, Frank?"

"I remember we laughed to humor Clara and her tall tales."

"Maybe *you* were humoring, but it always stuck with me, especially during those logical explanations we'd get when out-of-the-ordinary things happened here. And Samantha, you told me again to my face that you're a witch just after you had Adam – and made an ashtray fly through this very room, only to later convince me I'd seen things from taking hallucinogenics.[5] I knew better, though. I really did."

"You've always had good instincts, Mrs – Phyllis," Samantha said by way of confirmation.

Keith had trouble getting his words out. "What 'out-of-the-ordinary'? I've never seen anything like that here...until now. Dottie?"

"No, me either," Dorothy agreed.

"I have," Adam Newlarkin piped up. "But then again, I'm from Salem – Massachusetts, not the Salems in New Hampshire, Oregon, *et cetera*. When your town's whole culture is built around witches, you get this ingrained openness to the possibility."

"Yeah, well, I'm a Long Island lawyer. So what's ingrained in me is a need for proof," came Dave's response.

Gladys put in her two cents. "Proof? Proof? The proof's standing in front of you on four legs!"

"Don't start, Gladys," Abner admonished as the zebra butted his hand.

"Okay, Sam," Larry said chipperly, but with a clear indication he was annoyed. "This was a fun little initiation stunt with Darrin being allowed into the fraternity and all, but I think it's starting to go a little too far."

Louise seemed more troubled than anything. "And it's getting past Jonathan's bedtime. I want him back this minute!"

Seeing Darrin's hinting nod, Samantha declared, "I can't think of any better proof than that." Samantha reinforced her grip on her son. "All right, Adam, you change Jonathan back right now. And tomorrow we'll discuss how we're going to punish you for this little stunt. Go to it, young man."

"Yes, Mommy."

A lot less frantically than he had before, the little half-warlock pointed, and the black-and-white striped animal – in full view of everyone – became the tow-headed Jonathan Tate again.

Larry and Louise swallowed, pretty much at the same time. Jonathan turned to hug his mother. "Is what just happened to me what I think just happened to me?"

"Adam," Samantha told her youngest child, "what you did was

very naughty and you'd better tell Jonathan you're very sorry."

The angelic Adam managed to look cute even while looking guilty. "I torry, Jon-a-tin."

"There," Gladys said, satisfied. "You all saw that, right?"

"I might have seen it, but I don't believe it," Dave reported.

Betty finally contributed to the conversation. "I...I just don't know what to believe."

"Well, Sam, if we're in for a penny, we might as well be in for a pound," Darrin decided. "While we're on the subject of money... Dave, weren't you telling me you came back because you lost your wallet?"

Not understanding the relevance, Dave stammered a little. "Uh... well...yeah...like I said, I was trying to buy Betty a drink, and..."

"Then I think it's time we reunite you with your credit cards. Sam?"

Samantha set Adam on his feet and held his shoulder gently but meaningfully. "Stay right there." Straightening herself up, Samantha commanded, "Dave, hold out your hand. And everybody else... watch." With two fingers, she took a zap toward the attorney, who didn't have much to say when his billfold unmistakably materialized in his palm.

"There you go. And next time, don't leave home without it."

"That sounds like it should be a slogan for something," Darrin smirked.

"Maybe it will be."

Tabitha felt excluded. "Mother, you and Adam got to do something. I wanna prove myself, too."

"But your parents don't want you doing no-nos." Lisa's outburst earned an astonished reaction from her own mother and father.

"I think this one time we can bend the house rules," Samantha smiled. "What would you like to do for us?"

Tabitha surveyed the room, the witchlet looking quite serious... then suddenly, her eyes brightened. "I know! Lisa, happy early birthday."

Crossing her fingers together three times, Tabitha produced a singing thirteen-year-old Michael Jackson, all Afro and polyester suit. More than any of the other magical feats the newly clued-in mortals had witnessed that night, it was the sight of the teen sensation performing *Rockin' Robin* in close proximity that astonished them the most. Some stood with their mouths hung open, others found themselves bopping along in spite of themselves. And Lisa, of course, had to keep herself from jumping up and down, especially after she reached out to Michael, who took her hand for a moment.

"Oh, that boy's gonna go places," Samantha said with a little laugh. "That's enough, Tabitha. Send him on back to Motown."

Doing what she was told, Tabitha's triple-crossed fingers popped Michael out mid-chorus and left the Stephenses' living room – and their guests – amazingly quiet. Almost unsettlingly so.

Betty broke the silence out of unconsciously being unable to bear it. "Well, if it had been a week ago, we could have said this was all an April Fools' joke, but..."

Dumbfounded, Keith slowly looked down at Lisa.

"I told you, Daddy," she smiled.

"Yeah, baby," Keith said, feeling something sink in. "You sure did." Keith approached his friend. "Hey, D, that Christmas we had the office party here, that time Lisa first stayed over...you were with us in Tabitha's room when Lisa said Sam and Tabitha were witches."

Dorothy nodded in recollection. "We blew it off by telling Lisa she was our good little fairy."

"Lisa's not one of those kids who lives in make-believe," Keith continued, "so I didn't take her seriously. Or maybe I just didn't want to. It's bugged me a little ever since. I mean you hear that whole thing about witches being – "

"Ugly old crones," Samantha, Darrin, and Tabitha chimed in with Keith.

"Well, these guys disprove that theory," Darrin assured his co-worker, gesturing to his wife and kids and staying true to his vow to Hepzibah. "I mean, do they look like ugly old crones to you?"

"No," Keith admitted.

"You better believe they don't," Dorothy added.

"It's like I said," Lisa reminded her parents. "They're good witches."

Dave felt emboldened by the Wilsons' discourse. "So when you'd come to me drowning your sorrows about witches and witchcraft... that wasn't just pulling my leg, then."

Darrin nearly fell over. "You *were* listening!"[6]

"Pal, of *course* I was listening," Dave confirmed. "I started yappin' about other stuff whenever you'd bring it up because how was I supposed to respond to all this witch talk? Coulda been too much bourbon on your part for all I know. Then I don't hear from you for years...and now I find out everything you said about your wife being a witch is true. You know what? The jury may be out on this one for a while. But if I had to render a verdict right now..."

"Yes?" Samantha asked anxiously.

"Sam...I've always liked you. I guess you could say, uh, you cast a spell on me a long time ago.[7] By the way, you didn't cast one to get this lunkhead to marry you, did you?"

Samantha didn't know whether to be amused or offended. "Love spells aren't out of the scope of our powers," she confessed, "but no, Darrin acted all on his own. Besides, what fun would it be knowing someone only loved you because they had no other choice?"

"Case closed, milady. Darrin, she's a great gal. You've got great kids. If Sam being a witch isn't a problem for you anymore like it seemed to be when we lived on barstools together...then I'm not gonna stand here having a problem. It's *your* life, son!"

"Thanks, Dave," Darrin said, gripping Dave's extended hand.

As Tabitha got her kid brother to follow her to the sofa and returned to Samantha's side, Dave addressed the crowd. "Any other takers?"

Nobody seemed willing to grab the baton, so it was even more surprising when the usually shy Adam Newlarkin spoke up. "Well... when I was here, I had this curse on me[8]. A chair pulled out from under me by itself, a salad 'attacked' me...and I ended up going through this crazy ritual where I had to kiss a spotted dog and get dunked in the water three times. I won't even tell you about having to ride a horse through the marketplace. After that I figured Darrin and me just believed in the *possibility* of witches. So this really isn't that much more of a stretch. You know?"

"It would certainly explain a lot of things," Betty realized. "Mostly some of your bizarre behavior the years I worked with you, Mr. Stephens. Fretting over a teddy bear[9], suddenly chastising me over the most minute details[10], becoming this incredible cheapskate[11] – and once you were so courteous it got on everybody's nerves.[12] I didn't *think* you were behaving like yourself when things like that happened...and you weren't. It was this witchcraft."

Darrin sighed a little. "Yes, Betty. Most of that was behavior-altering spells put on me by Samantha's mother...I'll tell you about that some other time."

"I might not have been inclined to believe anything going on here," the former secretary continued, "except I can still see that picture floating through the reception area and winking at me.[13] After that, I knew something was up. I don't know about the rest of you, but...this makes sense as far as I'm concerned."

Phyllis, who as a matter of course looked a bit frazzled any time she visited her son's house, now seemed downright tranquil – without her tranquilizers.[14] "*I've* seen things floating through this *house*. And no offense, Samantha, but nothing about your mother would surprise me. Oh, Darrin, why didn't you just tell me from the beginning? You know with my family background I would have been the last person to pass judgment on you about anything occult."

"I'm sorry, Mom. I just made a decision after finding out about Sam that I couldn't tell my family.[15] And I wouldn't have – except I guess your grandson thought it was time for you to know."

"Wait a minute, Darrin, I don't know how I feel about this," Frank interjected. "You also know about *my* family background – your grandparents were devout Catholics. I'm not a particularly religious man myself, but I spent a lot of time in pews growing up and it always rubbed me the wrong way a bit when your mom would talk about her supposedly supernatural grandma.[16] I mean, the occult... witchcraft...isn't that all the same thing as demonism?"

Samantha held up her hand. "Let me put your mind at ease, Mr. Stephens," she said, "because we're not talking about *Rosemary's Baby* here. That movie did nothing to help our image. I'm sure you'd agree, among every walk of life, most people are inherently good. Yet there are always a few bad seeds. I do recall a time in witch history when some witches and warlocks practiced dark magic. And you know how it is when stories are told – they spread but get embellished with each retelling. That's why witches are still associated with cults and demons, especially in fiction. I have powers; I could use them for evil if I wanted to, but I don't. As with anything else in this life, Frank, it's what you do with it. Plain and simple."

"Sam, I adore you; you know that. I just have to put things in the think tank for a while."

"Then think tank this, too, Dad," Darrin told his father. "Is Samantha not the same person she was a half an hour ago, before you found out she's a witch? The same person she was a month ago, a year ago – eight years ago, when you first met her? The only thing different is that you know one more detail about her."

Frank scratched his chin.

"So this is why Jonathan and Tabitha haven't grown up together," Louise deduced.[17]

"And why you've always been so overprotective with Tabitha," Phyllis added.[18] "You were trying to keep people from finding out."

Samantha smoothed Tabitha's long, wheat-colored hair. "Yes, our daughter tends to be a little on the...precocious side. I always used to tell Darrin, 'it's awfully hard to break a child of doing something that comes naturally.'[19] And since we made a pact to keep my witchhood a secret..."

Louise glanced at Larry for a moment, as if for silent permission. "Samantha, I've never really said anything because I didn't feel it was any of my business. To answer a question Mrs. Kravitz asked me tonight, yes – I've seen strange things here...over and over again. But none of it came as that much of a shock to me. Not considering you also told *me* you're a witch when Jonathan was a baby."[20]

"I did?"

"Right there in the kitchen!" Louise exclaimed, pointing at its slatted doors. "We were fighting with our husbands, and they were fighting amongst themselves; while we were planning a reunion, you came right out with it. You probably don't remember my reply, either: 'Honey, you said it – I didn't.' Do you honestly think I didn't look at every unusual event through that lens after that? You're my best friend – we might have been closer still if you'd just truly confided in me instead of spending so much time trying to fake me out."

Samantha reached out and took Mrs. Tate's hands. Louise squeezed them back.

"Sam? Darrin..." Larry had a difficult-to-define gleam in his bright blue eyes. "This witchcraft stuff...if it can change Darrin's behavior and make him do all the strange things I've seen him do... can it change anyone? Anyone who's not a witch, that is."

Samantha answered cautiously. "It can..."

"I mean, you could make anybody do anything you want."

"Larry," an already exasperated Darrin said, "let's not open that door, shall we?"

"It'd sorta be like that book, *How to Win Clients and Influence People*..."

"That's *How to Win Friends and* – " Louise tried to correct her husband.

Larry rubbed his hands together gleefully. "Never mind the petty details."

"This is getting dangerously close to what Larry did in that dream spell I didn't know you put on me[21]," Darrin murmured in Samantha's ear.

"Now you know where I got the inspiration," Samantha replied just as clandestinely. Turning her attention to Larry, she couldn't help feeling like she did when had to scold Adam or Tabitha. "Larry, your knack for capitalizing on capitalism is legendary. Certainly I can understand the desire to turn bigger profits. But let me try to explain this to you...while we witches do possess nearly unlimited power, using that power for unfair enrichment is regarded as the height of unethical.[22] It kind of goes back to what I was saying before. A witch can use her powers for good, or she can use them for – "

"Sam?" Larry said.

"Yes?"

The gluttonous expression on Larry's face was replaced with one of mirth. "I was just teasing!"

Keith knew of Larry's lucre-loving ways as well as anyone. "You sure, Lar?"

Larry seemed almost hurt by the doubting eyes surrounding him. "Wow, my reputation is pretty air-tight in this crowd! I guess I can't say I don't deserve it. But listen, Darrin, this revelation about Sam isn't exactly new and out of the package. Come on! We had this client not long after you were married – he wanted to sell candy using an old crone as his symbol, and you started going on about how he couldn't because witches have feelings.[23] That wasn't the only time, either.[24] You've even looked me in the eye and said, 'She's a witch!'"

"You, too?" Louise couldn't believe she and her husband had kept the same secret.

"Twice![25] The number of times the word 'witch' has come up would be enough for any guy to start putting pieces together.[26] Hey, you two, of *course* in these last few minutes I've been thinking about doing some magical money-making. I have emoluments in my heart and greed in my soul. I wouldn't be me without it. But I'd like to think I've mellowed in recent years, at least a little. Like back when you came up with all that 'inside info' on the Bliss Cough Syrup account[27]...witchcraft, huh?"

"Yeah," Darrin concurred. "But I really wasn't acting on my own accord there. My father-in-law had given me this watch I could do magic with...and I think some of that magic went to my head."

"Then isn't what your father-in-law did...unethical?"

Samantha had never thought of that incident in those terms. "I guess it was."

"To tell you the truth," Larry went on, "I was uncomfortable with how I acted that day, talking about juggling the stock market and wanting to rule the world since I was a little kid. I mean, it's true...I *have* wanted to..."

"Called that one, too, Sam[28]," Darrin said of the dream spell, causing Samantha to look away mid-eyeroll.

"I'm gonna bottom line it for you. Samantha...when I walked in here tonight, I thought of you as one of my closest friends. Knowing what I know now...let's face it. Friends don't take advantage of each other, do they. Not even when one friend can conjure up a million dollars for the other friend. Ah..." Larry had a bit of a lost look for a moment. "Don't mind me. I'm just watching my ship that came in backing out of the harbor..."

Louise laughed. "He might be a pirate – but he's our pirate. And willing to give up the plunder? I'm more than a little impressed, honeybear."

"You don't know what a close call that was, Uncle Larry," Tabitha declared abruptly, mystifying the man.

"Hey, Tabitha," Jonathan unwittingly interrupted, preventing the Stephenses from having to explain their Hepzibah dilemma. "D'ya think you could get your brother to turn me into a zebra again? That was pretty fun. Or maybe a brontosaurus."

"You remember being a zebra, Jon?" Larry queried his son.

The candor in the room had Darrin feeling a little mischievous. "Don't *you* remember being a crow, Larry? In Salem?"[29]

Larry's face got that much closer to matching the white of his hair. "I thought I hallucinated that while knocked out."

Abner had been taking it all in, his demeanor not giving away his feelings on the subject at hand one way or another. However, he did allow himself to verbalize the one thought he kept coming back to. "You're awfully quiet, Gladys. I figured you'd be the first person we'd hear from."

Gladys stared down her husband. "I wanna hear what you have to say first."

"That may be some kind of world record." Abner's eyes toured the room, visiting upon Tates and Stephenses and Wilsons and secretaries and friends and children. "Everything I'm hearing tonight...I thought Gladys' cooking was hard to digest." Ignoring the resulting smack on his arm, Abner went on. "You don't know what I've been through with this one. How many nights she kept me up talking about what she allegedly saw over here. Animals stomping around and things flying all over the place. One time it was Santa and his elves.[30] And the workouts I got from her dragging me across the street to show me something bizarre! Of course I'd get to this living room window and everything would be normal.

"Gladys has always been goofy even on her best days, ever since we got married outta college in '35.[31] Here's something you'd never guess – I kinda liked that about her. But when Mr. and Mrs. Stephens were just *thinking* about buying this place, it was like Gladys poured gasoline on her goofy fire.[32] There's barely been a day I haven't had to hear about some strange thing or other happening under this roof. Psychiatrists[33], medicine[34] – nothing helped. Finally I sink a fortune into renting an RV just so's I can get her out of here and put her mind on something else. That's right, Gladys; I knew you'd figured out the reason for our trip before we even got outta Jersey.

"So we're here one night and it's starting up all over again. Only now I got all these other people saying Gladys was right and I was wrong. Watching a kid turn into a zebra – was that really Michael Jackson in here? – well, it's bringing to mind a few unusual things I saw myself, but wrote off. Once there was a mule that played chess..."[35]

"I told you there was," Gladys was happy to inform Abner.

"Another time Mrs. Stephens kept falling asleep when I was talking to her – "[36]

"That I didn't know. Why didn't you tell me about it?"

"And give you the satisfaction? We've been butting heads a lot more than we used to; at first I just thought because we're getting older and more set in our ways. Then a while back I started thinking I've been resenting you for upsetting the apple cart of my retirement – and you probably resent me because I've never believed anything that's come out of your mouth about this house.[37] So here it is...I can't deny what I've seen and heard tonight. I dunno if I'm convinced it's true, or if I'll ever be. But I guess I owe ya an apology for discounting you all this time. Don't get too used to it or anything, though."

Samantha felt a need to continue in that vein. "I owe you one, too, Mrs. Kravitz. I'm sorry for letting you believe you were crazy whenever you witnessed witchcraft or witchcraft-related things. It wasn't personal; we just...didn't feel safe telling anyone, and you had gotten so warm about it all, if not red-hot..."

Gladys Kravitz had waited eight years for this. Ever since she first saw Mrs. Stephens and her mother surround this then barren house with foliage of all descriptions[38], she knew in her heart there was something supernatural afoot. And only rarely had anyone supported her about it. She thought maybe she'd shake some believers from the tree when she went in front of a news crew to report that odd Aunt Clara conjuring up Benjamin Franklin[39], but no dice; the same when fellow partygoer Mr. Tate ended up taking back having seen nephew Tommy as a goat.[40] Gladys had only ever found a kindred spirit in that nice young Air Force captain who corroborated seeing aliens in the Stephenses' backyard.[41] She often wished he'd stuck around; the path of the nonconformist could be a lonely one.

Now, here was basically an entire room of people echoing what she'd had to believe in solitude for years. It was heady; she felt as though the floodgates inside her were finally getting a chance to open.

Very aware the spotlight was on her, Gladys let the water flow.

"Red-hot, was I? Well, you better believe I have a few things I wanna get off my chest – "

"That's it! I've seen and heard enough!"

All eyes gazed upon a severe middle-aged woman wearing her hair in a severe matronly bun who rushed into the room through the patio doors.

"I *knew* you were a witch!" the teacher Mrs. Peabody yelled, wagging her finger at Samantha as if she were sending a student to detention. "Thought you had me fooled with that story about your family being magicians, eh?[42] I was just waiting for you to slip up and it took the little boy to do it! We don't want your kind around here – you with your creepy spells and fiendish rituals. Mark my words, I am calling the police. I want this woman taken away! Right now!"

16 Making Zap Judgments

"I mean it, Mrs. Stephens," Maudie Peabody announced in front of her student and her student's friends and family. "The very notion of you stalking our PTA meetings looking for sacrifices – enrolling your child in my school to corrupt my class and expand your cult!" The teacher moved toward the phone stationed atop the Stephenses' TV set. "Well, it stops here. And I'm sure you won't object if I make my call from – "

"Why don't you knock it off?"

Samantha and Darrin's jaws nearly hit the floor – to say nothing of Abner's.

They saw Gladys Kravitz standing determinedly with her hands on her hips.

"You have no idea what you're talking about," the neighbor told the teacher. "Sacrifices? Cults? I don't know how long you've known Mrs. Stephens, but it's not long enough if you think *that* about her."

Maudie squared her eyes at Gladys. "At first I thought she was an alien, until she told me she was a witch – an assertion you all just confirmed. I heard you with my own ears."

"I thought she was an alien a couple times myself[1]," Mrs. Kravitz confessed. "You're a stranger, but already I see a lot of myself in you. Peeking through windows, listening in on conversations. Oh – and threatening to call the authorities. You're walking a trail I blazed long before the Stephenses even had kids. I've seen it all, take it from me. I assume you heard my husband saying he never believed a word of it; in no time at all, I became obsessed with the idea that something wasn't right with this family...maybe even more than I would have otherwise...because I was alone in my convictions.

"Tonight I found out I was right. For so, so long, everyone looked at me as if I'd lost my marbles, and it turns out they never left the bag. I'm gonna tell you something I've realized being here tonight: Samantha Stephens is good people. She's been a caring neighbor, and very tolerant of me coming over here to snoop all the time when she could have just as easily told me to go not to heaven, but the other place. I probably owe her a pantry full of bakery ingredients given how much I've borrowed just so I could get in here!

"I don't know much about witches, but Mrs. Stephens isn't at all like you describe. Neither are her kids. And I can't believe I'm saying this, but...it doesn't matter to me if they have magical powers."

Samantha looked as shocked as Gladys frequently had witnessing witchcraft. "Then why did you always act like it did?"

"I just wanted to hear I was right! The more people kept telling me I wasn't seeing what I was seeing, the more determined I became to verify it. Like I said, it sort of became a fixation with me. Maybe it took being away for a year, I dunno. It's clear now there's nothing here to condemn. So I'm not gonna let someone else try to."

"This is all well and good," Mrs. Peabody scoffed, "but a witch is a witch and nothing anyone can say is going to distract me from calling the police." Maudie reached for the phone.

"Samantha, can't you do something?" Phyllis asked, almost begging.

Approaching the enraged educator, Samantha told her party guests, "Well, I could..."

Samantha snapped her finger in Mrs. Peabody's face, which suddenly lit up. "Why, Mrs. Stephens!" Putting the phone down, Maudie continued, "I seem to have interrupted a party! I'm so sorry for the inconvenience." Her tone had changed completely, rendering her friendly and solicitous. Too friendly.

"Yes, Mrs. Peabody; we're celebrating my husband's promotion," Samantha said through a forced grin.

"How lovely! I remember how proud I was when Mr. Peabody, bless his soul, advanced through the district and became vice principal of Towner's Elementary. I couldn't have been happier for him if I – "

Samantha specifically addressed Dave...and Frank. "See, what I just did to her is up there with casting a love spell to make someone fall in love with you. Mrs. Peabody is completely under my power; nothing she's saying is of her own free will. She might want to call the law on me in her true state, but at least those are her own feelings; knowing what they are, I can deal with them directly and honestly. Just because I *can* control someone doesn't mean I should.

"That's one of the main things I've learned living like a mortal. Oh, now, who said it...'With great power comes great responsibility.' Franklin Roosevelt? Someone from the French Revolution..."

"Naw, it was Spider-Man," Jonathan the former zebra chimed in.

"Anyway, possessing the power of witchcraft is awe-inspiring, I'm not gonna lie – but there's even more power in knowing when not to use it. And I don't really want to be defined by it. That I'm a witch is just one part of me. When all is said and done, I'm just Samantha. I want to be known and loved for who I am as a person – not treated better or worse because I happen to be a little different than most people. You know?"

Samantha twitched her nose, taking her spell off the teacher. Maudie's cordial expression became stern again, with a little confusion added. "I don't know what you just did to me," she said stiffly, "but I am still calling the police." Once more, she picked up the Stephenses' receiver.

"Do that," Dorothy dared. "I won't cover Sam being a witch, but I'll sure as shootin' tell any officer that shows up there's nothing evil or creepy about her."

Betty joined Mrs. Wilson at her side. "Same. Mrs. Stephens has always been good and kind to me."

"The Torah has conflicting views about anything supernatural," Abner revealed, "but I don't. Not about this particular neighbor."

Larry made his way to Samantha and put his arm around her. "I would sooner have Sam make all the money in my bank account disappear than turn my back on her." Louise blew Larry a kiss.

Frank said nothing, instead grabbing a warming bottle of champagne from its half-melted bucket of ice and refilling his glass resolutely. He looked up, studied Samantha intensely...then raised the flute in her direction. "To the nicest woman – and witch – a guy could hope to have for a daughter-in-law. To Samantha!"

Those who retrieved their drinks, and those with none, repeated Frank's toast with verve: "To Samantha!"

Keith watched the outnumbered Mrs. Peabody; by now the phone she still held in her hand was generating a loud off-hook tone. "We don't do no gatecrashers at this party – dig?"

As stately as she was still able, Maudie Peabody replaced the receiver and headed straight for the front door, not looking behind her while exiting and closing it. Keith and Dave actually whooped. Betty, Abner, and Adam Newlarkin applauded. And Darrin drew nearer to his wife, giving her a kiss on one cheek while Larry bussed the other.

Samantha couldn't help laughing. "Wow...how 'bout that. Thank you all for your support – I often wondered what it would be like telling everybody. I feel more relieved than I thought possible. I'd gotten used to keeping that part of myself a secret; I don't think I realized until right now how much of a strain it's been."

"A strain I put you through," Darrin said, feeling regret.

"We both agreed to that decision, sweetheart," Samantha reassured her husband, "and I'm not sorry I did. Made life interesting, anyway!"

Louise found herself looking toward the door. "Why do I get the impression you haven't heard the last of Mrs. Peabody?"

Samantha whistled. "You may be right. Tabitha, you wanna change schools Monday?"

"Aw, I can handle Mrs. Peabody. Besides, if I change schools I won't be able to see Charl – "

Raising an eyebrow, Samantha gently asked, "Charlton Rollnick?"

Tabitha seemed to be struggling not to turn red. "Mother," came her subject-changer, "now that everyone knows about us...are Adam and me allowed to use our powers as much as we want instead of having to do things the mortal way all the time?"

Samantha clicked her tongue. "No, Tabitha, we still have to function in the mortal world. After all, there's nearly four billion people out there who don't have the first idea about us."

"So," Gladys started, kneeling down to the young witch, "what Sidney said about you turning him into a mushroom[2]...that was true?"

Tabitha crinkled her nose and tilted her head to the side, uttering a word she'd heard inflected a certain way all her life. "Well?"

Hearing Samantha's catch phrase issue forth from her daughter caused smiles and chuckles among the entire group.

"All righty, then," Samantha called to everyone. "Since nobody's readying to burn me and my kids at the stake, I think it's time we relight the fire of our party instead. Just two quick bits of housekeeping first. One: I don't have to tell you that not everybody will be as understanding as you've proven yourselves to be, especially those who don't know me personally. I think I can safely speak for Darrin when I say we would really appreciate keeping my witchly identity just between us in this room."

Darrin winked. "Consider yourself safely spoken."

"My lips are sealed," Phyllis promised.

Adam Newlarkin nodded. "I've no issues with that."

Keith sported a playful grin. "You mean we could make a club of it? Secret handshakes, decoder rings, and that stuff?"

"Whatever makes you happy, dear," Dorothy replied, pecking his forehead in mock exasperation.

"Listen, if any of you need instruction on how to keep witchcraft from the world, I have enough chapters to create a very thick textbook," Darrin kidded.

"Yeah, I've seen pages from your textbook," Larry smirked. "Claiming you switched Sam and Endora on live television using something you learned in an electronics manual.[3] Giving me that song-and-dance about making a unicorn by sticking *papier-mâché* on a horse.[4] And that time you guys sat for Jonathan, when Louise thought she saw him in London..."[5]

Louise had total recall of the event. "You did everything to stall getting us back here to the house. To keep us from finding out Jon really *was* in London!"

"I was?" came the transfixed Jonathan's response. "*Cool*."

"Gotta hand it to you, Darrin," Larry conceded. "You sure learned how to think fast on your feet."

Darrin snickered. "Think how well that's gonna serve me at McMann, Tate and Stephens."

"So, you said two bits of housekeeping, Samantha." Betty hoped to get the night back on track. "What's the second?"

Samantha passed the couch, scooping Adam up and stationing herself at the head of the group. "I was thinking...in the spirit of unity we have going on tonight, this might be a good time for you all to meet some other witches I know. I mean, technically, most of you already have met them; you just didn't know they aren't human."

"Wait a minute," Darrin said. "Are you sure? How many witches are we talking about?"

"Just the major players, sweetheart," Samantha assured.

Jonathan clapped his hands together. "You mean there are other witches besides you guys?"

"If you only knew," Darrin deadpanned as Samantha handed him their son.

"I'm not sure how many we number," Samantha reflected. "This is just what you might call a representative sample." Snapping both fingers, she made the couch, coffee table, and chairs vanish. "If I can just get you to fan out a little," she told her guests, who complied. Samantha then put French manicured fingers to temples.

> *"Not like the kind you see in covens*
> *Or baking children in fairy tale ovens*
> *To prove you're real and not a myth*
> *Kindred witches, appear forthwith!"*

Mortals less familiar with the magical goings-on of 1164 Morning Glory Circle, like Lisa's parents, Dave, Betty, and Adam Newlarkin, retreated involuntarily upon seeing huge plumes of smoke erupt from the living room floor. The more seasoned mortals – Kravitzes, Tates, and elder Stephenses – still registered shock, but somehow had an easier time accepting what was happening before their eyes. For their part, Lisa and Jonathan stood rapt.

The evaporating billows revealed Endora, Maurice, Serena, Uncle Arthur, Esmeralda...and Dr. Bombay.

"Apologies for the *small* representative sample, darling," Endora said cheerily, having traded in her flying suit for a vibrant purple and orange gown accessorized by giant lavender pearls. "But this was all your father and I could muster, even after we amplified your spell, since you originally wanted those of our ethnicity to stay away from your soirée tonight."

"We leapt into action as soon as we saw that these mortals showed a willingness to accept you," added Maurice, who would sooner go naked than not don one of his Victorian tuxedoes.

"Well, I would have appreciated you leaping a little later, Uncle Maury," said Samantha's lookalike cousin Serena in her trademark, high-pitched voice. "I was skydiving near the Great Barrier Reef in Australia. Though if it hadn't been for the foxy Aussie pilot, I wouldn't have bothered with a plane!" Serena then let out an ear-shattering cackle.

Maurice plugged his ears, giving Darrin a woeful look. "Darryl, I take back what I said about no one ever daring to call me 'Maury,'" he conceded, reminding Darrin of the time he and Samantha tried to get out of naming their son after the warlock.[6]

"I was interrupted doing something far more important!" the booming Bombay insisted. "I was carefully concocting a cure for a new witch disease that causes one to sprout feathers. I suppose you could say I'm working on a wing and a prayer!" The mustachioed doctor had himself in stitches until he realized his humor wasn't being appreciated. His response was to simply sigh, "Nothing."

Samantha turned to the family comedian. "No snappy comeback, Uncle Arthur?"

"I never work with amateurs," came Arthur's droll reply. "Good to see you again, Sammy."

Though no one asked her, Esmeralda volunteered her whereabouts. "I wasn't far," she said witheringly. "But if I don't sit down soon, my feet are going to go numb from these ditzy shoes." The yoo-hoo maid caught the amused Darrin's expression. "Oh, *dear*. I meant 'glitzy.'"

Samantha spoke to her mortal party guests. "Let's get everybody acquainted. These are my parents, Maurice and Endora...my cousin, Serena..."

* * *

Being the common denominator, and now serving as unofficial witch-mortal ambassador for this very mixed group in her living room, Samantha discovered the introductions were a little more involved than she'd envisioned. Halfway through, she found herself wishing she'd simply zapped up "Hello, I'm _____" tags. After essentially keeping the people from her witch world separate from her mortal world all this time, the crossovers were both awkward and liberating. Fortunately, the Tates, Darrin's parents, and Mrs. Kravitz had met nearly all the supernaturals at some point anyway, so it was just a matter of familiarizing folks like Abner, Betty, Dave, the Wilsons, and Adam Newlarkin with them.

It was a surreal experience. Now able to let go of the long-held fear she had stuffed down about whether mortals in her inner circle would react badly to her being a witch, Samantha experienced a sort of converse fear about her relatives, maid, and doctor, considering they themselves hadn't always taken the kindest view of humans. But any fog of discomfort that might have hovered in the room started to dissipate, and faster than Samantha would have bet on. Those amassed under her roof were interacting peacefully and cordially, and it didn't seem to matter that some had magical powers while others didn't.

"Hi, Cotton Top!"[7] Serena vamped to Larry, unable to resist patting his coarse white hair.

Larry hoped Louise wouldn't notice his cheeks flushing a bit. "Ah, Serena; last time I saw you, I said you were unique.[8] I'm not surprised that extends to you being more than human."

"That explains the Vitamin V you gave him," Louise remarked. "I knew even a pill you can't get in a pharmacy couldn't make a man grow younger. That funny kid we saw was Larry, wasn't he, Serena."

Jonathan was intrigued. "You were a kid like me, Dad?"

"I thought I dreamt that, but yeah," Larry affirmed. "A little older than you are now."

"Bet that was the morning you made me go to school half an hour early," Jonathan pouted to his mother, "'cuz I never saw him. I miss everything neato."

Dr. Bombay looked perturbed. "What is this Vitamin V you were handing out, Serena? You didn't get it from me – don't tell me that skirt-chasing apothecary[9] has been dispensing medicine without my approval again."

"How do you think I get my exercise, Bomby?" Serena replied playfully, again launching into her shrill laugh.

"I shall have to dispense hearing aids soon if you keep that up. And need I remind you, you shouldn't have given witch medication to a mortal."

Seeing the doctor brought things back for Larry. "You mean like those 'Cold Bombs' of yours we almost marketed?[10] The common cold didn't stand a chance against those pills...man, too bad about that side effect that made our voices pitch up."

"Is that how come my ears hurt when she laughs?" Jonathan asked regarding Serena. "She took some?"

Louise shushed him, hoping the now-confirmed witch wouldn't be insulted. "So, I recall you having blond hair at one point...and playing guitar.[11] Have you kept up with it?"

"Oh, I'm still known to grind my axe when the mood strikes," Serena boasted.[12]

"Maybe later you could play Jon that tune you did for us," Larry suggested. "What was it...*The Iffen Song*?"

Serena's eyebrows raised. "Huh? Never heard of it."[13]

Keith shook Arthur's hand just slightly cautiously. "Good to meet you! Darrin's told us a bit about your legendary...sense of humor."

Uncle Arthur flashed his ironic smile. "If Digby's[14] throwing around words like 'legendary', Sammy must've gotten him a dictionary for Christmas!" Then he spied Dorothy's uncomfortable look and Tabitha's scolding one. "Sorry about that; we're supposed to be building bridges to help Sam and Darrin. Bear with me – I can't break such a good habit in a matter of minutes."

"Just don't pull any practical jokes on Lisa's parents, okay?" Tabitha asked earnestly. "You'll give Adam here ideas."

"I don't get to see enough of you kiddies." Now including Lisa, Arthur asked, "How do you all know each other, anyway?"

Lisa hooked arms with Tabitha. "Our daddies work together at McMann and Tate – well, now, McMann, Tate and Stephens. We already called ourselves sisters, but we've been even more sisters since Tabitha covered us with black-and-white polka dots."

"Polka dots? When did that happen, honey?" Dorothy asked, not a little surprised.

"Before you and Mr. Wilson came back for the Christmas party," Tabitha explained. "I was trying for a color between hers and mine so we could really be sisters, but I got dots instead."[15]

Arthur's bottom lip jutted out thoughtfully. "Sounds like something that happens when my witchcraft's on the fritz. But if you really wanted to make it so color wouldn't be an issue, you should have done this." The warlock zapped, and suddenly Lisa and Tabitha were completely desaturated – literally black-and-white. "It's just as well – color TVs are still too expensive." Arthur roared buoyantly. "Hey, I said I wouldn't pull jokes on Lisa's *parents*! I'm too much."

"This is groovy, too, Tabs," Lisa grinned, taking in her monochrome state.

Using the hand Tabitha wasn't holding onto, Adam waved at himself and instantly became colorless as well. He giggled cherubically as Keith and Dorothy looked on.

Tabitha sighed. "I told you you'd give him ideas," she lamented to her prankster great-uncle.

Phyllis touched Samantha's arm. "Remember you told me once that your whole family was 'wacky as witches'?[16] I'm a little disappointed you felt you had to drop hints like that. There was no need to make me believe I was hallucinating[17] or that *I* had floated that antique doll I gave to Tabitha."[18]

"She made you think you had powers, too?"[19] Gladys questioned animatedly. "Well, Mrs. Stephens, you sure came up with some doozies to throw us all off the scent. Though if I'd known it was really you who could do magic and not me I wouldn't have stood outside in a downpour trying to turn the rain off."

"I admit I did rather elevate hiding anything witchy to an art form," Samantha said, unconsciously straightening the foyer mirror. "It's going to take a little while to get unused to it." Seeing Esmeralda floundering her way across the living room with empty ashtrays, Samantha waved her over. "Esmeralda, don't worry about cleaning anything. After all, this is a party you weren't even invited to at first. I just want you to know I didn't mean to hurt your feelings when I said you couldn't come."

Esmeralda seemed to be using the ashtrays for balance. "You didn't hurt my feelings, Samantha. I understood why you wanted this to be a mortals-only affair. Of course, who knew it was going to turn out the way it did."

Samantha smiled. "Adam, apparently. Are you still having trouble standing up on the platforms? Why don't you take them off?"

"Because they look so good on my feet. At least I found somewhere to wear them on a Saturday night."

"You put them on just to come over here when Samantha called?" Phyllis wanted to know.

The usually shy Esmeralda looked as if she knew something. "You could say that. Actually, I've been here the whole time."

"The whole time?" asked a confused Gladys.

"Oh, yes. I was invisible." Esmeralda glanced at Samantha warmly. "And you thought I couldn't stay out of trouble."

Samantha put her arm around the yoo-hoo maid's shoulder. "Will miracles never cease."

Gladys was still having a hard time absorbing everything. "What do you mean, 'out of trouble'?"

"Nothing, I just have a little magical issue when I sneeze.[20] Luckily I finally found a really good mortal antihistamine. For a while I thought the party was done, but once everybody was back I just faded right onto the dance floor again."

"Back?" Phyllis was lost.

Samantha sensed a need to soothe blown minds. "Maybe we'd better stick to one event you didn't personally witness at a time," she suggested to her mother-in-law and neighbor.

"By the way," Esmeralda added, "I was having so much fun dancing with you all that I got a little carried away giving you that booty bump."

Phyllis gawked at Esmeralda. "That was you?"

"I forgot myself for a moment. Then again, if I hadn't given you and Mr. Kravitz the tiniest little zap, you would have stayed too scared to dance, even though you both wanted to."

Samantha tittered to herself and gave up trying to be Esmeralda's translator. "I haven't had a chance to refresh the ice for quite a while. I'll be right back." Gladys and Phyllis were left to fend for themselves as Samantha headed to the kitchen.

Endora toyed with Frank's tie. "I still can't believe it sometimes – that I almost broke up your marriage."[21]

"Oh? How did this happen?" Maurice inquired inquisitively.

"We had a little bit of a flirtation, Frank and I."

"It wasn't that serious," Frank replied, eyeing Maurice carefully.

"Wasn't it, though! He ended up flying to Miami while Mrs. Stephens took a train to Phoenix. But once Samantha and I got them together in that Angel Falls, it was all's well that ends well – in language of the Bard you'd understand, Maurice."

Frank looked increasingly uneasy. "I always wondered how a big ol' jetliner could land in a tiny place like Angel Falls. But," he went on for Maurice's sake, "I was just enjoying Endora's attention because it made me feel young again. I didn't even realize she was married. I wasn't trying to – "

"You wanted to feel young again," Maurice said understandingly. Then his tone became menacing. "So it's only *a propos* I turn you into a drooling one-year-old!" Endora's husband raised his hand, and Frank actually cowered. A moment later, Maurice was all smiles and laughter. "Not a bad performance for the only warlock to graduate from London's Royal Academy of the Arts, eh, my boy? Of course, considering it opened in the 18th century, I was far older than the rest of my classmates. You have nothing to worry about, Frank," he assured, rolling his Rs. "Endora and I have what the young people today would call an 'open marriage.' Have had for centuries. We were the envy of many a medieval king, let me tell you!"

Samantha didn't think only filling the ice bucket would be enough, so she poured most of the remaining bag into a large mixing bowl. But the cubes sat there melting as Samantha peered into the living room from her side of the counter that separated the kitchen and dining room, watching as beings from two realms seemed to be chatting amicably – which had always seemed impossible before now. The scene almost had her in a trance.

Suddenly, Hepzibah popped in behind her, snapping her out of it.

"Your Majesty!" Samantha managed a mini bow in her awkward position. "No fanfare?"

Standing in a mortal kitchen made the High Priestess no less severe. "Even we are schooled in the fine art of subtlety, Samantha."

"If it please," Samantha said, hoping to stay a step ahead of the sovereign, "I'd just as soon not introduce you to my human guests just yet. I think they have enough to take in for the moment."

"We did not traverse the atmospheric continuum to further fraternize with those of this other culture – though one day that would make a fascinating addition to our research on it. No," Hepzibah clarified, "we have come to inform you of our decision regarding the matters debated in front of the Council tonight."

Samantha felt hopeful and like the world was dropping out from under her feet at the same time. "Which is?"

"Judging by what we have seen of these mortals' reactions to the news that you are a witch..."

"Yes?"

"We have decreed...that perhaps there is hope for witch-mortal relations after all. A decree with which the Witches' Council concurs."

Eyes wet with tears, Samantha could only say, "Thank you, Your Majesty. You know, they really are making an effort out there."

Hepzibah waved the subject away. "There's hardly more need for discussion, Samantha. We have seen for ourselves that perhaps we witches need to open our minds as well, as so many mortals are calling for today in politics, movies, music..."

"Today, tomorrow...it's a concept that should never go out of style. It can just be such an easy one to forget." Samantha suddenly remembered something that threatened to be the ultimate party pooper. "Ooh...what about Mrs. Peabody? I mean, your condition was that all mortals were supposed to accept me and the children, and she made no secret of her – "

The High Priestess leaned in closer to Samantha. "One rotten apple need not spoil the entire barrel, Samantha. We...have taken care of it."

"I don't know that I understand what you're – "

"Well, we were primed to erase *somebody's* memory tonight."

Samantha tried to hide her shock. "I thought no witch was supposed to interfere in the outcome – "

The smallest smile played on Hepzibah's lips. "We ordered the Witches' Council and your parents not to interfere," she stated. More quietly, the High Priestess added, "I never said I couldn't."

Trying not to laugh, Samantha didn't know what to be more flummoxed by: Hepzibah's action or the fact that she finally didn't refer to herself in the third person.

As if catching her pronoun peccadillo, Hepzibah regained her regalness. "As for the other mortals, what we have witnessed from them this eve is a satisfactory start. Time will tell if they hold true to their convictions or not."

Samantha collected her containters of ice. "Yes. Time will tell."

"We do only have one more question to submit to you, and this is off the record. Might you consider taking a seat on the Council? Witches of your veracity and persistence are hard to come by – and I could pass a resolution to rename the entity the 'Noble Nine.' That does rather roll more easily off the tongue."

"I appreciate the invitation; truly, I do. But I'm definitely done with governing. I only want to be empress of this palace."

"To each his own, Samantha."

"Exactly, your Majesty."

17 Witches' Lib

Abner and Gladys Kravitz strolled through the living room arm-in-arm, each taking in the scene of mortals in conversation with witches. "So, I'm still waiting for it, Gladys," Abner told his wife.

"Waiting for what?"

"The chorus of I-told-you-sos. I expected you'd hire the Vienna Boys' Choir to sing it in five-part harmony."

Abner's one-of-a-kind attempt at appeasement upstaged any urge Gladys had to crow. "Let's just say, you finally believing me about our neighbors is enough. You have to wonder, though..."

"Wonder what, Gladys Gruber, now Kravitz?"[1]

"Now that I no longer have to convince you there are unusual things going on across the street...what are we gonna talk about?"

Passing Darrin and Endora at the entrance to the patio, Abner simply said, "Getting you into a cooking class."

Gladys again thwacked Abner's arm with her free hand – only more tenderly than she did before.

Endora looked up at Darrin almost coquettishly. "So you really thought I would have five eyes?"

"Silly now, I know," Darrin acknowledged. "And that's how we began.[2] We've had some battles royal since then, haven't we?"

"I saw worse at Hastings in 1066," Endora said measuredly, "but we've come close a few times."

Darrin tip-toed up to the wall that had always existed between himself and his mother-in-law. "I suppose I started it by calling witchcraft 'nonsense'. Do you think things would still have escalated the way they did if you hadn't been following Hepzibah's directives?"[3]

Endora waved a hand. "Who can tell? We probably would have

clashed anyway – given how strongly we two feel about Samantha and what's best for her. I'll never understand why she regards you with such fascination, but I'll credit you this...not many mortals have gone toe-to-toe with me, let alone as many times as you have, knowing I'm capable of so much more than...verbal comebacks."

"Well, I'll credit you this: you are exasperating, antagonistic, vindictive, captious..."

"Captious? What in the name of all that's witchly does that even mean?"

"Yet...no one can say you're not a witch of your convictions. You're fiercely protective of those you love. And no one knows more than I that your imagination has no peer. There are times I almost... admire you."

Endora paused. "Don't start making me like you, Durwood."

"And that's the one thing I've never understood – why you never use my actual name."

"I've called you 'Darrin' before, Endora insisted.[4] "A handful of times, anyway..."

"Yeah, I guess you're right...*Eudora*." Darrin said with a hint of a roguish smile.

Endora's eyes rolled beneath expanses of turquoise eyeshadow. "Touché, Durwood...touché."

Samantha and Uncle Arthur slowly made their way down the carpeted stairs. "Thanks for restoring the color to the girls' cheeks – and everywhere else."

"Love the way Adam was able to take care of his own restoration. Can't quite fathom why the little mortal boy wanted to go grayscale, too, though."

"So, are you satisfied that none of your practical jokes are still in residence upstairs?[5] I can't believe I haven't seen you since you deposited them here trying to impress that witch Aretha. How many months ago was that?"

Arthur was cavalier. "It's no big deal, Sammy. I just decided that, after Aretha, I needed to do a little soul searching...over the rainbow."

"Well, I'm glad you're back. Have you heard from her since you went your separate ways?"

"No," Arthur said, not looking at all unhappy. "But I've heard from her brother."

"Well, hello there, Kinky Top!" Serena said in oozing greeting to Keith, patting his dark locks. Detecting Dorothy's icy reaction, she added, "I meant his hair. Yours is so wonderful, too, Mrs. Wilson. Maybe you can teach me to make my own into an Afro. After all, it's practically there already!" Serena lightheartedly said of her own teased brunette 'do.

"It really is uncanny how much you and Samantha look alike," Dorothy admitted, trying to overlook Serena's flamboyant friendliness.

"Oh, we get that all the time," Serena pooh-poohed. "But we're very different, too. For example, I don't think Sammy could even begin to appreciate that *with-it* record collection you have!"

"Thank you!" Keith beamed. "We're proud of it. We're always on the lookout for new grooves."

"Greenwich Village, SoHo...shops all over New York, really," Dorothy expounded.

"Well, they don't have nothin' on the shops where I feel the funk in the real Soho, on the West End," Serena said of her experiences in England. "Have you ever been?"

Keith and Dorothy shook their heads.

"Oh, you would *love* it! The nightclubs, the concerts! Maybe once this ho-hum meet-and-greet is over I'll pop you two over there with me and give you a real taste of far-out!"

The Wilsons didn't know whether to be excited or unnerved.

Frank carefully studied Tabitha's other grandfather. "It's a little daunting knowing I'm talking to a man who could turn me into something at any moment."

"Welcome to my world," came Darrin's knowing response. "I've been a veritable zoo over the years."[6]

Maurice took it all in stride. "Well, Darryl, at least we do have one thing in common besides Samantha – we've both been mules."[7]

"Yeah – except you didn't have to be one on your birthday," Darrin commented. "Come to think of it, Dad, you were a mule, too, at one point."[8]

"I was?" asked the astonished Frank.

"Samantha turned you into one to convince Mom to stop using her 'powers'. You don't remember, do you."

"I never even told Phyllis, but...I've always wondered if that was real. Because I have a vague recollection of doing something not too pleasant to your rug."

"Good thing for me the agency created a campaign for a new carpet cleaner that isn't on the market yet."

"It's crazy," Abner finally chimed in. "I feel strangely left out.

You've all been mules but me."

Maurice breathed on his knuckles and rubbed them against his formal suit coat. "Would you like me to round out the set?"

"No, no, that's not necessary." Abner suddenly froze. "Wait a minute. That chess-playing mule I saw...you?"

"And quite the adversary you were, too, struggling with me for supremacy of the board. I've never seen a mortal execute a fork move with such dexterity."

Abner smiled, thinking how his years of practice against himself paid off. "Any time you want a rematch...just bray."

The group was joined by Dave and Adam Newlarkin, who definitely had something on their minds.

"Hey, Dar, this has been one of the most fascinating nights of my life," Dave told his old friend, "and believe me, next time you talk, you will know I'm listening. But all this kind of took the focus off a different fascinating night I was hoping to have."

Adam's sheepish look said it all. "We've been keeping the Bettys waiting an awful long time."

Darrin thought the former secretaries must have gone home hours ago...until he looked at his watch. "Oh, right. It's just barely ten...for you guys," he added *sotto voce*.

"They probably think we fell into a sewer somewhere," Dave worried. "Confidentially, this is the first date I've had in eons, and I don't want Ms. Ashmont to think I stood her up."

"Or I Ms. Moorehead. And we still have to drive all the way back there," Adam realized.

"I've got a roadster," Dave bragged. "Get us there faster than anything you've got."

Maurice shifted into a surprising fatherly role. "Gentlemen, where are these ladies typecast in their roles as ladies-in-waiting?"

Adam wasn't sure how the question connected. "Um, La Petite Maison[9]...it's on the other end of town..."

"Then these ladies shall wait no more. Prepare to be sent there directly."

"You can do that?" The bookish Adam became amazingly animated. "How do I even begin to thank you?" Looking at Darrin, he said, "Listen, I haven't had a date in eons, either..."

"Tell Samantha 'good night' for us, and come by my practice sometime soon, okay?" Dave patted Darrin's shoulder, then Maurice's. "Much obliged, sir. Witchcraft is cool!"

Flicking both his wrists, Maurice made the mortal bachelors disappear.

"If I hadn't seen it for myself," the amazed Frank said, shaking his head, "I'd never have believed it."

"That's for sure," Abner agreed.

"Warlock or mortal man, the pursuit of female happiness should bring us all together in solidarity," Maurice proclaimed.

"Only one thing. Their cars are still parked outside," Darrin noted.

"Well, I can't do everything for them. Let me tell you fellows about the time I romanced Mary Pickford. Before that dolt Douglas Fairbanks stole her from me, that is..."

While Larry and Endora were deep in conversation, Betty Wilson was deep in concentration. "I should have seen it from the beginning when I met you in Paris[10]," Larry allowed. "I always thought it wild enough that you and Sam visited the same time Louise and I were there – but when she was in the restaurant one minute and I talked to her on the phone at home the next...well, the signs were there, weren't they? There were countless others, too; I guess I just didn't let myself add them up. All things considered, though...knowing you're a witch doesn't make you any less enchanting. It makes you more so, really."

"You may recall at one point I deemed you a man of taste and judgment[11]," Endora replied, exuding glamor as always. "I see I wasn't wrong in that assessment. Now, you're sure you have no plans to take advantage of my daughter and her powers for your own material gain? You *have* had a rather consistent pattern of avarice over the years."

Larry showed a rare earnestness. "Listen, no matter how you slice it, Endora, I'm still human. I can't say I won't be tempted. But I have Darrin and Sam – and I presume you – to keep me in check if I try to pull anything. Plus Louise. She's got powers I'm sure even witches haven't heard of," he chuckled.

"No doubt," Endora grinned. "Ms. Wilson," she continued, turning to the former secretary, "you look as though you're trying to memorize my face. Perhaps a picture would make that easier."

"Picture!" Betty felt as if the tumblers of the safe in her mind had finally clicked into place. "*Now* I remember where I know you from. You're the one in that winking, floating picture frame!"[12]

"I always did photograph well," Endora said with delight.

"So you really are her family doctor," Phyllis asked Dr. Bombay, who looked like he had come down with a case of terminal boredom. "I've been wondering ever since that time I met you – in my son's bathroom, of all places[13] – it means you're a witch doctor, then, doesn't it?"

The warlock just barely escaped being impolite. "Madame, that idiom may be technically accurate, but its syntax is ghastly."

"My apologies. There's one more thing I'd like to ask, if you don't mind, now knowing you're of the supernatural persuasion."

"If you must."

"Do you have anything for a sick headache?[14] Whenever I get one, the pills my mortal doctors give me never seem to help."

Dr. Bombay brushed his fingers against his substantial mustache. "Next time you're so afflicted, have Samantha find me. I might be prevailed upon to write a prescription for you." The image of the apothecary doggedly giving chase to Darrin's mother provided Bombay with some much-needed amusement. "Excuse me."

The doctor made his way through the throng of conversing witches and mortals, arriving at the table of food where Esmeralda was standing.

"Hello, Dr. Bombay. Exciting turn of events tonight, isn't it?"

"I haven't decided. Accepting mortals makes sense in priniciple... but it's going to take more than one evening to get past how dull so many of them can be."

"No one said it would happen overnight," Esmeralda supposed. "Remember, for as much as they were taught we're nothing but creaky hags, we grew up always hearing that mortals are inferior to us. And I don't really find that to be true, the more time I spend among them."

"The journey of a thousand miles, I wager. Any of these earthly tidbits worth consuming?"

Esmeralda pointed to a plate. "These *kourabiedes* are actually not terrible. It's good to see you, doctor, because it gives me a chance to finally thank you for trying to cheer me up after Ramon Verona threw me over. You know, by introducing me to your friend Norton."[15]

"As I recall, you and Norton didn't look anywhere close to snogging."

"I know," Esmeralda sighed, "but that love potion you whipped up enlivened things there for a while." The maid couldn't help thinking of her brief, resultant fascination with Samantha's husband, which she had never completely lost and would never, ever reveal to anybody. "Um...how are your nurses? It seems you're barely seen out without one on your arm anymore."[16]

The doctor took pleasure in being reminded of his prowess. "Well, aside from making my practice run more smoothly, they do shave a few centuries off a warlock." But something about Esmeralda unexpectedly cast his assistants in a different light. "However...I also find them terribly superficial at times. I often ruminate on whether witches with any depth exist in this cosmos."

"I see." Esmeralda was not skilled at interacting with those of her kind – especially the male of her kind – so she couldn't be completely sure she was sensing what she thought she was sensing. She was hardly aware of herself when she asked, "Doctor...do you have a first name? I've never heard anyone use it."

Clandestinely, without the slightest trace of his usual bravado or bluster, he looked his one-time patient in the eye. "It's Foxworth," he replied. "Foxworth Bombay."

Esmeralda wasn't wrong in sensing it.

"Hmm," Samantha said, inspecting the small plot under the outside bay window. "Seems Mrs. Peabody tramped down some of my marigolds."

"I can't believe the High Priestess Hepzibah made her forget the whole thing – like she almost did me." Darrin pulled his wife into a tight hug. "Thanks for not waiting until after the party to tell me about Hepzibah's reversal. Though admittedly, the suspense about whether or not I'd still know you tomorrow was about the only thing keeping me awake. It must be at least two in the morning to us."

"The party's in full swing again or I'd put Tabitha and Adam to bed. Not that Adam will remember most of it."

Darrin kept his arm around Samantha as they strolled through their backyard. "I dunno...if Tabitha can remember things that happened before she was born, Adam may have a photographic memory, too. Now...about that dream spell you put on me..."[17]

"Yes, said cautionary tale...which I built around the world finding out I'm a witch. As long as our friends and family don't break the pact – and I don't think they will – we should be all right."

"A dream spell, a forgotten trip to the North Pole[18]...a forgotten attempt to live by your witchcraft[19]..." Darrin started playfully. "Any other memory erasing you did on me that I should know about?"

"No," Samantha answered sheepishly, "that was about it. And I'm sorry you had to hear it from the Council and not me."

"I get now why you reacted so strongly those few other times I wanted to trade in the mortal life for your powers[20] – you already knew how it would turn out. That I wouldn't be able to control myself."

"You've come a long way since then – and you've mellowed so much about witchcraft in general[21]. The slightest bit of magic used to make your blood pressure spike."

"Too many examples to count; not terribly proud of that. I guess it's only natural witchcraft doesn't upset me like it used to, not after being around it this long," Darrin surmised. "And you! Who knew this worldly witch who couldn't manage scrambled eggs in the early days[22] – yeah, I saw you zap 'em back to an edible state once – would end up not only acing mortal housewifery, but day-to-day mortal life. I'd say we've kind of met in the middle, wouldn't you?"

Samantha embraced Darrin and kissed him affectionately. "Not such a bad place to be."

From their vantage point on the patio, the Stephenses peeked into the living room and watched Arthur and Maurice chatting with Larry, Keith, and Phyllis. Betty and the Kravitzes were laughing with Serena and Esmeralda. Dr. Bombay was bending Frank's ear while Dorothy and Louise discussed fashion with Endora. And Lisa was showing Adam how to play Battleship against Jonathan and Tabitha.

"Look at them," Darrin smiled. "We've *all* come a long way, haven't we?"

Samantha exhaled, satisfied. "Mmm-hmm. And I have a feeling this is just the beginning."

The marrieds' attempt at a second kiss was interrupted by the loud clinking of metal against glass, perpetrated by a celebratory Larry. Samantha and Darrin returned to their parlor to hear what the orating ad man had to say.

"Okay, everybody," Larry announced. "This whole United Nations for Witches thing has been great, but, lest we forget, we still have Darrin's promotion to celebrate. And the night is still young. Now that there are more revelers to revel alongside us, let's all lift up our glasses and – "

Samantha gasped. "Glasses! I'm so sorry, Mother, Daddy...the rest of my non-mortal clan...I never offered you drinks."

"Don't blame us for her lack of manners," Maurice droned jokingly.

Serena's high voice commanded attention. "Not to worry, Sammy! I'm the best bartender in the solar system!" One exuberant zap later, everyone was holding expensive goblets filled with fine reddish-brown liquid. "Ta da! Some of Uncle Arthur's sherry.[23] With Shirley Temples for the kiddies, of course."

"Serena, how many times have I told you to stop raiding my wine cellar?" the annoyed Arthur asked. "Especially when you don't serve up booze any better than you did those frozen chocolate covered bananas at that mortal job we had."[24]

"Oh, lighten up, Arturo. I did it for Phyllis! See, I remembered,

Mrs. Stephens! You thought Arthur's weird sense of humor came from being a tosspot. Well, it just so happens there are no tosspots in our family. Just crackpots!" Serena's characteristic laugh bounced off the living room walls.

Larry raised his goblet. "Well, Keith, why don't you get another one of your records ready while we all drink to – "

Suddenly there was a loud thud and a jangling of metal that had everybody wheeling around.

It was Aunt Clara, covered in ash and soot and sitting in the fireplace opening.

"Oh, hello, dears!" greeted the kind-hearted witch. "Am I late?"

Samantha ran to her long-absent aunt. "Oh, my stars! Where have you been? Darrin and I haven't seen you since you zapped up that UF[25] – I mean, we stopped hearing from you even before we found out I was having Adam..." Samantha couldn't hold back a few alleviating tears. "And I thought maybe something terrible had happened to you...or that I'd never see you again." Samantha helped Clara up and hugged her hard.

"Oh, what a darling. I...I didn't mean to stay away so long, Samantha," Clara explained. "I'm sorry. You see, after that incident with the...the UHF, I decided to unwind by taking a trip around the world to add to my doorknob collection.[27] And I was having a ball, simply a ball...until I got a little lost flying through the Bermuda Triangle. No harm, dear; I got an excellent tan! But I heard your summons thanks to your parents making it more detectable, so I concentrated as hard as I could to get back here to you. Of course this engine doesn't have as much horsepower as it once had, you know!"

Darrin approached and gave his aunt-in-law a warm hug of relief. "It's good to know you're okay, Aunt Clara."

"It's been far too long, Darrin. Far too long!" Coming out of the embrace, Clara studied her favorite mortal. "Well, I...I hope you don't mind my saying this, but...you look different than you used to somehow. I really can't quite place why."

"That's what I always thought, too," Tabitha said, surprising everyone by agreeing.

Endora stood with Arthur. "You might have sent a message so we wouldn't worry."

"For the benefit of those who haven't already met her," Arthur tried to make clear, "this is Clara. Our sister."[28]

Betty and the Wilsons made Clara's acquaintance, while the others in attendance got reacquainted.

"And here when I met you I didn't believe you telling me you're a witch[29]," Phyllis had to admit.

"Well, what else would I be?" Clara replied merrily.

"Here, Aunt Clara, let me get you cleaned up," Samantha offered, not for the first time feeling bad that her aunt's trademark black dress, fox stole, and flowered hat were covered with gray smudges.[30]

"No, no, I got myself all the way here – I can certainly handle freshening up." Clara waved confidently, but immediately found herself cloaked in swaths of colorful material and strand after strand of vibrant beads befitting an African tribeswoman. "Oh! That wasn't exactly what I...well, it's...it's fashion-forward, now isn't it..."

"I think I'm gonna like Aunt Clara," Dorothy smiled.

Clara's second attempt was more successful, putting her in a clean version of the clothes she arrived in. "Better than the washing machine any day." she giggled.

One redhead introduced herself to the other redhead. "So you're Clara! I've heard so much about you. I'm Esmeralda...I've sort of been filling in for you as babysitter the last little while."

"Well, then," Clara beamed, "I suppose when it comes to that particular school, we're both graduates!"

"Samantha!" Louise called, aiming her index finger at the fireplace. "What's that shiny thing over there?"

"On the floor?" Samantha scanned the area. "Those are some of Aunt Clara's doorknobs that fell out of her bag. I guess some items shifted during flight – "

Louise walked to the fireplace foundation. "No...*here*."

A brick had dislodged as a result of Clara's landing. In the rectangular hole it had left, something dingy yet decidedly sparkly lay between dust and cement powder. Samantha reached for it and brought it up to the light...

It was her diamond heart necklace.

Samantha needed a moment to catch her breath. "Darrin, look! I thought I had lost this forever!" Further examination filled in at least one blank. "The clasp is broken. But how did it end up – "

"It must have slipped off when we did the renovations around here a couple of summers back[31]," Darrin reasoned. "We did overhaul the fireplace ourselves. Who'd've thought?"

"I told you it would show up in a way you wouldn't expect," Dorothy affirmed.

"It's like I used to tell you, Dumbo!"[32] Serena shrieked. "Love power conquers all!"[33]

"A mystery worthy of Agatha Christie – solved by Aunt Clara." Samantha kissed her beloved aunt's now clean cheek.

Clara carefully took the chain so the heart wouldn't slip off. "This always occupied a place above your own heart, Samantha – and it shall again. But first let me snazz it up a bit for you."

"That's okay, Aunt Clara; I'll take it to the jewelers next week..." Darrin could just see Clara mistakenly filling the room with diamonds. It would almost be worth it to see Larry's reaction.

Gently passing her hand over the charm, Clara instantly made it shine more brilliantly than it had the day Darrin bought it for Samantha. Into the bargain, she had repaired the clasp. Handing it back to its owner, Clara's look was pure self-congratulation. "Not to worry, children – I still gots it goin' on." Her eyes widening, she added, "Did I get that right?"

Keith had to shout above the warmhearted laughter. "Listen, all – that dance floor out there has gotten stone cold. So it's our civic duty to warm it back up again. It'll just take me a second to load another stack of discs – "

"Don't bother," came Serena's declaration. "I want to take a turn deejaying this affair. But take comfort in the fact our tastes in music play on nearly identical stations." With two fingers, Serena made a record appear in mid-air, which began spinning on its own.[34] It was Curtis Mayfield's *Keep On Keepin' On*.

Everyone metabolized the lyrics that spoke of taking a stand and the promise that there was still a lot of faith and trust in the world. "Sweet," Keith nodded. "I almost brought that."

Serena brandished her goblet high. "To love, love, love!"[35]

"Love, love, love!" everyone toasted, including the children.

"Oh, Sammy!" Serena exclaimed. "This could be a whole new movement, like Women's Lib. It's *Witches'* Lib – only instead of burning bras, we'll burn brooms!"

Most of the group followed Serena and the levitating LP out to the patio. Larry, on the other hand, approached the fireplace and meaningfully gripped Darrin's shoulder. "Congratulations again, you son of a gun. Can't wait to partner up with you starting Monday. And it's lovely you could join us, Aunt Clara. Any other mysteries you can solve while you're here? Like why I have the strong feeling Morning Glory Circle was in Patterson but now it's in Westport?"[36] Larry emitted his signature hearty guffaw and headed outside with the others.

"Oh!" Aunt Clara blurted out. "I did it again."

Darrin and Samantha escorted Clara to their makeshift dance floor, where Curtis Mayfield's silky message of unity had witches and mortals swaying to its beat. Even the more stodgy supernaturals like Maurice, Endora, and Dr. Bombay got into its hypnotic groove. This time, Esmeralda gave Phyllis a booty bump in plain sight. Frank was inspired to do the same. The Kravitzes shimmied with Arthur and Betty. Jonathan, Lisa, Tabitha, and Adam joined hands and danced in a circle around the radiant Aunt Clara. Dorothy and Keith, who had created an unintentional, unconscious space between them, were magically pushed into an embrace by an approving Serena. And Larry and Louise moved lovingly to the exhilarating strings and horns.

Samantha made ready to cut a rug, but Darrin stopped her. His eyes glued to his wife, he took the recovered and restored diamond heart from her, opened its chain's clasp, and closed it devotedly behind her neck. Her hand lingered down the chain, stopping at the encrusted pendant that rested above her very full heart.

She had only one word for him. "Good!"

The Stephenses joined hands and became aware that they had somehow drifted to the center of the jiving throng. They found it appropriate, since their marriage was the reason everybody was here. It now seemed somehow mortals had always known about witches, and that this knowledge had never been a problem, couldn't be a problem. For whatever else had been, and whatever was to come, there was only harmony here tonight, and a distinct sense that the differences people focused on out of fear weren't differences at all, but simply unique ways of being that made up this miraculous, right-on universe. Samantha and Darrin Stephens, almost psychically, made an agreement that they would keep on keepin' on, like the song said, with more love and support than they'd ever had, made easier in the certainty that they had each other – and always would.

Cassettes on which Adam-Michael James recorded *Bewitched* as a child in 1979 and 1980 by placing a tape recorder in front of the television speaker. The correct titles are "Take Two Aspirins and Half A Pint of Porpoise Milk" (#42), "Darrin Goes Ape" (#222), and "The Truth, Nothing But the Truth, So Help Me, Sam" (#254).

To Michael!
Happiness!
Elizabeth Montgomery

and "Emma"
says thanks
for you nice words
about "Second
Sight"

ELIZABETH MONTGOMERY
B.K.M.

LOS ANGELES, CA 90069

MARINA DEL REY, CA 902

1984
APR
PM

Elizabeth Montgomery's response to a fan letter the 14-year-old
Adam-Michael James wrote to her in 1984, following her appearance
in the television movie *Second Sight*.

ENDNOTES

CHAPTER 1

1. "A Good Turn Never Goes Unpunished" (#252)
2. "I, Darrin, Take This Witch, Samantha" (#1)
3. "Charlie Harper, Winner" (#99)
4. "No Zip in My Zap" (#113)
5. "Serena's Youth Pill" (#247)
6. "I, Darrin, Take This Witch, Samantha" (#1)
7. "How Not to Lose Your Head to King Henry VIII" (#229-#230)
8. "Samantha's Thanksgiving to Remember" (#119)
9. "Mother Meets What's-His-Name" (#4)
10. "How Green Was My Grass" (#131)
11. "Daddy Comes for a Visit" (#180)
    "Darrin the Warlock" (#181)
    "The Return of Darrin the Bold" (#217)
12. "...And Something Makes Three" (#12)
13. *The Bewitched Continuum*, pg. 150
14. "Is It Magic or Imagination?" (#148)
15. *The Bewitched Continuum*, pg. 576
16. "I Get Your Nanny, You Get My Goat" (#122)
17. "Samantha's Pet Warlock" (#209)
18. *The Bewitched Continuum*, pg. 605
19. "Solid Gold Mother-in-Law" (#120)
    "The Warlock in the Gray Flannel Suit" (#239)
20. "...And Something Makes Three" (#12)
    The Bewitched Continuum, pgs. 579, 604
21. "Eat At Mario's" (#35)
22. "The Truth, Nothing But the Truth, So Help Me, Sam" (#254)
23. "What Makes Darrin Run" (#191)
24. *The Bewitched Continuum*, pg. 552
25. "The No-Harm Charm" (#138)
26. "Man of the Year" (#139)
27. *The Bewitched Continuum*, pg. 442

CHAPTER 2

1. *The Bewitched Continuum*, pg. 207
2. "The Warlock in the Gray Flannel Suit" (#239)
3. "How to Fail in Business With All Kinds of Help" (#104)
4. *The Bewitched Continuum*, pg. 533
5. "I, Darrin, Take This Witch, Samantha" (#1)

6. *The Bewitched Continuum*, pg. 10

7. *The Bewitched Continuum*, pg. 420

8. "Be It Ever So Mortgaged" (#2)

9. *The Bewitched Continuum*, pg. 7

10. "To Go or Not to Go, That Is the Question" (#201)

11. *The Bewitched Continuum*, pg. 439

12. *The Bewitched Continuum*, pg. 436

13. *The Bewitched Continuum*, pg. 436

14. "The Salem Saga" (#203)

15. "Be It Ever So Mortgaged" (#2)

16. "Sam in the Moon" (#91)

17. "George the Warlock" (#30)

18. "Once in a Vial" (#125)

19. "Samantha's Pet Warlock" (#209)

20. "Mrs. Stephens, Where Are You?" (#160)

21. *The Bewitched Continuum*, pg. 20
     "Samantha's Good News" (#168)

22. "I, Darrin, Take This Witch, Samantha" (#1)

23. "I, Darrin, Take This Witch, Samantha" (#1)

24. *The Bewitched Continuum*, pg. 261

25. "To Twitch or Not to Twitch" (#132)

26. "Be It Ever So Mortgaged" (#2)

27. "Driving Is the Only Way to Fly" (#26)
     "Super Arthur" (#190)

28. *The Bewitched Continuum*, pg. 4

29. "Eye of the Beholder" (#22)

30. "Marriage, Witches' Style" (#161)

31. "Samantha's Yoo-Hoo Maid" (#172)

32. "George Washington Zapped Here" (#249-#250)

33. "Adam, Warlock or Washout?" (#242)

34. "Okay, Who's the Wise Witch?" (#195)
     "Turn on the Old Charm" (#199)
     "Make Love, Not Hate" (#200)

35. "Samantha's Magic Mirror" (#226)

36. "Samantha's Not So Leaning Tower of Pisa" (#232)

37. "Samantha's Magic Sitter" (#243)

38. *The Bewitched Continuum*, pg. 544

39. *The Bewitched Continuum*, pg. 222

40. "To Twitch or Not to Twitch" (#132)

41. "Samantha's French Pastry" (#147)

42. "Samantha's Secret Is Discovered" (#188)

43. *The Bewitched Continuum*, pg. 586-587

44. *The Bewitched Continuum*, pg. 577
45. "My Baby, the Tycoon" (#55)
    "Three Men and a Witch on a Horse" (#241)
46. "To Twitch or Not to Twitch" (#132)
47. "Be It Ever So Mortgaged" (#2)
    The Bewitched Continuum, pg. 579, 604
48. "I, Darrin, Take This Witch, Samantha" (#1)
    The Bewitched Continuum, pgs. 579, 604

CHAPTER 3

1. "Love Is Blind" (#13)
2. "I Remember You...Sometimes" (#97)
3. "What Makes Darrin Run" (#191)
4. "Sisters At Heart" (#213)
5. *The Bewitched Continuum*, pg. 468
6. "Tabitha's Weekend" (#163)
7. "The Dancing Bear" (#58)
8. *The Bewitched Continuum*, pg. 342
9. *The Bewitched Continuum*, pg. 342
10. "I, Darrin, Take This Witch, Samantha" (#1)
    "Samantha's Secret Is Discovered" (#188)
11. "Samantha and the Antique Doll" (#228)
12. "McTavish" (#130)
13. "Out of Sync, Out of Mind" (#116)
14. "Samantha's Secret Is Discovered" (#188)
15. "Samantha and the Antique Doll" (#228)
16. "It's Wishcraft" (#103)
17. "Samantha's Double Mother Trouble" (#182)
18. *The Bewitched Continuum*, pg 411
19. "Samantha's Supermaid" (#154)
20. "A Nice Little Dinner Party" (#19)
21. *The Bewitched Continuum*, pg. 506
22. "Samantha's Witchcraft Blows A Fuse" (#253)
23. *The Bewitched Continuum*, pg. 555
24. "Mrs. Stephens, Where Are You?" (#160)
    "Tabitha's Weekend" (#163)
    The Bewitched Continuum, pg. 342
25. *The Bewitched Continuum*, pg. 498
26. *The Bewitched Continuum*, pg. 538
27. "Three Men and a Witch on a Horse" (#241)

28. "Follow That Witch (Part I)" (#66)
    "A Bum Raps" (#68)
    "Man's Best Friend" (#70)
29. "Is It Magic or Imagination?" (#148)
    The Bewitched Continuum, pg. 311
30. "Splitsville" (#140)
31. "Weep No More, My Willow" (#152)
32. "Samantha for the Defense" (#88)
33. "Soapbox Derby" (#90)
34. "Nobody But A Frog Knows How to Live" (#106)
35. "Tabitha's First Day In School" (#248)
36. "School Days, School Daze" (#251)
37. "Tabitha's First Day In School" (#248)
38. "School Days, School Daze" (#251)
39. "Sisters At Heart" (#213)

CHAPTER 4

1. "Sisters At Heart" (#213)
2. "Accidental Twins" (#78)
    "Mixed Doubles" (#221)
3. *The Bewitched Continuum*, pg. 389
4. *The Bewitched Continuum*, pg. 205
5. *The Bewitched Continuum*, pg. 379
6. "The Safe and Sane Halloween" (#115)
7. "Splitsville" (#140)
8. "Samantha the Dressmaker" (#60)
9. *The Bewitched Continuum*, pg. 471
10. "Little Pitchers Have Big Fears" (#6)
11. "Baby's First Paragraph" (#62)
12. "Soapbox Derby" (#90)
13. "The Safe and Sane Halloween" (#115)
14. "Tabitha's Very Own Samantha" (#189)
15. "Santa Comes to Visit and Stays and Stays" (#184)
16. "Mary, the Good Fairy" (#215)
17. "We're In For A Bad Spell" (#39)
18. "The Salem Saga" (#203) to "Samantha's Bad Day in Salem" (#207)
19. *The Bewitched Continuum*, pg. 483
20. "It's Wishcraft" (#103)
21. "To Trick-or-Treat or Not to Trick-or-Treat" (#177)
22. "Sisters At Heart" (#213)
23. *The Bewitched Continuum*, pg. 302

24. "The Moment of Truth" (#76)
   The Bewitched Continuum, pgs. 150, 155
25. *The Bewitched Continuum*, pg. 378
26. "Naming Samantha's Baby" (#176)
27. *The Bewitched Continuum*, pgs. 4, 74
28. "The Safe and Sane Halloween" (#115)
29. *The Bewitched Continuum*, pg. 94
30. "The Corn Is As High As A Guernsey's Eye" (#94)
31. "That Was No Chick, That Was My Wife" (#117)
32. "Samantha Loses Her Voice" (#150)
33. "What Makes Darrin Run" (#191)
   "Mixed Doubles" (#221)
34. *The Bewitched Continuum*, pg. 336
35. "Playmates" (#133)
   The Bewitched Continuum, pg. 273
36. "Samantha's Double Mother Trouble" (#182)
37. "Hansel and Gretel in Samanthaland" (#238)
38. *The Bewitched Continuum*, pg. 530
39. "Eye of the Beholder" (#22)
   The Bewitched Continuum, pgs. 579, 604
40. "A Chance on Love" (#196)
   The Bewitched Continuum, pgs. 436, 605
41. *The Bewitched Continuum*, pg. 127
42. *The Bewitched Continuum*, pg. 506
   "Samantha on Thin Ice" (#246)
43. "Samantha's Witchcraft Blows A Fuse" (#253)
44. *The Bewitched Continuum*, pgs. 493, 527, 566
45. "I, Darrin, Take This Witch, Samantha" (#1)
   to "The Girl With the Golden Nose" (#73)
46. "The Girl With the Golden Nose" (#73)
47. "Red Light, Green Light" (#23)
48. *The Bewitched Continuum*, pgs. 415-416

CHAPTER 5

1. "School Days, School Daze" (#251)
2. *The Bewitched Continuum*, pgs. 6, 261
3. *The Bewitched Continuum*, pg 107
4. "Red Light, Green Light" (#23)
5. "Help, Help, Don't Save Me" (#5)
6. "No Zip in My Zap" (#113)
7. "Samantha's Old Man" (#210)
8. "The Good Fairy Strikes Again" (#216)

9. "Samantha's da Vinci Dilemma" (#124)
10. "Hoho the Clown" (#92)
11. *The Bewitched Continuum*, pg. 436
12. "A Nice Little Dinner Party" (#19)
13. "I, Darrin, Take This Witch, Samantha" (#1)
    "Samantha's Secret Is Discovered" (#188)
14. "Double Split" (#64)
15. "Illegal Separation" (#32)
16. "Three Men and a Witch on a Horse" (#241)
17. "...And Something Makes Three" (#12)
18. "Fastest Gun on Madison Avenue" (#57)
19. "I, Darrin, Take This Witch, Samantha" (#1)
    "The Girl With the Golden Nose" (#73)
20. "Samantha for the Defense" (#88)
21. "The Short Happy Circuit of Aunt Clara" (#83)
    "Nobody But A Frog Knows How to Live" (#106)
    "The Safe and Sane Halloween" (#115)
22. "What Makes Darrin Run" (#191)
23. "Mixed Doubles" (#221)
24. "Samantha's Secret Is Discovered" (#188)
25. *The Bewitched Continuum*, pgs. 364, 421
26. "Endora Moves in for a Spell" (#80)
27. "Samantha's Secret Saucer" (#137)
    "Splitsville" (#140)
28. "Out of Sync, Out of Mind" (#116)
    "Samantha and the Antique Doll" (#228)
    The Bewitched Continuum, pg. 500
29. "Samantha's Old Man" (#210)
30. "Junior Executive" (#46)
    "Out of the Mouths of Babes" (#224)
31. "Just One Happy Family" (#10)
32. "A Vision of Sugar Plums" (#15)
33. "A Nice Little Dinner Party" (#19)
    The Bewitched Continuum, pgs. 37-38
34. "The Girl With the Golden Nose" (#73)
35. "We're In For A Bad Spell" (#39)
36. "Charlie Harper, Winner" (#99)
37. "Which Witch Is Which?" (#24)
38. *The Bewitched Continuum*, pgs. 120, 225
39. "My Baby, the Tycoon" (#55)
40. *The Bewitched Continuum*, pg. 288
41. "Samantha's Double Mother Trouble" (#182)

CHAPTER 6

1. "We're In For A Bad Spell" (#39)
2. "I Confess" (#135)
3. "Instant Courtesy" (#153)
4. "The Ghost Who Made A Spectre of Himself" (#235)
5. *The Bewitched Continuum*, pgs. 506, 568
6. *The Bewitched Continuum*, pg. 406
7. *The Bewitched Continuum*, pg. 576
8. "Man of the Year" (#139)
9. "Samantha and the Antique Doll" (#228)
   The Bewitched Continuum, pg. 500
10. "School Days, School Daze" (#251)
11. "Baby's First Paragraph" (#62)
12. "What Every Young Man Should Know" (#72)
13. "Samantha's Secret Is Discovered" (#188)
14. "Sisters At Heart" (#213)
15. "The Witches Are Out" (#7)
    The Bewitched Continuum, pgs. 579, 604

CHAPTER 7

1. "Hoho the Clown" (#92)
2. *The Bewitched Continuum*, pgs. 74, 186
3. "Darrin, Gone and Forgotten" (#144)
4. "If They Never Met" (#127)
5. "To Go or Not to Go, That Is the Question" (#201)
6. "Salem, Here We Come" (#202)

CHAPTER 8

1. "Be It Ever So Mortgaged" (#2)
2. "Salem, Here We Come" (#202)
3. *The Bewitched Continuum*, pg. 406, 528
4. "Tabitha's Very Own Samantha" (#189)
5. "TV or Not TV" (#236)
6. "Samantha and the Beanstalk" (#171)
7. "Hansel and Gretel in Samanthaland" (#238)
8. "I, Darrin, Take This Witch, Samantha" (#1)
9. "Sisters At Heart" (#213)
10. "Little Pitchers Have Big Fears" (#6)
    "Samantha's Curious Cravings" (#174)
11. "Long Live the Queen" (#108)
12. *The Bewitched Continuum*, pg. 297
13. "Salem, Here We Come" (#202)

14. *The Bewitched Continuum*, pg. 223
15. "Salem, Here We Come" (#202)
16. "To Go or Not to Go, That Is the Question" (#201)
17. "The Salem Saga" (#203)
    "Samantha's Old Salem Trip" (#208)
18. "Samantha's Secret Is Discovered" (#188)
19. "Samantha's Bad Day in Salem" (#207)

CHAPTER 9

1. *The Bewitched Continuum*, pg. 306
2. "It's So Nice to Have a Spouse Around the House" (#145)
3. "How Not to Lose Your Head to King Henry VIII (Part I)" (#229)
4. "Adam, Warlock or Washout?" (#242)
5. "George the Warlock" (#30)
6. *The Bewitched Continuum*, pg. 520
7. "Long Live the Queen" (#108)
8. "The Trial and Error of Aunt Clara" (#95)
9. "Samantha's Secret Saucer" (#137)
    The Bewitched Continuum, pgs. 294, 369
10. "Serena's Richcraft" (#245)
11. "Darrin, Gone and Forgotten" (#144)
12. "Man's Best Friend" (#70)
13. "The Witches Are Out" (#7)
14. "The Leprechaun" (#63)
15. "Follow That Witch" (#66-#67)
16. "The Catnapper" (#71)
17. "Darrin the Warlock" (#181)

CHAPTER 10

1. "I Confess" (#135)
2. "The Battle of Burning Oak" (#164)
3. "Samantha's Secret Is Discovered" (#188)
4. "Just A Kid Again" (#193)
5. "School Days, School Daze" (#251)
6. "Samantha's Caesar Salad" (#173)
7. "I'd Rather Twitch Than Fight" (#84)
8. "Aunt Clara's Victoria Victory" (#100)
9. "Samantha's French Pastry" (#147)
10. "Paul Revere Rides Again" (#206)
11. "George Washington Zapped Here" (#249-#250)
12. *The Bewitched Continuum*, pg. 439
13. "George Washington Zapped Here (Part II)" (#250)

14. "My Friend Ben" (#87)

15. *The Bewitched Continuum*, pgs. 371-372

16. *The Bewitched Continuum*, pg. 223

17. "Mrs. Stephens, Where Are You?" (#160)

18. "Samantha on Thin Ice" (#246)

19. "The Witches Are Out" (#7)

20. "Humbug Not to Be Spoken Here" (#123)

21. "A Vision of Sugar Plums" (#15)

22. *The Bewitched Continuum*, pg. 30

23. "Abner Kadabra" (#29)
   "Samantha's Secret Saucer" (#137)

24. "Samantha for the Defense" (#88)

25. "The Safe and Sane Halloween" (#115)

26. "I, Darrin, Take This Witch, Samantha" (#1)

27. "Mother Meets What's-His-Name" (#4)

28. *The Bewitched Continuum*, pgs. 4, 27

29. "Your Witch Is Showing" (#20)

30. "George the Warlock" (#30)

31. "School Days, School Days" (#251)

32. "...And Something Makes Three" (#12)
   The Bewitched Continuum, pg. 4

33. "A Is for Aardvark" (#17)

CHAPTER 11

1. *The Bewitched Continuum*, pg. 578

2. "It Takes One to Know One" (#11)

3. "The Eight-Year Itch Witch" (#240)

4. "To Go or Not to Go, That Is the Question" (#201)

5. "Endora Moves in for a Spell" (#80)

6. "Long Live the Queen" (#108)

7. *The Bewitched Continuum*, pgs. 228, 305

8. *The Bewitched Continuum*, pg. 306

9. "Samantha's Good News" (#168)

10. "Just One Happy Family" (#10)
   "Paris, Witches' Style" (#234)

11. "Samantha and the Beanstalk" (#171)

12. "Tabitha's Weekend" (#163)

13. "A Plague on Maurice and Samantha" (#237)

14. "Tabitha's First Day In School" (#248)

15. "A Plague on Maurice and Samantha" (#237)

16. *The Bewitched Continuum*, pgs. 158, 486

17. "Alias Darrin Stephens" (#37)

18. "And Then There Were Three" (#54)
19. "Nobody's Perfect" (#75)
20. "The Moment of Truth" (#76)
21. "If the Shoe Pinches" (#197)
    The Bewitched Continuum, pg. 423

CHAPTER 12

1. "George Washington Zapped Here (Part II)" (#250)
2. "Mother Meets What's-His-Name" (#4)
3. "Darrin the Warlock" (#181)
4. "The Salem Saga" (#203)
5. "Samantha's Power Failure" (#165)
6. "Be It Ever So Mortgaged" (#2)
7. "Mother Meets What's-His-Name" (#4)
8. "Trick or Treat" (#43)
9. "To Trick-or-Treat or Not to Trick-or-Treat" (#177)
10. "Which Witch Is Which?" (#24)
11. "Once in a Vial" (#125)
12. *The Bewitched Continuum*, pg. 588 (Ron Randell)
13. "George the Warlock" (#30)
14. "The Battle of Burning Oak" (#164)
15. "Daddy Does His Thing" (#167)
16. "Samantha's Not So Leaning Tower of Pisa" (#232)
17. "A Majority of Two" (#136)
18. "Marriage, Witches' Style" (#161)
19. "The Return of Darrin the Bold" (#217)
20. *The Bewitched Continuum*, pgs. 476-477
21. "Serena's Richcraft" (#245)
22. "George the Warlock" (#30)
23. "Pleasure O'Riley" (#25)
24. "Salem, Here We Come" (#202)
25. *The Bewitched Continuum*, pg. 441

CHAPTER 13

1. "A Vision of Sugar Plums" (#15)
2. "A Vision of Sugar Plums" (#51)
    The Bewitched Continuum, pg. 102
3. "Just A Kid Again" (#193)
4. *The Bewitched Continuum*, pg. 416
5. "Junior Executive" (#46)
    "Out of the Mouths of Babes" (#224)

CHAPTER 14

1. "Charlie Harper, Winner" (#99)
2. "Splitsville" (#140)
3. "Man's Best Friend" (#70)
   "Darrin, Gone and Forgotten" (#144)
   "George the Warlock" (#30)
4. "How Not to Lose Your Head to King Henry VIII (Part I)" (#229)
5. "How Not to Lose Your Head to King Henry VIII (Part II)" (#230)
6. *The Bewitched Continuum*, pg. 223
7. "Samantha's Thanksgiving to Remember" (#119)
8. "Samantha's Old Salem Trip" (#208)
9. "Santa Comes to Visit and Stays and Stays" (#184)
10. "The Witches Are Out" (#7)
11. "To Trick-or-Treat or Not to Trick-or-Treat" (#177)
12. "Samantha's Bad Day in Salem" (#207)
13. *The Bewitched Continuum*, pg. 440
14. "Salem, Here We Come" (#202)
15. *The Bewitched Continuum*, pg. 223
16. "Witches and Warlocks Are My Favorite Things" (#77)
17. "Salem, Here We Come" (#202)
    The Bewitched Continuum, pg. 442
18. *The Bewitched Continuum*, pg. 347
19. "Witches and Warlocks Are My Favorite Things" (#77)
20. "Nobody's Perfect" (#75)
    "The Moment of Truth" (#76)
21. "Sisters At Heart" (#213)
22. "To Go or Not to Go, That Is the Question" (#201)

CHAPTER 15

1. "The Battle of Burning Oak" (#164)
2. *The Bewitched Continuum*, pgs. 365, 436, 506
3. "Samantha Goes South for a Spell" (#142)
4. "Samantha Meets the Folks" (#14)
5. "Samantha's Secret Is Discovered" (#188)
6. *The Bewitched Continuum*, pg. 142
7. "Red Light, Green Light" (#23)
   "And Then There Were Three" (#54)
8. "We're In For A Bad Spell" (#39)
9. "My Boss, The Teddy Bear" (#49)
10. "I Remember You...Sometimes" (#97)
11. "Cheap, Cheap" (#112)
12. "Instant Courtesy" (#153)

13. "Solid Gold Mother-in-Law" (#120)
14. "Samantha's Secret Is Discovered" (#188)
15. "I, Darrin, Take This Witch, Samantha" (#1)
16. "Samantha and the Antique Doll" (#228)
17. *The Bewitched Continuum*, pg. 273
18. *The Bewitched Continuum*, pg. 335
19. "It's Wishcraft" (#103)
20. "Double Split" (#64)
21. "I Confess" (#135)
22. "My Baby, the Tycoon" (#55)
    "Three Men and a Witch on a Horse" (#241)
23. "The Witches Are Out" (#7)
24. "To Trick-or-Treat or Not to Trick-or-Treat" (#177)
25. "That Was My Wife" (#31)
    "The Corsican Cousins" (#211)
26. *The Bewitched Continuum*, pg. 88
27. "Darrin the Warlock" (#181)
28. *The Bewitched Continuum*, pg. 276
29. "Samantha's Bad Day in Salem" (#207)
30. "Santa Comes to Visit and Stays and Stays" (#184)
31. "Illegal Separation" (#32)
32. "Be It Ever So Mortgaged" (#2)
33. "And Then I Wrote" (#45)
34. "Be It Ever So Mortgaged" (#2)
    "Ling-Ling" (#21)
    "Red Light, Green Light" (#23)
    "Samantha's Pet Warlock" (#209)
35. "Daddy Does His Thing" (#167)
36. "Samantha's Lost Weekend" (#186)
37. *The Bewitched Continuum*, pg. 94
38. "Be It Ever So Mortgaged" (#2)
39. "Samantha for the Defense" (#88)
40. "The Safe and Sane Halloween" (#115)
41. "Samantha's Secret Saucer" (#137)
42. "School Days, School Daze" (#251)

CHAPTER 16

1. "Abner Kadabra" (#29)
   "Samantha's Secret Saucer" (#137)
2. "Santa Comes to Visit and Stays and Stays" (#184)
3. "The Mother-in-Law of the Year" (#214)
4. "Samantha's Yoo-Hoo Maid" (#172)

5. "My Grandson, the Warlock" (#40)
6. "Naming Samantha's Baby" (#176)
7. "Serena Stops the Show" (#192)
   The Bewitched Continuum, pg. 412
8. "Serena's Youth Pill" (#247)
9. "Samantha's Lost Weekend" (#186)
   "A Plague on Maurice and Samantha" (#237)
   "Samantha's Witchcraft Blows A Fuse" (#253)
10. "There's Gold in Them Thar Pills" (#107)
11. "Hippie, Hippie, Hooray" (#128)
12. "Serena Stops the Show" (#192)
13. *The Bewitched Continuum*, pg. 412
14. "The House That Uncle Arthur Built" (#218)
    The Bewitched Continuum, pg. 578
15. "Sisters At Heart" (#213)
16. "Samantha's Double Mother Trouble" (#182)
17. "Samantha's Secret Is Discovered" (#188)
18. "Samantha and the Antique Doll" (#228)
19. "Abner Kadabra" (#29)
20. "Samantha's Yoo-Hoo Maid" (#172)
21. "A Nice Little Dinner Party" (#19)

CHAPTER 17

1. "Illegal Separation" (#32)
2. "Mother Meets What's-His-Name" (#4)
3. "To Go or Not to Go, That Is the Question" (#201)
4. *The Bewitched Continuum*, pg. 577
5. "The House That Uncle Arthur Built" (#218)
6. *The Bewitched Continuum*, pg. 597
7. "Daddy Does His Thing" (#167)
8. "Samantha and the Antique Doll" (#228)
9. "I Confess" (#135)
10. "Witch or Wife" (#8)
11. "Samantha's Curious Cravings" (#174)
12. "Solid Gold Mother-in-Law" (#120)
13. "Out of Sync, Out of Mind" (#116)
14. "Samantha Meets the Folks" (#14)
    The Bewitched Continuum, pg. 581
15. "Make Love, Not Hate" (#200)
16. *The Bewitched Continuum*, pg. 565
17. "I Confess" (#135)
18. "A Vision of Sugar Plums" (#15)

19. "A Is for Aardvark" (#17)

20. "The No-Harm Charm" (#138)
    "Daddy Comes for a Visit" (#180)
    "Darrin the Warlock" (#181)
    "Samantha's Magic Potion" (#212)

21. *The Bewitched Continuum*, pg. 506

22. "Be It Ever So Mortgaged" (#2)

23. "Mrs. Stephens, Where Are You?" (#160)

24. "Samantha's Power Failure" (#165)

25. "Samantha's Secret Saucer" (#137)

26. *The Bewitched Continuum*, pgs. 294, 369

27. "The Witches Are Out" (#7)

28. *The Bewitched Continuum*, pgs. 156, 163

29. "Samantha Meets the Folks" (#14)

30. "Samantha Meets the Folks" (#14)
    The Bewitched Continuum, pg. 579

31. "To Go or Not to Go, That Is the Question" (#201)

32. *The Bewitched Continuum*, pg. 578

33. "Hippie, Hippie, Hooray" (#128)

34. "Serena Stops the Show" (#192)

35. "Hippie, Hippie, Hooray" (#128)

36. *The Bewitched Continuum*, pgs. 415-416

ABOUT THE AUTHOR

Photo by Irene Doyle

Author, actor, singer-songwriter – the only life for Adam-Michael James is a creative one. While he loves performing (his favorite role to date is *Beauty and the Beast*'s Lumière), AMJ segued to the other side of the stage in writing the book and lyrics for *The Nine Lives of L.M. Montgomery*, a multimedia musical drama based on the life and characters of the famed "Anne of Green Gables" author. In addition to having analyzed scripts for several Hollywood production companies, AMJ has been a columnist for SoapCentral since 2009, where his commentaries about *The Bold and the Beautiful* reach an estimated quarter of a million readers. "I, Samantha, Take This Mortal, Darrin" is AMJ's fourth book, a de facto spin-off of previous offering *The Bewitched Continuum*, his critically acclaimed "linear guide" that explores the continuity of the supernatural sitcom's 254 episodes. More awaits at adammichaeljames.com and facebook.com/bwcontinuum, where AMJ invites you to become a part of his bewitching community.